INNOCENT ECHOES

Josefine Fowler

Copyright © 2021 J.A. Fowler

This book is a work of fiction. Names, characters, places, and incidents either are the product of the author's imagination or are used fictitiously, and any resemblance to actual persons living or dead is entirely coincidental and not intended by the author.

All rights reserved. No part of this publication may be reproduced, distributed, or transmitted in any form or by any means, including photocopying, recording, or other electronic or mechanical methods, without the prior written permission of the publisher, except in the case of brief quotations embodied in critical reviews and certain other noncommercial uses permitted by copyright law. For permission requests, write to the publisher, addressed "Attention: Book Rights and Permission," at the address below.

Published in the United States of America

ISBN 978-1-953904-61-4 (SC)

J.A. Fowler
222 West 6th Street
Suite 400, San Pedro, CA, 90731
www.jafowlerauthor.com

Ordering Information and Rights Permission:
Quantity sales. Special discounts might be available on quantity purchases by corporations, associations, and others. For details, contact the publisher at the address above.

For Book Rights Adaptation and other Rights Permission. Call us at toll free 1-888-945-8513 or send us email at admin@stellarliteray.com.

Contents

Prologue vii
1 8
2 10
3 12
4 15
5 18
6 21
7 24
8 27
9 30
10 33
11 36
12 38
13 42
14 49
15 51
16 53
17 55
18 59
19 63
20 65

21	69
22	72
23	75
24	80
25	85
26	87
27	92
28	95
29	99
30	102
31	106
32	109
33	116
34	119
35	122
36	125
37	127
38	129
39	132
40	136
41	139
42	142
43	145
44	147
45	149

46	151
47	155
48	158
49	161
50	164
51	168
52	170
53	173
54	175
55	179
56	183
57	186
58	189
59	191
60	194
61	197
62	200
63	203
64	207
65	210
66	213
67	216
68	219
69	222
70	224

71	227
72	230
73	232
74	235
75	237
76	239
77	241
78	244
79	247
80	249
81	252
82	254
83	256
84	259
85	261
86	264
87	267
88	270
89	272
90	275
91	278

PROLOGUE

The temperature was 110 degrees with the sun beating down on the long deserted road. The landscape was dry and barren. No sign of clouds for miles with a 100% chance of no rain. Miles of dead, pale grass that looked more like flattened wheat was the extent of the view. Dust was tossed around by the occasional gust of warm air. Maria, a frightened and confused ten-year-old immigrant, sat in a white Lincoln town car. "It's okay," a woman's voice consoled her. "You'll be so much better off. A new life awaits you. A life where you can be anything you want to be." Gentle hands pushed Maria's hair behind her ear then the woman kissed her on the forehead. The woman patted Maria's hand and said, "Everything will be just fine."

Minutes later, a car almost identical to the one Maria was sitting in, pulled up alongside them. A gust of wind tossed up a thick cloud of dust that settled slowly. Next to Maria, the woman grabbed her bulky purse from beside her and quickly exited the town car's back seat. She approached the driver's side window of the arriving vehicle, and the driver rolled his window half-way down. "Everything is set," the woman assured as she leaned in to speak to the driver. "Does she come with instructions?" the thin-faced driver asked.

"Instructions included," the woman replied as if discussing a new toy or piece of equipment. The thin-faced man grinned, displaying yellow decaying teeth, and handed her a very thick, brown envelope. The woman opened the envelope and examined the contents. She closed the envelope with a satisfied expression, carefully slipped it in her purse and returned to the car where Maria waited. She opened the car door, smiled, and held out her hand for Maria to take. She walked Maria to the white Lincoln that had just arrived. The tall, thin driver now stood by the back door, holding it open for Maria. She stood in front of him with bewildered eyes. Maria looked up at the thin driver standing by the door. "Where I am going?" She asked in her mixed up, broken English.

She was nervous and afraid. She needed to urinate. Tiny tears were forming at the corners of her big brown eyes. She looked up at the thin-faced man and waited for an answer. There was silence. She climbed in the car, and the door closed.

1

It was a clear hot, Saturday afternoon. I was enjoying my last weekend at Crystal Lake with some of my friends and my big brother Jim. I was sitting at a large concrete picnic table located under a large oak tree that provided more than enough shade. My friends were swimming and engaging in some horseplay, laughing and splashing water. All was going great as I sat there relaxing and observing a game of volleyball happening to my right. I glanced over at my brother as he stood over the grill, appearing to be carefully studying the burgers and skillfully flipping a rack of ribs. Suddenly, my attention was drawn to a small boy hollering out. "My ball, my ball!" he was pointing toward the lake. I was a powerful swimmer, so I never stopped to think that I was wearing jeans, a muscle top, and sneakers. Without hesitation, I dove into the lake and started to swim. The blowing wind had already floated the ball out about 100 yards. That distance was a mere fraction of what I could swim without even beginning to feel tired. My friends and brother knew this, which was why no one paid much attention to me swimming out to get the ball.

When I was close enough to grab the ball, both of my legs cramped up; in horror, I was suddenly paralyzed from the waist down. I began sinking like lead. In a panic, I tried to cry for help, but I only released mute bubbles. I swallowed water and breathed in water through my nose. The pain in my chest was excruciating. On that day, I was going to die, of that I was sure. No one could tell I was drowning because no one witnessed frantic splashing or heard cries for help. As I descended, I raised my head to see the sun slowly moving farther and farther away. My eyes were open, but I only saw darkness.

A sense of clarity and quiet comforted me. I remember thinking, "God, you're the only one who can save me. If you can see me, please help me now." Everything was silent. All was black, and I felt peaceful as I continued to drop into the abyss of darkness.

Suddenly, my body felt a surge of energy, and an unseen force tossed my body up from the depths of the lake. In what seemed like seconds, my body shot above the water. I took in a deep breath the instant I felt the sun and breeze on my face. When I reached the surface of the water, I was surprised and thankful to find the small blue and gray ball floating a couple of feet next to me. Without wasting any time, I lunged and grabbed it. I rested for a minute, clinging to the ball with both my arms. I don't know what happened. What I do know is that I should have died on that clear, summer day. I held on and hugged that beautiful blue and silver football like someone who finally found a long lost friend. I looked up at the clear, blue sky in awe and smiled with tears welling up in my eyes. I took a deep breath and, in an almost inaudible voice, I whispered, "Thanks." I slowly began paddling toward the shore.

My legs were no longer cramped, and I did not feel the water in my lungs. My breathing had returned to normal. I calmly walked out of the lake and gave the ball to the little boy, who ran to me and grabbed it. After giving me a big smile, he ran to his mother. She was standing at the edge of the water staring in the direction I had come from, looking as if someone or something was still there. She was blowing a whistle. Beep, beep, beep.

It was my alarm, waking me up from a nightmare. No. Not a nightmare, a memory that I see and recall as if it happened just yesterday.

2

It was time to get ready for work. As a school teacher, I can't be late, tired, upset or lazy. I love my career as a teacher, but it is not always easy, especially for me. My name is Jennifer Knoes. What's so special about me? Well, I believe the last time I was just me was the day of my accident. I have another name, but I do not know what it is. The thing is, after that eventful summer day of drowning, I noticed right away that things were not going to be as they were. My way of viewing life changed entirely after that summer. I became academically motivated and started making all A's and B's in school. I graduated with honors, and a college scholarship, something no one could have ever guessed would happen. In an 18-year old's body, I often thought like a 30 or 40-year-old. For this reason, I skipped a lot of the foolishness most 18-year-old kids would typically get into.

It also meant I managed not to get caught when I did cross the lines between right and wrong. After college, I worked at a Breast and Cervical Cancer clinic, which was challenging and rewarding. I was always able to guess which clients I needed to appoint stat and which clients I could allow rescheduling without any problem. I planned on staying there for a while and making that my last career. Unfortunately, I don't dictate my future. Changes just come to me, and I do what I feel I should do.

It was July when I woke up one morning wanting to do something else. I was getting ready to go to work when the teaching idea came about. I don't know why; All I know is that I decided I wanted to be a teacher. Two years before that date, I had laughed at the idea. I had a friend who worked at the same clinic try to talk me into becoming a teacher. "Come on, Jennifer, it will be fun. You can join the same program I am joining," my friend Nancy pleaded as she stood in my office doorway. I glanced at her and continued reviewing my medical files. "Imagine me, a teacher of small children? Are you kidding? Surely I would hang a child by the toes or crack an idiot parent across the jaw before the closing of the first six weeks." I replied.

I have learned to accept new avenues in my life and just do and go where I am led. In other words, I follow my instinct. I don't argue. I do, however, sometimes question my destination. Somehow, things always work out. That week in July, I called around and found an alternative certification program. It was a type of program that trained a person to take and pass the Teacher Certification exam. That was all I needed since I had already completed a Bachelor's degree years before choosing to be a teacher. One month after applying for the alternative certification program, I scheduled an interview and landed a job at Coronado Elementary. Two weeks after the interview, I held the key to my first classroom. A year after enrolling in the alternative certification program, I took the Teacher Certification exam. I was able to take my exam and pass it the first time. Even with questions, I did not understand, I knew which answers to choose. Tests were not stressful for me. When I realized how easy testing came to me, I tested for five other certifications and succeeded.

I dressed in a casual outfit of a tan blouse and black slacks. With my hair up in a French roll and my makeup neatly applied. I washed and refilled the cat dishes and placed them down on the floor as my two little ladies raced for breakfast. I headed for the door of my small apartment, clutching my book bag in one hand and my purse and lunch tote in another.

3

I had begun my fifth year of teaching 1st Grade, and I was a little worried. Since the first day of school, something in my subconscious warned me to be prepared. But prepare for what? What was heading my way? I was not aware that my world would soon be shattered and changed forever.

It was now three months into the school year. Christmas was fast approaching, as was our field trip to The Casa Manana Theatre. Every year we embarked on a journey to a theatrical presentation of *The Polar Express*. The school district has strict policies about permission slips, media releases, etc. Every November, I begin to send the forms home for signatures and updates for any child that has re-located since school begins. Before the event date arrives, I will have collected a slew of consent forms and personal information forms that have to be kept on file and taken with me on the field trip in case of an emergency that involves having to contact parents.

It was after 3:00 pm, and the kids were gone for the day. This year I am blessed with twenty-one little ones, two of who enrolled just a few days ago. The children are all precious, and by now, I knew which parents came in stoned or on some prescription drug. By the look on my little children's faces, I could tell who had dinner the evening before and who had a rough night. Those who had a rough night were usually the ones who did not have anything to eat once they left my classroom at 3:00 pm the day before. Bill, my smallest boy, was being neglected, and he was a hot mess, but I had no evidence. I noticed Bill's mom was wearing sunglasses twice already in the early morning while dropping him off. I am aware that a little one's life can be very stressful, so I treat all of my students with the dignity and respect they deserve. They trust me. In several cases, I'm probably the only one they trust. What my students don't tell me, I already know. For this reason, I look out for them and worry about their safety once they leave my classroom.

I sat at my desk, finishing up some lessons, when my coworker, Claire, poked her head into my classroom. "Hey Jen, have you received the field trip permission forms on all your students yet?" she asked, leaning in the doorway.

"Only my two new students, Mike and Leslie Cardenas, have not returned their permission slips," I answered. We had noticed that the same lady picked up the students after school. Like clockwork, she would show up right at 3:00 pm to collect the children.

Claire looked at me and said, "My new student has not returned his forms, either."

It was curious that they all had the same last name, address, and parents, but they did not look alike. All three students listed Mr. and Mrs. Walker as their legal parents.

I looked at Claire. "Tomorrow, let's provide a new permission form for each child."

"What is so difficult about completing one darn form?" Claire said, sounding agitated.

"Well, we still have a couple of weeks before the Christmas program and field trip, so let's be patient. If we get nothing back, then I will talk to the lady that picks them up and ask that forms be completed and return promptly, okay?" I gave Claire a reassuring look. She smiled.

"Okay, I am finishing up and heading out. If I am not out there tomorrow at dismissal when she shows, let me know if you have any trouble. If she gives you any grief, we will have to notify Mrs. Phillips and make arrangements for them to stay behind with another teacher." Claire said.

"Okay," I replied.

Claire was leaning in the doorway with her arms crossed. She suddenly looked at her watch and shouted, "Oh, snap! I just remembered I have to go. I have to figure out what to get for my big sister's birthday. I'm going over to her workplace to probe her for clues about what she would like as a gift. That way, I will have a chance of getting her something she might want. It's hard to buy a gift for her. I mean, she pretty much has everything she needs. The moon is full tonight, so maybe I will get lucky." She raised her eyebrows and smiled.

"You did not tell me you had a big sister," I said surprisingly.

"Well, she just recently moved here, and she is managing the new Halston Hotel downtown. I figure since she's the head honcho, it won't be a problem if I drop in. Who knows, I might even get a free dinner from big sister." She raised her eyebrows again. "Don't work too late, Jen. See you tomorrow." Claire waved her right hand, turned, and headed down the hall in the direction of her classroom, no doubt to collect her things and lock up.

Something about Claire attracted me to her the minute I met her. She was the quiet type and very smart. She was into learning new languages. This year Italian was at the top of her list. She and I decided to learn the language ourselves. I have not been very successful. Some days I am motivated, and others, I'm just not interested. It might be that deep down inside; I have no desire to speak Italian. Italian only strikes me as desirable when it comes as a tall, dark-haired, blue-eyed male or as a main dish of pasta, meat sauce, and garlic bread.

Claire has this natural beauty about her. Unlike me, she is calm all the time and soft-spoken. Her classroom is always quiet and peaceful, which I found creepy in the beginning, then I realized they do all the things the other 1st grade classes do; they just do them quietly. After work, when everyone is gone, and she lets her hair down, literally speaking sometimes, Claire becomes a little more open. If you add a glass or two of wine, she becomes downright funny, down-to-earth, and sometimes dangerously straightforward with her words. That is what I like best about Claire. She stands at a long and lean 5ft 8in. She doesn't wear makeup. What for? The girl has beautiful skin. Her big green eyes, dark brown hair, and light skin make her look more like an English teacher from France, not the native Spanish speaker from Monterey, Mexico, that she is. At first glance, parents would wonder about her Spanish speaking skills. That, of course, always diminished when she opened her mouth. She has a very heavy Spanish accent. Ironically, it does not affect her Italian accent when she is practicing her new Italian phrases.

Innocent Echoes

It was still light outside, and echoes of laughing children came from the playground outside my classroom windows. I sat at my desk for a while, finishing up some grading, and glanced out the large windows. To my surprise, there were no children on the playground. "Odd, I couldn't have imagined the laughing of so many children." I thought to myself. I stood to look out at a still and eerily quiet playground.

On the opposite side of the street, I saw a shiny motorcycle without its rider. At least twice a month, a motorcycle police officer would have a heyday putting long pink citation forms under windshield wipers of illegally parked cars. I still can't figure out why people park there. There are signs plain as day with the words "No Parking from 2:00 pm to 5:00 pm." The first time I saw the officer, my intuition told me he was there for a purpose, and it was not to write citations. It felt like I was watching a friend. If he has been my friend in my dreams, chances are he will come to me. He will say something I will recognize or remember hearing. I watched him methodically work at his ticket-writing ritual. On my side of the building, I counted 14 vehicles holding a pink slip pressed to their glass windshields. The fourteen citations on the vehicles looked like whipping pink tongues.

While observing this officer, I noticed that he did not walk like other police officers; he walked taller, although he could not have been taller than 6 feet. One thing that caught my attention was the fact that he was not lean. He was kind of chunky and, even from a distance, his uniform appeared flawless, and his motorcycle was beyond shiny. I enjoyed watching him as he ritualistically went about his work.

Before I headed home, I decided to check my work e-mail. Mrs. Phillips made it an unwritten rule that all teachers were to check their mail during the day and again before leaving the building. First in my row of the new e-mail was an e-mail from our principal. It was a request for someone to volunteer to be the Invention Convention Coordinator.

Invention Convention is an event that encourages young inventors to participate by inventing something they believe consumers will purchase. It requires quite a bit of time outside of the regular teaching hours. The e-mail noted the process, from beginning to end, would be from November 5th to January 8th. Attached to the e-mail was a timeline from the Invention Convention Coordinator of what documents would be due from every school representative. That task would be performed by the lucky volunteer. I stared at the e-mail and decided the task was not for me.

I pushed the delete button, and to my surprise, my computer locked, and I could not delete it nor exit the page to read another e-mail. For those who don't pay attention, this would simply be an old computer and the bad ending of a good day. For people like me that listen and respond, it's a clear message that this is what I need to be doing before the winter break arrives. I pressed the reply button to find my computer functioning again. I responded to the e-mail with an enthusiastic, "Yes! I will be happy to take this task on". I sat at my computer for a few minutes after sending the reply, wondering what awaited me. I was excited about the new people I would meet and nervous about the future's adventure. That's the beauty of life. It's loaded with surprises. I like and fear that the most. I do not doubt that I will meet some new people and learn something new.

I went on to read the rest of my e-mail after saving flip charts in my drafts folder and deleting all the junk mail that managed to sneak through our district filtering system. It was 5:30 pm when I finished grading papers, filing important documents, and preparing center materials for the next day. I looked out the window to find the motorcycle cop gone. I scanned my classroom for the last time; all was clean and organized just how I like it. I smiled with approval, grabbed my purse, flicked off the lights, and headed home.

5

That evening, instinct told me to drive by the Walker's house. I had made a copy of their paperwork when they arrived. I keep all of my student's phone numbers and addresses on my phone for quick reference. What I was sure of was that their adoptive guardians were Mr. and Mrs. Walker. I was not sure of what I was looking for, nor whether I would recognize it if I found it. It was almost twilight, and the streets were quiet now. Lights in the houses indicated that most people had arrived home and were having dinner. I could see the beautiful full moon with a reddish-yellow hue, and I wondered how Claire was making out probing her sister for birthday gift clues. I silently wished her luck.

To some people, a full moon means bad luck. To others, it is the prime time to turn something terrible into something new. For example, if there were an unresolved quarrel, a full moon would be an excellent time to make amends. If you took something or accidentally broke something belonging to someone else, a full moon evening would be a good time to return items because it helps with understanding. Some superstitious beliefs are that if you sleep under a full moon, you may fall ill for a long period of time. A very popular superstition about the full moon is that it brings havoc, fills emergency rooms, and has police officers swamped with emergency calls. There is also a superstition that if the full moon is seen over the right shoulder, it brings fortune and good luck to that person. The full moon seen over the left shoulder brings bad luck. I hope Claire has good luck with her sister. I smiled.

I arrived at the neighborhood where the kids lived to find rows of quiet, well-manicured lawns. Some homes were already decorated with strings of Christmas lights. The street was lined with trees that had begun to embrace winter. Without hesitation, the trees shed their leaves in a dramatic dance with every breeze that blew. As I drove past the Walker's house, I noticed something odd. It was strange because the temperature had dropped into the 40s this evening; it was too cold for being outside longer than a few minutes.

By the light of the full moon, I could see the lady that drove the white van sitting on a white wooden swing made for two. She was dressed in a black coat and wore gloves. She was reading a large book. It was a children's book with large pictures, but she was not reading to herself. She was reading it out loud because her mouth was moving, and she was making facial expressions, but from where I was, I could see no one out there but her.

I begin to think that maybe she was on some learning English program, where they promise that you will speak a foreign language just practicing fifteen minutes a day. What is really guaranteed is that you will lose your patience, you won't use it daily, and your credit card will be charged for the program. Perhaps she was reading in the direction of the garden to help the plants grow faster. Some people do believe that if you talk to your plants, the plants will be happier. Why anyone would care if a plant is happy or not is beyond me. Still, she was not reading to plants. She was reading to a patch of dirt that had already been tilled for a new crop. Perhaps she was engaging in some ritual, and the big book was a cover-up for different words she was reading. I've read that some wealthy people practice a variety of good luck and wealth rituals during a full moon.

As I drove by, I slowed down and looked at the lady. I thought it could also be that she was practicing her reading before she read to the children. Yes, those books in the bright blue milk crate by the swing were for reading to the children. I was sure of it, positive. Those are for reading to the children. Why then, did her face look so sad?

In the driveway were a BMW, a Lincoln Continental and a white van probably used to transport the children to and from school. I did not see any children frolicking inside the house, but perhaps they were busy in other areas of the house that did not have outside windows. It's times like these that I wish I had access to the spy gadgets some spies use on T.V. What I would give to have a long rifle gun with a listening device that would allow me to hear all of the conversations happening in the house by simply pointing it in the direction of each room. Now that would have been perfect. Of course, if caught, I could face serious

Innocent Echoes

consequences that could negatively impact my teaching certification. No, no spy gadgets for me, thank you.

I reached the end of the street, turned the corner, and headed home. Perhaps tomorrow I will find meaning in what I have seen this evening. Other than the lady sitting outside reading, I did not see anything I would consider unusual.

6

The next morning all went smooth, and routines fell into place. I checked the student's folders for returned permission slips and found nothing in Mike and Leslie's folders. At dismissal, while lining the children up at the door, I noticed Esperanza Gomez coming down the hall. I quickly moved away from the door and started rushing to the back of the line as if someone had called me. I listened for her noisy heels to pass by and away from my door.

Little Leo looked up at me from the line and asked, "Can you help me shove my jacket in my backpack?"

"I most certainly will not, young man! Put that nice jacket on. It is very windy and cold out." I said in a chastising tone.

He sighed and began to pull the jacket out of the backpack to put it on. I looked at my door and could see no one standing by it or coming toward it. I walked the kids out single file to the pick-up area beside the school.

The street is a one-way from 2:00–5:00 pm. It made it easier for parents to drive up and collect their children. I saw the lady driving up to pick up the children. Since the three kids had the same last name but did not resemble each other in the slightest, I concluded they were undoubtedly adopted. Both Claire and I sent the permission slips home again. This time we attached a red note for parents. We were both hoping this would prompt the parents to complete and return the forms. Before I released Mike and Leslie to the lady in the van, I reminded them to have their parents check their folder tonight. They both smiled and agreed.

I knew something was not right, but I didn't know what. I don't mean your basic adoption mix-up or relatives adopting relative's children. I knew something was very wrong.

"Well, you think this is the last batch of forms we will have to send?" Claire asked as we walked back into the building.

"I hope so," I replied. I looked up to see Ms. Gomez scrambling through some paperwork she held in her arms, walking down the hallway heading straight for us. "Walk faster," I told Claire. "We are making a quick left into the copy room before Esperanza notices us," I whispered. We walked into the copy room.

"Why are you avoiding her? What if she comes in here?" Claire asked suspiciously.

"I'm going to the restroom. If she comes in here looking for me, tell her I feel sick, I have diarrhea, and I'm probably puking my guts out. I don't care what you tell her as long as she doesn't wait to talk to me. She creeps me out!" I said and began closing the restroom door.

"I can't tell her that; it's stupid!" Claire protested. The door to the restroom slammed, and the loud bolt lock sounded. Claire sat on the large blue couch and waited.

It must have been 5 seconds between the door slamming and Ms. Gomez walking in. "Hi, Ms. Alaniez," she said, still holding a pile of papers.

"Hi, Ms. Gomez," Claire replied and pretended to be reading a magazine from the center coffee table.

Ms. Gomez stood in the middle of the room, looked around, and frowned. "Where is Ms. Knoes? Wasn't she with you?" She asked suspiciously.

"Oh, Jen is not feeling well," Claire answered. "If you came in here to use the ladies' room, I would recommend the one down the hall. She has diarrhea really bad. She's probably in there puking too." Claire said as she wrinkled her nose.

"Oh gross," Ms. Gomez replied, making a sour frown. "I just wanted to touch base regarding the Christmas program. It's important to start rehearsing on stage. It's early, but when dealing with little ones, the sooner the practice begins, the better." She hugged her stack of papers and sighed, No worries, I will touch base with her later," Ms. Gomez said in a low tone. She hugged her papers again and left the lounge.

Claire took her phone out of her pocket and typed a text to Jen. "It's all clear. Come on before she comes back!"

Jen opened the door. She stepped out of the restroom.

"Thanks, buddy. What did you tell her?"

Claire broke out in a laugh and said, "That you had really bad diarrhea, and you were practically crapping in your pants. That you were probably puking your guts out too."

We exited the lounge laughing. Walking down the hall, Claire deliberately bumped into me and sighed. "What was that about?" Claire asked.

"She creeps me out, Claire. I don't know what it is, but something just tells me to avoid her like the Black Plague. I'll figure it out, but for now, I just want her away from me." I replied.

At the end of the hallway, I entered my classroom, and Claire continued to hers. Ms. Gomez does not hide her amazement at me. Whenever we have staff meetings after school, it seems she is always staring at me when she knows I am not looking her way. I do not know Ms. Gomez since this is her first year at our school. I am sure I have never met her before, and I'm even more certain that she gives me the creeps.

Part of my uniqueness is that I can feel trouble even days before. I can also read people, sometimes by just looking at them. I can usually spot the bad ones right away. The thing is, I don't always know why I do things; I just know I am supposed to do them. Things turn out perfect in the end, but it's confusing while I am waiting to see what happens. I cleaned and organized my classroom for the next day. It was a daily ritual to wipe the tabletops clean, pick up the crayons, markers, and pencils from the floor, and organized my reading table.

7

I usually don't mind working late since it's such a short drive home. It's not like I have a spouse or a family waiting on me to get home as some other teachers do. Being married can get complicated for me, so I take one day at a time. I do have a boyfriend of six months that I spend my time with. For the time being, my family consists of my two cats, Chloe and Kayla. They are pretty self-reliant as long as their food dish is full. They don't rely on me for much. They have a doggie door (I'm sure they would be offended to know that). I don't like knowing that my pets are cooped up in a small apartment while I am gone, so I had the door installed for them. On perfect days they go out and enjoy the sun and cool breezes. I believe they like the freedom they get while I am out. As a single female, I would have never opted to have pets, but two years ago, out of nowhere, I decided I wanted a pet for a companion. It was getting stale just coming home to an empty apartment and no one to snuggle with or talk to. A pet was as close as I could get at that time. I must admit it was one of my best choices that year. My two cats make great listeners and rarely complain. They also make great snuggle companions.

I adopted my cats from the animal shelter when they were eight weeks old. I remember walking into the shelter with my I.D. and $55.00 in my pocket. I wanted to make sure I would not adopt more than one kitten. Something in the back of my mind told me I would have two cats. I, going against this idea, brought just enough money for one. A young lady in a blue smock approached me while I sat in the waiting area, completing some paperwork the receptionist had handed me, and asked, "Are you adopting a dog or cat?"

"A kitten," I replied enthusiastically.

"Great!" she said with a white smile and gestured for me to follow her. I stood with my clipboard in hand and handed it to the receptionist as I passed by. She smiled and took it, glancing to make sure all areas were complete.

The young lady made a hand gesture. "This way, please," she said as we walked down a long hall. We entered a large room of cages. The odor of cat litter, cat food, and sanitizer lingered in the air. We turned the corner of the first aisle and, to our immediate right, sat a large cage containing a momma cat and seven kittens snuggled around her. I was only interested in one kitten, and I spotted it immediately. It was a calico kitten with patches of gray, black, orange, and brown. "I would like this one," I said, and I pointed to the kitten I had already mentally named Chloe.

My mind was made up, and I was about to leave the area when a change in my plans happened. Another kitten from the same cage came pouncing as if saying, "Hey, if my sister goes, I go!" It was a Tabby cat with black and gray stripes like a tiger with huge emerald green eyes and fluffy as can be. "Aww, look at this little rascal. She wants to go with you," the attendant said.

I smiled, "Actually, I only have $55.00 cash and did not bring my checkbook, so I am afraid I can only afford one today." I said, sounding regretful. I had prepared myself for this one. I looked over at the kitten. It was so beautiful with its pleading eyes. It stood with its face touching the cage that held its mother and five other siblings. It tilted its head and released a sad, low pleading meow. The attendant glanced at the plastic hanging folder that was fastened to the cage with a zip tie and looked at me with the biggest smile yet.

"Well, wouldn't you know? This kitten is paid for, so you can take it for free," she said enthusiastically. I knew she was lying. It was her desperate attempt at finding the kittens a good home. I couldn't resist the kitten's plea and the good deal.

The final outcome developed itself as it should have been. Although I try to change outcomes that I don't agree with, it seems that someone or something of a higher power is always there to make sure things go as planned for me.

Fifteen minutes later, I was the proud owner of both kittens. Like loving sisters, they snuggled together in the small brown carrier I had purchased from a thrift store just days before. I could tell they were delighted. Chloe was showing her elation by cleaning her sister, then pouncing on her with playful gladness. Two cats was a good plan; I just did not know it before I entered the shelter. Now,

Innocent Echoes

I was in love with both of my little rascals. That day I brought them to my small garage apartment they have always called home.

I arrived home with enough time for a quick frozen dinner, a hot bath, and a glimpse at the evening news before it would be time for me to get some sleep. I decided on a can of chicken and wild rice soup for dinner. I poured the contents into a glass bowl and heated them in the microwave. Canned soup certainly does not fall into any of the six food groups of the Food Pyramid but, for this evening, it would have to do. After eating my dinner, I rinsed my bowl and placed it in the dishwasher. I cleaned up the kitchen counters and wiped the stainless steel sink. I always clean the kitchen before I go to bed. One thing I can't stand is walking into a filthy kitchen first thing in the morning. Oh, and bugs. I hate bugs of any kind.

I turned off the lights and headed to the bathroom to prepare for bed. I took a nice long hot bath, then brushed and flossed my pearly whites. When I walked into my bedroom, towel drying my hair, I noticed I did not have a bottle of water on my nightstand. Water is my usual nightcap and my morning drink. I returned to the kitchen to get a bottle of water from my refrigerator. It's a healthy habit I picked up after watching a video our counselor shared with the classroom on the importance of keeping a body hydrated and how it makes a person's skin look vibrant and younger-looking. The magic word was younger. Being a female in my thirties, I was trying to hold back time in any way I could.

I decided maybe I did have time for some evening news. I opened my water bottle, plopped myself on my large brown sectional, and clicked on the T.V. This evening's headline focused on the Mexican Border. "This evening, a patrol officer reported two bodies found in a parked car found close to the Mexico border. Authorities believe it may have been a drug deal gone wrong. Back to you, Angela," the news anchor concluded.

Angela, who was reporting on local news, continued. "Sometime early this evening, a couple was robbed at gunpoint at their home in North Lake Worth. After what looked like an apparent robbery, both the husband and wife were shot in the head." I could see officers in the background going in and out of the home. Then I did a double-take on the officer exiting the house. There she was, Rachel Brinks, in a Lake Worth Police Officer's uniform.

"Well, I'll be damned," I said out loud in a low tone as I held my water bottle away from my lips. Rachel was my high school best buddy in American History class. She was quiet and stood at about 5ft tall in high school. She sat in front of me in the last row closest to the door. She had long curly hair that she wore in a tight bun. We did not talk much during class, but after school, we usually got together to do homework in the library. You might say Rachel and I worked in a cooperative pair way before collaborative pair studying was thought of as cool. In those days, it was called cheating. If you so much as mentioned to a peer what your answer was, or how you came about it, and the teacher found out, you would be punished—getting caught sometimes meant being ridiculed by the teacher and given extra work. Rachel was kind, helpful, and always went by the rules. It took me a whole month to convince her to work with me. "What if we get caught?" she asked.

"We won't," I replied.

"How do you know we won't get busted?" She asked again.

"I just know, okay, trust me." I gave her a mischievous wink.

"If I get busted by Mr. Cadena, I am going to be so embarrassed. He happens to be my favorite teacher," she said.

Rachel and I had our own code words and signals we often used to get through the trials and tribulations of high school. If we were talking about something and needed to meet somewhere without anyone following us, we just claimed to have a headache. We both understood that the last location given by the one with the headache would be the meeting place after school. It worked out really well. If others were around, I would say, "I have a headache, I'm thirsty, and I still have to return my library books." Rachel would know to meet me at the library after school. I never let Rachel down and, up until we parted ways after high school graduation, she always had my back. Rachel looked shy and meek but, like a Cobra, if you stepped on her, she would strike without hesitation.

Tomorrow, I will call Rachel and catch up on current events. I could not help but smile; finding Rachel was a great way to end my night. I put the cap on my water bottle and turned off the T.V. I was tired and needed to rest. If I were lucky, I would not dream.

Claire drove her convertible into the hotel parking, parked her car close to the front entrance, and grabbed her purse just in case big sister was not treating for dinner. She walked into a large lounge area, clearly made for those waiting to check-in or out, whichever would be the case. The receptionist was checking out a middle-aged man who seemed to be in a hurry going by the times he glanced at his watch. Claire looked over to the back of the lounge area and noticed a beautiful silver coffee pot on the large counter. Next to it were clear glass domes covering an assortment of pastries. When the receptionist finished with the man, Claire walked up to the desk.

"Yes, how can I help you?" the receptionist asked with a smile.

"Can you tell me where I could find Jackie Stone?" she asked.

"Yes. Is she expecting you?" the clerk inquired.

"No, but hopefully, she will have a minute for her little sister. Tell her Claire Alaniez is here to see her."

She picked up the phone, pushed three numbers, and said, "Mrs. Stone, there is a Claire Alaniez here to see you."

"Oh, send her down to my office," she said in a cheerful tone.

Claire walked down the long hall, with its classic wallpaper of pale beige floral design and walnut wainscoting. The hallway was very clean and lined with five-foot abstract paintings separated by an occasional brown upholstered bench. The long hallway was quiet and vacant of guests. Claire continued toward the hotel restaurant. The delicious aroma of perfectly grilled steak and Italian seasonings greeted her before she arrived at the restaurant entrance.

The restaurant was small but very elegant with its wine-colored tablecloths and white napkins folded between silver rings. A large round table close to the entrance displayed crystal goblets next to each place setting. The Italian music playing in the restaurant faded as she continued to the end of the hall and took a sharp right. There, around the corner, in a small but plush office, she found her big sister sitting behind a mahogany desk. In front of it sat two square leather chairs, but against the back wall and opposite the desk sat a long French velvet chaise.

"Hey you!" she said as she stood and gave Claire a warm sisterly hug. Jackie motioned for Claire to sit down in one of the chairs. Instead, Claire chose the chaise. Jackie grabbed one of the chairs, turned it to face the chase, and sat down. "To what do I owe this visit?" she asked with concern. "Are you okay?"

"Yes, of course. Everything is fine. Can't I visit my big sister without anything being wrong?" Claire asked. "How is your new position as the big honcho?"

Jackie sighed, stood, and turned the chair around so that she was straddling it, and folded her arms across the top. "This new position is never boring, to say the least!" she laughed. "This damn weather change brought with it some surprises. From one day to the next, some doors don't close right, or the lock hinges don't align. Last week, I was walking down the 2nd-floor hallway when I heard a man's voice coming from a room with a door that hadn't closed properly. Naturally, I stopped to listen in case someone needed help or something. No, he was saying, "I missed you. I missed you so much. Six months is a very long time." After that came the pounding of the headboard on the wall. Obviously, he was very happy to see her! I could hear her gasping and moaning. To be honest, I was jealous of the bitch." Jackie laughed. "I calmly shut the door that had slipped open. I swear after that, I walked out to the patio and had a cigarette." She laughed again.

One thing Claire loved about Jackie was that she says things just like they are. She enjoyed talking to her big sister, although sometimes it could be embarrassing. Claire had forgotten that she smoked on occasion. She decided for her birthday that she would buy her a gift she could definitely use. "Actually, big sister, I came to visit you to see if you would be working on your birthday. If you are, I will bring your gift here. If you are not working, I will bring it to your house." Claire said, sounding offended.

"I will probably be here," Jackie said. "Thanks, that's very sweet of you. Are you getting me something expensive?" Jackie asked. Claire laughed. "Oh, hell no, not on my teacher's salary!" They both laughed.

Jackie looked at her watch. "I'm starving." She stood and turned the chair facing the desk again. "Come on; let's grab a bite at Avanti's. I have not had dinner, and it's time. If you came directly over here from school, chances are, neither have you."

Claire smiled. "Right, you are big sister, right you are." She stood, adjusting her top.

Jackie grabbed her navy blue jacket off a coat hook behind the door. Avanti's was the name of the restaurant on the first floor of the hotel. When they walked into the restaurant, the host immediately approached them. "I've got this, Mary. I'll be at my usual table." Jackie said. The hostess smiled and said, "Yes, ma'am. I will get your server."

She vanished through some red velvet curtains. In a few minutes, she reappeared and returned to her post. They were sitting at a corner of the restaurant that allowed a view of almost every table, easily giving them a clear picture of everything happening in the restaurant. This was undeniably the executive corner.

The view of the entire space was impressive. All of the tables were round, some meant for four, and bigger tables for six or eight parties. Through the intercom came violin music with a taste of Italy. Claire relished her sister's offer of a nice meal and ordered her favorite, a Ribeye steak cooked medium-well, a potato with all the fixings, and a side of asparagus with a creamy butter sauce. The food was delicious. Claire enjoyed her visit with her sister. Although their different schedules did not allow them to spend a lot of time together, they kept in touch. Like sisters, they managed a movie night or a day at the spa once or twice a month.

10

I was standing at the entrance of a famous dance club, surrounded by laughter and loud talking. Glancing back, I could see the line of about one hundred people behind me. A tall, African American bouncer, in a tight black muscle top and fitted black slacks, looked like he could sign up for the next Mr. Olympia bodybuilding competition. He smiled at me like a person would a good friend. "You look very sexy tonight. Come on in, beautiful," he said as he unhooked a thick burgundy and gold rope while looking at another muscled up male, who opened the solid black wood and marble door that led me inside.

    I walked in and went straight to my usual table. At least in my head, I knew this was my table. This place was familiar to me. The scent of expensive colognes and perfumes, along with smoke, was in the air. Ironically, it was not unpleasant. The scents added to the excitement of the place. The music was loud. The dance floor was a large square made up of lights flashing underneath; it was long and wide. Surrounding it was a white marble wall with a top wide enough to serve as a narrow bar. Although I could not see any faces, something told me all of these people were currently or formally in the book of Who's Who in elegance and money.

    Everyone was full of energy and excitement. People were dancing with and without partners. Some ladies danced in groups, while others danced in a combination of male and female threesomes. The retro sound reminded me of the music played in the vampire movie *Blade*, except there were no sprinklers attached to the ceiling that were set to spill blood on the dancers. The beat, however, was equally wild and nostalgic. I looked up to encounter a tall male body leaning down to me. He was wearing a black jacket, a white shirt, and a skinny black tie, which hung loose. The cologne he wore was spicy and fresh, very sexy. Men's cologne turns me on like nothing else. "Here you go, baby." I turned to him and noticed an Ace of Spades tattooed on the skin between his thumb and index finger as he handed me a gin and tonic. I had just taken a short sip when he extended his hand to me and led me with his other hand on my waist to the dance floor.

We danced very close, his hands never leaving my body curves. I knew he was with me. We kissed on the dance floor, at first a short string of slow kisses, and then he held me close enough for me to feel his excitement in his nicely tailored slacks. "Come on," I said as I nipped his neck. I took him by the hand and led him down the hall into the ladies' room.

"Really," He asked.

I smiled, "Really."

I headed to the Accessible stall at the end. Before we had even reached the door, his hands had pulled my skin-tight dress up and had exposed my bottom. I could hear him moan. "Oh baby, you are one hell of a firecracker."

I turned to kiss him. I could feel our tongues tangling and teasing one another, and my body heat ready to burst. I loosened his slacks and took out what I would call a woman's best friend. Or at least it was mine. I turned my back to him and bent my body over, with my forearms on the wall, as to invite him in. I anticipated him pulling me to his body and caressing my full breasts with his large, soft hands. I felt his body meeting mine. Like an addict receiving their fix, I was oblivious to everything. Pleasure, that's all I wanted. The pleasure was what I felt and what I needed so badly. My heart was racing. I could feel the beginning of my climax, at first, a small tingle, then a buildup with every thrust. "Ooohhh," I moaned as my body convulsed under the command of his final thrust and his tight grip. I felt a hotness fill me. My body collapsed, but he held me gently before I felt his body slowly leave mine. "Oh God, I love you," he said as he held me against him.

Beep, beep, beep! My alarm was going off and waking me to the reality of school and children. I don't know the people I see in my dreams. Even the male I had sex with. The only thing I do know is that when I dream, I am well aware that I am on another level of consciousness. I do things I would not normally do in my waking life. What I do when I dream is as real as what I do during the day. All of my senses are heightened. The pleasure is real. I never see the people's faces, but somehow I know who my best friends and my boyfriends are supposedly and vice versa, who I need to stay away from and who will hurt me. This gift has saved my life several times.

It was time to get myself ready for work and feed my two precious cats before I headed out the door. I showered, lathering my body with candy apple body wash, and sprayed my body with a candy apple body splash before slipping into black slacks and a gray silk pullover.

I applied my natural makeup look, taught to me by the attendant at MAC Cosmetics. Of course, this makeup lesson came with a $152.00 price tag after purchasing what I needed to look fabulous daily. I wrapped my thick hair into a professional-looking French bun. Once I was pulled together, I filled the cat's food and water bowls. Both cats were sprawled on the entryway table. I kissed them on the head and grabbed the book bag I routinely left by the door.

11

I arrived early to school, hoping for a smooth day. I drove into my usual parking space and grabbed my bags. Claire's car was not in the teacher's parking lot, so I would have time to prepare for the day before she stopped to chat at my doorway as she routinely did before heading to her classroom. The cafeteria staff begins placing our breakfast bags outside our classrooms at 7:00 am daily. I opened my classroom door to bring in the breakfast bags before I did anything else. I put my purse in the closet and turned on my computer to check my e-mail for any important messages. I found nothing interesting in the mail, a teacher asking for old Christmas cards and a reminder from the counselor that Christmas Angel forms must be submitted by the scheduled deadline.

Like clockwork, the director of the Invention Convention contest had e-mailed the packet I was to distribute to the teachers. I also received a great big Thank you! from Mrs. Phillips for taking on the task. As soon as I read the Invention Convention guidelines, I printed a copy for each classroom teacher, in addition to forwarding the information via e-mail. This gives the teachers the liberty to print the number of copies they need without wasting ink and paper. As far as the timeline went, that was my first step.

Invention Convention allows students to create an invention of their own choosing. The great part of the Invention Convention is that students can enjoy being creative and have a chance of winning first, second, or third place in their grade level. The first-place winner in every grade level is then entered in the district competition. This competition takes place at another elementary school. Students whose invention wins in the district receive a small trophy and media recognition. This year a monetary prize of $500.00 will be awarded to the most scientific and the most creative inventor. It's exciting to see all of the inventions created by all of those young innovative minds.

I moved on to earlier e-mails I had received and came across a reply from Mrs. Phillips letting me know that if the Cardenas kids did not submit their permission forms, they would be staying with our music teacher, Ms. Gomez. I finished with the computer work and set it up with the school literacy program. Both of my computers were ready to go, and I was preparing the breakfast bags on the table when Claire knocked on the door that stood open. "Good morning," she said in a cheerful voice.

I turned and smiled. "Hey, how was your visit with sis? I asked.

"It was nice. It's always nice to see Jackie," she said, then changed the subject. Her expression went from cheerful to somber.

She told me that Bill would not be coming to school today. When I asked her how she knew, she said she had just seen mom enter the building leaving Bill in the car. She said when she looked over at him, he smiled and waved. She said he looked to have a black eye and some scratches on his face.

"I don't think mom will bring him to school until he looks better. She probably went to the office to tell them he would be out with the flu or some kind of virus to cover her ass from Child Protective Services."

I took a deep breath and relaxed. "Thanks for letting me know."

Claire gave me a half-smile and waved before she headed to her room.

When everyone was sitting at their seats, eating their breakfast, I reviewed the kid's folders for homework, parent notes, and in Leslie's and Mike's case, for permission slips. No permission slips. I decided that if I did not receive the forms by tomorrow, I would have to ask that they be filled out when I dismissed the kids. Maybe the driver could at least sign for the kids. I mean, it's a field trip permission slip. It's not like we are taking them out of the city. For heaven's sake, we are not even taking them out of the school zip code since the theatre sits only a few blocks away. What was it with these people? I thought to myself.

12

At 3:06 the next afternoon, Claire and I were standing at the curbside where we dismissed our students, waiting for the parents to pick up their children. At 3:05, I spotted the lady in a white Town and Country van as she drove up to the pickup area. I motioned to Claire to watch my remaining students as I approached the van. "Excuse me," I said as I raised my hand to get the driver's attention.

She was a thin Hispanic lady in a short black Bob haircut. "Good afternoon. My name is Ms. Knoes. I am Mike and Leslie's teacher. I have sent field trip permission slips home a number of times and, as of today, I have yet to receive them back. Would it be possible to take the time to fill them out now?" I raised my hand and revealed two permission slips. "I also need the form for the student in Ms. Alaniez's class."

She looked at me as if I had just held up a gun. She said, "No, no time today, maybe tomorrow. I come tomorrow," as she shook her head and looked back at the kids. As soon as they had all piled in, she maneuvered the van to move forward. I was still close enough to the van to feel it rub on my body slightly as she drove away. I stepped back quickly to keep from losing my balance.

"What was that all about?" Claire asked as she walked up to me.

My other students were picked up while I was attempting to get permission forms signed.

"I don't know. If I had to guess, I would say that driver was afraid of something."

Claire frowned. "Let's see if the secretary has anything on those kids."

We walked straight to the administrative office. Samantha pulled the kid's files and examined each one separately.

She sighed and said, "Well, the Birth Certificates look authentic, and we know they all live at the same place. They were adopted by Mr. and Mrs. Walker."

"Very well then, I will make a call and let them know that the students will be staying with Ms. Gomez if they do not want the children to attend the field trip. Their other choice would be to have the forms signed and returned tomorrow or receive new ones to complete." I smiled at Sam in frustration.

She winked. "Hang in there," she said.

"Thanks, Sam," I answered and turned to head out of the office.

Samantha is one of the most thorough clerks I have ever encountered. She has been doing her job for two decades, and she is very competent. Samantha was charming, a petite brunette with a pearly white smile, and always dressed professionally. Although she was in her late 50's, she could pass for her early '30s, easy.

Claire and I walked out of the office, satisfied, and headed toward our classrooms as if we were on a mission. Down the same hall, heading toward us was Mr. Brooks. Mr. Brooks is our school counselor. He has worked here for almost ten years. He usually wears a gray suit, skinny black tie, and white shirt, his signature look. I slapped him a high five as we passed.

"Have a great day, Ms. Knoes." he said as he continued walking in the opposite direction.

Mr. Brooks has a healthy appetite for alcohol. Most people couldn't tell if they did not know what to look for. He's what you would call a high functioning alcoholic. He stands at 5ft 11 inches, is husky, and he combs his dark hair with enough hair grease to keep every hair strand in place. He reminds me of a character straight out of a classic Italian gangster movie. The thing about Mr. Brooks is that he has many connections due to having various other careers before becoming a school counselor. He is very good at what he does, and the kids love him. He is always able to get sponsors for the school functions and speakers for our Career Day. He even has sponsors that donate food during the Thanksgiving and Christmas holidays. He has a stack of forms and a long list of calls to make every year, not to mention the significant number of families that come to the school for Thanksgiving dinner grocery boxes and Christmas gifts. The holidays are a massive task for a counselor working solo. Still, I don't recall Mr. Brooks ever complaining about his duties as our counselor.

We arrived at the turning point of the hall where I head to my classroom, and Claire continues to hers.

Claire asked, "Well, Jennifer, what do you say we call it a day?"

"Sure. Let me check my e-mail first. I have to send a trifold count to the Invention Convention Coordinator."

Claire continued to her classroom to set up for the next day and collect some work she wanted to take home. I sent an e-mail requesting 140 trifold boards. "More than enough," I thought to myself. I finished reading my e-mail and signed off my computer.

I wiped down the tables and organized the centers for the following day. I packed some papers to Grade, my lesson plans, and math Teacher's Edition in my black leather book bag. I reached Claire's room and waited for her at the doorway of her classroom.

"Come on, slowpoke, it's not like we practically live here as it is," I said, glancing at my watch.

"Go on without me; I still have to set up my centers for tomorrow," Claire hollered.

"Okay, see you bright and early," I replied and headed out the building. There were three cars in the parking lot, Mr. Brooks', Claire's, and mine. There was still daylight left, and I wanted to go by the kid's house to see if maybe, by chance, I could get a glimpse at something unusual. Perhaps I would find something that would give me a reason to visit their home. I now knew that the lady that picked them up was just a ride like a taxi. I also knew she had a lot to hide, and she was afraid.

Five minutes later, I was again approaching a middle-class neighborhood that looked quiet and serene. All of the lawns were immaculately groomed. Not one single car was parked in the street. The whole block appeared too perfect. I drove by the address of the home, which sat on a large corner lot, only to find a home with manicured landscaping and a friendly-looking snowman, obviously welcoming the holiday season. There were two huge red Poinsettia plants by the porch. Hanging in the center of a large wooden door was a colorful wreath sprinkled with small multicolored lights. As I drove around the side of the home, I could see a large playground that made the house look like Paradise Park to any child. In one corner of the large gated yard sat a huge green turtle filled with what appeared to be white sand. On the opposite side was the white sitting swing for two.

Beside the swing, I could see the large patch of dirt. Every few feet of it held up what looked like a seed packet, perhaps showing what was planted in that area, But what plants grow in the winter? I was a little confused by this scene, but since I don't know much about planting and crops, perhaps some plants will grow in freezing weather. Who knows? I thought to myself. I could see another patch of land that looked tilled. Perhaps that was for another crop to be planted later.

The garden looked cared for and picturesque. It looked creepy neat. Something about it made my headache and my stomach turn. What was going on? After circling the block a couple of times, I found nothing unusual. I decided to drive home. By now, the sun was setting. The neighborhood was still and quiet. Yet in my head, I could hear someone screaming, crying, and pleading.

"Please! Please! Please!" Innocent echoes of laughter that suddenly turned to cries, but that was just my head. I am aware of reality and imagined events. The sounds of the children could be from a distant past. They could also be from the future. Everything in the neighborhood was eerily still.

13

As I drove up the drive of my small garage apartment, I could see Jack sitting on the couch with his feet propped up, no doubt waiting on me. Oh, snap! I completely forgot we had arranged a dinner date. Fortunately, I had prepared lasagna the night before and had it ready to bake. All I had to do now was just pop it in the oven. Fixing the French bread would be a snap, and we could spend time snuggled up on the couch while dinner was in the oven. The living space consisted of a large brown sectional that made it easy for us to snuggle and relax. For my last birthday, Jack gave me a 42-inch T.V. to mount on my living room wall. He enjoys it more than I do since he spends a lot of his free time at my place.

When I walked in, I noticed that Jack was watching some home improvement show about twin brothers that sell and remodel homes. The brother dressed in a suit was clearly, the real estate agent. The other brother dressed in jeans and a plaid shirt was the builder. They were showing clients different floor plans for their new home.

I placed my black book bag and purse by a long wooden table in the entryway and dropped my car keys in a crystal bowl that sat in the center of the table. The sound of keys dropping redirected Jack's attention away from the television and toward me.

"Hey, sorry I'm late," I said apologetically. Jack opened his arms to me as he laid himself back on the couch. "Come over here, you," he said with his pearly smile, indicating he understood and all that mattered was that I was home safe. Somehow, being in his arms made the world better. My worries could wait. I wanted to forget about work and enjoy a nice quiet evening with the person I loved the most. Jack was a dream come true for me. He stood at 6'4" with short blonde hair, a body that would make a Greek god jealous, and a gorgeous smile. The best part about Jack was that he was very down to earth. I had never known what it was like to be in love and trust someone until I met Jack. Still, Jack does not know about my abilities. Someday soon, I will have to explain, but not tonight. Tonight was our time.

I met Jack on a Sunday afternoon that I will never forget. I went to Ted's Tools, the neighborhood home improvement store because I needed a blade for my small jigsaw. I was cutting large sheets of white-board at home to make little dry erase boards for the kids. I stood there, staring at the hundreds of blades for what seemed like forever. I ended up staring at the last row from the bottom. With one knee on the floor and the other up and level with the row, I was having trouble figuring out which one I needed to buy. "Can I help you?" I heard someone ask. Then I saw Jack kneel next to me in the same position. "What kind of saw do you have? I'll bet I can fix you up," he said reassuringly. I described my saw, and he handed me a small pack of blades. "This ought to do it," he said as he stood and offered his hand to help me up. He was gorgeous, and something about him made me feel completely at ease. "I'm Jack," he said with a nervous smile as he held my hand.

"Oh, I'm Jennifer," I replied and made no attempt at retrieving my hand. Jack asked me out to lunch the next day after I deliberately came in for some more blades, telling him I wanted to stock up. Jack and I have been in love since then. I adore him, and I know I am blessed to have him. Now, six months later, he can still melt my worries away with one single kiss. He tells me he wants me forever, but I have yet to hear the word marriage. The one thing that I will have to work on is changing his mind about children. We have had a heart to heart talk about someday starting a family to which he said, "No, let's not focus on babies until after the first two or three years." Perhaps he just wants to make sure we get to enjoy each other for the first few years.

We ate our lasagna and drank red wine. After dinner, we snuggled together on the couch by the fireplace. Within minutes, we were undressed and tangled with each other. We were first moving in a gentle rhythm, then in a heavy fast pace before we both collapsed with sexual release. "Oh God, I missed you," he said as he fell beside me, almost falling off the couch. We laughed and snuggled comfortably.

The next morning I arrived at school with my regular twenty minutes to spare to organize my desk, drink my thermos of coffee and take a bite of my cream cheese bagel that I managed to pack even on mornings when I am on a time crunch. I grabbed the clipboard I kept hanging right inside my classroom door that held my list of 20 tasks to do every morning. I went through the list and completed my tasks well before the little ones showed up. At 7:40, I heard the school's public address system call me. "Ms. Knoes, can you please come to the office?" "Absolutely," I replied and headed toward the administrative office.

Like a rerun of the evening before, here comes Mr. Brooks down the same hall in the opposite direction.

"Hey, fancy seeing you here," I said. I high fived him and kept walking toward the office. Upon arrival, I greeted the office staff.

"Good morning, ladies. Did someone call?" I asked with a smile on my face as I walked into the administrative office.

Samantha, the secretary, was busy at the desk greeting students and parents. She looked over at the principal's office door. "Go on in," she said, as she pointed at the door with the flower pen she held in her hand. I entered to find Mrs. Phillips and Claire talking.

"Jen, we have the field trip forms you need; all of your students will be going with you."

"Okay," I said. "We are all done with that and can now focus on other important matters."

"Ms. Knoes, thank you for your diligence. You must have made quite an impression with the driver to bring the forms signed by the parents. We even received Ms. Alaniez's student form. I appreciate the way you and Ms. Alaniez work together."

She handed me two completed field trip forms, and she gave Claire the one for her student, David. We both thanked her once again and began walking out of the office, but before we turned to exit the office, Samantha said, "Take attendance first thing, Ms. Knoes."

Poor Sam always had to remind me to take attendance. I was getting better at it, but the reminders did not hurt.

"I'm on it," I answered and headed down the hall.

Although Samantha was very patient with me, she's not one on whose hit list I would like to be on. Crazy things could happen when the head of the office is not on your side. Things like not getting supplies requested, having the purchase order for our next field trip delayed, or worse, misplaced. Lost forms would be very, very possible if you ever got on her bad side.

Claire and I walked side by side down the hallway. "Let's get ourselves to our class before the last bell rings, and we have a slew of kids out in the halls," I said. We walked down the hall at a fast pace and arrived at our classroom door right on time.

Two of my parents had brought in the breakfast bags and had begun serving the kiddos for me. One parent was walking around with a pair of scissors opening small waffle syrup tubes, while the other helped them open their waffle packages. My classroom parents are lifesavers. The kids ate their breakfast at their desks and cleaned up when they finished. They had the morning routine down to a science: eat breakfast, clean up, and complete the morning work on their desks. As soon as the children were all seated and eating, I took attendance; Bill was absent. After about twenty minutes, the children had finished with their breakfast, cleaned their area, and turned in their completed morning work.

I rang a small brass bell to indicate to the students that it was time to start our morning. Every morning began with a get- ready song to get the kids into school learning mode. "Okay, kids, turn and find a partner," I said enthusiastically. The kids paired up and followed the song instructions of clap-clap, shake hands with your partner, hug your partner, and get ready to learn. When the song ended, the kids automatically dropped onto their designated space on the carpet and prepared for the morning reading lesson and this week's vocabulary. This week we were learning about weather and the winter season.

While my Promethean board read the literacy book of the morning, I walked around and monitored. Promethean boards were introduced to our classrooms five years ago. It is a full-screen board 7 feet wide and 6 feet tall. I program it to read the book of the day for the week. Today it was "Wilber the Penguin." Once the board has read the story in its entirety, it will ask questions I have programmed in, followed by introducing the weekly vocabulary. The Promethean board is used for numerous classroom tasks that include grading, testing, interactive games, and photoshoots. It allows face chat with classrooms in other parts of the world. Looking back, I don't know what I did without it.

All was going well. Students were diligently working on their alphabet letter, Ww. Snow was in the weather forecast for today, and I recalled the weatherman on the radio stating snowfall would begin after 9 am and continue until noon. The snow was expected to stick. Inside, I was feeling almost as excited as my students get when they see snow. My classroom has an entire wall of windows, so this morning I kept the blinds up so the children could witness the snowfall as part of their winter weather lesson. As predicted, the snow flurries began falling like thick white feathers at 9:05 am. The kids were enjoying watching the falling snowflakes through the window. They enjoyed it so much that I had to ask them to start counting the snowflakes. When they counted twenty snowflakes, they were to add two more. At least if they were going to look out the window, they would be practicing their counting.

After an hour of heavy snow, the playground was a winter wonderland. I decided I would take the students outside to enjoy the snow for 3 minutes. What better way to learn than to experience what we are learning?

"I want to make a snow angel," I heard little Leo tell Leslie.

Mike hollered, "I'm gonna make me a snowman!"

"Okay, listen up!" I said in a firm tone. "I will give you three minutes to make a snow angel."

I knew the principal would not see us because she was in a meeting in a windowless room for the next hour and the vice principal was out of the building until tomorrow. I also knew I had to time it perfectly so other teachers would not see my little ones running around in the snow.

"When I blow my whistle, I want all of you lined up and ready to come back inside. Does everyone understand?"

In unison, they answered, "Yes, ma'am."

I lined up the students and headed down the hall toward the courtyard. Coming out of a classroom and walking in the same direction, I met the PTA president.

"Hey Nicole, how's it going?" I asked.

"Oh great!" she replied. "I am setting up baskets of fruit in the lounge for teachers to take and use for their Christmas classroom activities."

"Wow! That is so sweet and cool of the PTA to do that for us." I said thankfully.

"Oh, it's not us. We have this very cool parent that sends fruits and vegetables every season, it seems," she said.

I had noticed the apples and pumpkins in the fall and the tomatoes, strawberries, and peaches in the spring.

"I always just thought it was the PTA providing those for us," I said with surprise.

"Oh, they have been doing this since their kids registered a few years ago. Now that is a parent dedicated to keeping the teachers happy," she said, displaying her large yellow stained teeth that looked too large for her mouth.

Perhaps her teeth looked too big because her body and face were so thin. She stood at about 5ft 9 inches tall, but her figure type was spaghetti: long, skinny and plain, which reminded me of a tall Goldie Hawn on crack. The fact that she liked wearing pastel colors in vertical stripes did not help any.

"Okay, I'll talk to you later, Nicole. Thanks for doing all this work for us." I smiled and waved as I escorted my students out of the building.

The children laughed and frolicked into the courtyard. As soon as they reached a large flat patch of snow, they began to throw themselves in the snow and move their tiny arms in a flapping motion to make angel wings. They ran, laughed, and jumped around in delight. In groups of two and three, they would stand and find a clear patch and repeat the process of making snow angels. A group of three girls stuck out their tongues, trying to catch the fat icy flakes. I asked the kids to limit themselves to 2 snow angels. Most obeyed my request; others lost all control once they were outside. After five minutes, I brought the children in and lined them up to hang their jackets and wash their hands before starting their lesson.

They were to draw the winter scenery outside the window and think of the clothes people wear in cold weather. After drawing their scenery, they were to write two or three sentences describing their picture. While some drew and colored, I called the children five at a time to my table and helped them with brainstorming ideas for what to write in their journals. We talked about beginning their sentences with a capital letter and ending each sentence with a period. Some students went to the word wall, an alphabetical wall I keep with vocabulary picture cards. Leo took the picture of a snowman from under the letter S and a picture of mittens from under the letter M. After forty minutes, everyone was finished with their writing and colorful picture of their winter scenery.

"Okay, children, on the carpet. I'm going to read a very exciting book about winter,"

The students listened and shared how some of the pictures in the book looked like the scenery they drew in their journals. After a discussion of the book and reviewing vocabulary, I allowed them time to discuss with a friend what they liked most about winter.

I realized it was almost time for lunch. The kids all lined up to use the restroom and wash their hands. When everyone was back in their seat, I called the

Innocent Echoes

students to the lunch line. Leslie and Mike always brought their lunch, so they usually line up first and lead the rest of the class single file to the cafeteria. Today, I carried my lunch that I had prepared this morning. On days when chicken nuggets are the main course, I bring my lunch. Today I brought a Peanut Butter and Jelly sandwich, a banana, and some almond milk in a short silver thermos. I am not crazy about fried foods, let alone chicken nuggets that don't even look like chicken. The kids, however, love it when chicken nuggets are on the menu. Today I can be sure they will eat all of their lunch, and I will have nobody playing or getting out of their seat. I sat between Leslie and Mike and enjoyed a quiet lunch. I noticed that they had packed a pretty healthy lunch for both of them. Their lunches consisted of a turkey sandwich, a pouch of grapes, 100% orange juice, baked potato chips, and a bottle of water. Since lunch was only 30 minutes, the students ate quickly and quietly. The rest of the afternoon went pretty smoothly.

After lunch, the students went to P.E. (Physical Education). Once I pick them up from specials, they only have 1 hour of Math and thirty minutes of Science and Social Studies, which consists of a ten minute lesson and twenty minutes at their designated centers. Before I knew it, it was time to line up for dismissal.

I walked out into the hallway to find Delmon, our custodian, rolling a cart piled with trifold boards straight toward me.

"Ms. Knoes, I believe these are for you. Sam said she did not have space for these in the office and asked me to bring them to you."

"Okay, thanks. Will you roll the cart by my door? I will be back in later to distribute them to the teachers."

"Sure thing Ms. Knoes, sure thing," Delmon replied. My students were still in line and followed me out of the building to the pickup area. Like a rerun of the days before, the lady in the white van drove up, picked up the students, and sped off.

I arrived home from school tired and ready to relax for a while. I lay down on my very comfortable sectional for all of ten minutes before I received a call from my best friend, Katy. Katy is the only one who knows I am a little unique. I have never told her the whole story about anything. I keep that to myself. Perhaps someday she will figure it out; then again, what does it matter?

"Hey, can I ask you a question?" she asked.

For some strange reason, she took the liberty of using me like an Ouija board. She would call me once or twice a day to ask me questions until she was satisfied. Then she would hang up. The good thing about Katy is that when I needed anything, she was always able to help. She had rich friends, average friends, friends in low places, and unique friends in low places if you understand my meaning.

"What's up, Katy?" I asked.

"I have a question," she said.

"Do you think I will meet my Mr. Right this year?"

I laughed and answered, "Katy, you met one Mr. Right three months ago, remember? You kicked him out over some ridiculous argument."

"Oh yeah, well, what are the chances he'll come back?" she asked.

"Next month, you'll run into another Mr. right. He will have green eyes, so dress well when you go out to eat with your friends."

"Okay, thanks," she said, and hung up the phone.

I waited by the phone. It rang again. I picked it up and said, "In two weeks!"

"Okay!" Katy replied, and she hung up the phone.

Lately, she forgets to even say hello or how are you. It's all about her. I get upset sometimes, but then I let it go because I know that she is not aware of how her attitude has changed. She is delightful and always does her best to help. Perhaps I feel it's a one-way road because I have been lucky enough to not need anything from her lately. Last year, I was watching an infomercial about an exercise program that helped lift your butt. I called Katy the next morning, gave her the exercise program's name, and told her it was a six-disc set. I wanted to know if she could get me the program cheaper. "No problem," she said. "I will have it for you in a week." She always delivers. I have never asked her how or who. I do know that she has a dark past, but I also know she will never hurt me.

Katy is single and works as an office coordinator in a medical clinic. She stands at 5 foot 4 inches and is small framed. Petite, you might say. Her bust line, on the other hand, is not so petite. She and Dolly Parton would be running a close race if anyone ever compared the two. She wears her dark brown hair in a professional French Roll that always looks tight and neat. Katy is very smart and has excellent people skills. She is definitely in the right profession, but as smart as she is, Katy has one major problem. The problem is that she rejects good men and falls for the complete losers. She finds the ones looking for a mother, not a wife, or the ones that want a mistress whose money they can spend on other women. Last year, she fell for an alcoholic. Not just an alcoholic, but an alcoholic who was married and had children living in another country. I believe that in her innocent, naive way of thinking, she thought she could change him. She started to see his true colors when he began to threaten to beat her. When the beatings during his drunken fits of rage began, she realized that she was in a cesspool of crap. Unfortunately, the poor choices flaw is something only she can fix. Until now, she has not been able to separate the good, the bad, and the ugly when it comes to men. I love Katy like a sister, and I am always there for her, but I also do my best to stay out of her business as a good sister should. She seems to attract drama, and losers like lights attract insects and nasty bugs.

15

After talking to Katy and leaving her satisfied with the answers she was seeking, I made myself comfortable on my couch and dialed the Lake Worth Police Department. I was unsure if I would find Rachel, but I figured now was the best time, if any, to try.

The phone was answered on the second ring with, "Lake Worth Police Department, is this an emergency?" a woman with a raspy voice asked.

If I were asked to guess, I would say she was in her 50s and smoked a pack of unfiltered Camels a day.

"I would like to speak to Officer Rachel Brinks, please."

"May I ask what this is about?" she asked.

"No, ma'am, you may not," I replied sternly.

"Stand by, please," she said.

She clicked a button or switch that did not cut her off completely because I heard her very irritated voice yell out, "Hey Jason, tell Officer Brinks there is a smart-ass on the phone who wants to talk to her."

Minutes later, I heard Rachel's unforgettable voice.

"Officer Brinks speaking, how can I help you?"

Just the sound of her voice made me smile.

"You know, with your straight-arrow attitude, I pictured you becoming a nun or marine animal activist saving whales somewhere in the Pacific," I said.

There was a short silence, and then she laughed that crazy laugh I have missed for so long. I knew she would recognize my voice.

"With your collaborative learning and rule-bending, I pictured you being incarcerated by now. I see your bedside manner hasn't changed. It took you all of two minutes to piss off our dispatch," she replied.

We both laughed.

"Jennifer! How the hell have you been? I have missed you, old friend! It seems like a million years since I last saw you! A partner in crime like you is hard to find, you know? My life has been lacking adventure since graduation. How did you know I was in Lake Worth? I just transferred here from D.C. a couple of weeks ago."

"I didn't know you were here. I saw you on the 10 o'clock news investigating that robbery that ended with two people dead," I answered.

"Oh, that's an interesting case, to say the least. We have our work cut out for us on that one," she said.

"So, what's your situation?" I asked. "Married? Single? Divorced with kids? What?"

Rachel laughed, "No way to married! Hell no to divorced! A big no way in hell to divorced with kids!

"Come on, girl, you taught me better than that!" she said. "Single. That's me, and I love every minute of it. In a few years, maybe not so much, but for now, I'm okay as a party of one. What about you?" she asked.

"I'm single also and, like you, I like it. I do have a boyfriend that allows me my freedom." Rachel laughed. Well, I'm in no big hurry to clean up after someone and wash extra laundry. I'm good," she said.

"Rachel, can we meet to talk and catch up?" I asked

"That would be great, Jen. Just say when and where," she said enthusiastically, "I am glad you called, girl; I can't wait to see you."

I could tell by her tone that she was smiling. I pictured her with her tight bun and pink lipstick. "Hey, just do me a favor. Don't call and piss off our dispatch again. She is a royal pain in the ass on a good day. Besides, she deliberately screws up our coffee when she is in a bad mood. If I could make it myself, I would, but I burn water." she said and laughed. "Okay, I promise to be nice," I assured her. We set our meeting time and place. I said goodbye and hung up the phone, still smiling.

16

The first few months went smoothly, but school days were moving fast. I had volunteered to help with the holiday program before I knew Ms. Gomez would be in charge. I figured I would survive two hours. Besides, we would be so busy Ms. Gomez would not have time to chat with me. There aren't many teachers that offer to stay after hours to volunteer. Most of them have young children, and I don't blame them for trying just to get home. Since the program is last week before our Christmas break, I will not be bombarded with tests and grades. Grades will be due two weeks after we return, so as long as I'm caught up, I will be able to stay on schedule. I don't like being behind on posting grades, and staying aligned with what should be taught and when is very important. Some people don't understand the rigid schedule and how critical it is until they are affected by a move to a new school. Our curriculum is aligned so that if a child leaves and begins class in a new school, it will be as if he never left. The lessons will be covering the same concept. That prevents a child from going to another school and being completely lost, not understanding what is being taught because he did not receive the foundation for it. Grades are another task that can't be taken lightly.

Today, we have parent portals that allow parents to stay informed regarding student's grades. If a teacher gets too far behind, inevitably, there will be a handful of parents complaining about unposted grades to the principal, or worse, the school superintendent. Some parents don't give teachers a break, so I work late every single day. Some days it's a miracle I stay sane and in control. Our last Republican presidents, considering their wealth of education from Ivy League Colleges, didn't understand that every child and family is different. Sometimes the more educated people are, the faster simple common sense goes out the window. After all the training, meetings, hundreds of grades, parent/teacher conferences and intervention for failing students as well as extended hours spent on lesson preparation and center preparation, "No Child Left Behind" seems to translate to "No teacher left with a behind after sitting for hours doing paperwork."

To my surprise, the day went well. Mike and Leslie showed up with their backpacks and homework ready. During the day, routines went as scheduled, and the children were now at a level where they felt comfortable with each other. I noticed they didn't whine or bicker about partners. They just seemed to turn, choose a partner, and enjoy the morning. Mike and Leslie were never a problem. They always had a partner, and they both worked well with the other children. They were both very polite and considerate of the others.

Although the day was uneventful, I was still worried about Bill. I asked the children to put up their math puzzles, and I lined them up for dismissal.

It was quitting time for me. I grabbed my purse and noticed the Christmas Angel forms on my table that I forgot to place in the kid's folders. I will need to do it first thing in the morning to meet the deadline for returning the forms. I better not forget, I thought to myself. I locked my door and headed to the front exit. I encountered Mr. Brooks coming down the hall. The holidays were always stressful for school counselors.

"Good to see you, Mr. Brooks!" I smiled and held out my hand for our usual high five as we crossed paths. I stopped briefly as I felt emptiness come over me. The feeling I usually get when a good friend or family member moves far away.

17

The next morning started like many other days. The breakfast bags were sitting on a small table, and the children were trickling in. They placed their folder in a tub by the door and walked straight to the board where they choose their lunch for the day. Bill came to school today in a long sleeve shirt. The scratches on his face had healed, and the black eye Claire had mentioned was gone. He had taken and eaten his morning breakfast, and now he came up to me as I sat at my computer preparing to take roll.

"Teacher, may I have another breakfast if we have extra?" he asked in a whisper.

"Sure, just give me a minute to check something, okay?" I whispered back.

"Okay," He whispered and smiled as he walked back to his seat at his table.

After everyone who was going to have breakfast had eaten, I checked the breakfast bag. My breakfast was still available. I called Bill and gave him the thumbs up. He knew what that meant. He smiled and went to the breakfast bags. He took a package of waffles, an apple sauce cup, and a small box of raisins and put them in his backpack.

Ms. Bernadette, our librarian, who was walking by the classroom, noticed Bill putting breakfast in his backpack. She peeked in.

"Hey Jen, are kids supposed to take food home? They're not supposed to, right?" she asked, gesturing over at Bill with her head.

"You are correct, Ms. Bernadette, but all children are supposed to have dinner daily as well," I replied.

"Ahhh, I get it, "she said, smiling as she walked away.

School policy is that breakfast food should not be removed from the classroom. What the kids do not eat goes in the trashcan, or I return it to the cafeteria, and they dispose of it. I figure if I am going to get in trouble for giving food to a child whom I am certain does not eat once he leaves my classroom at three, then so be it. Ms. Bernadette had learned to understand my rule-bending actions, and I am sure sometimes even agreed with them.

This week we were studying shelters in Science and families in Social Studies. We had discussed shelters early in the week, and now we were going to discuss families and the shelters they live in.

"Okay, everyone to the carpet," I said, motioning the kids to come and sit around my rocking chair.

I was reading a short picture book about shelters and families from around the world to refresh their memory about what we were studying. After the read aloud, we began discussing families.

"Who would like to tell us about their family? Andy, would you like to go first?" Andy was slim and tan with big brown eyes. He wore a haircut that looked like someone hand placed a bowl on his head and cut around it. He stood up and said in a monotone voice, "I have two parents that love and take care of me. I live in a big house close to the school. That's all." Then he plopped himself down on the carpet.

"Thank you, Andy, good job," I said.

The kids were playing with their feet when one of Leslie's black canvas shoes slipped off. It was then that I noticed the letter "B" written on the bottom of her toe.

"Who would like to go next?" I continued as if I had not seen a thing.

Everyone shared something about their family except Mike and Leslie, who appeared nervous about the subject and did not volunteer to speak. We finished in time to line up for lunch. The students walked single file, and I walked next to the last one, keeping an eye on the group. I stood at the entry of the cafeteria and watched them march into the serving line.

"There you are," I heard Claire's voice behind me.

"What's up, Claire?"

"Jen, my student David, you know Mr. and Mrs. Walker's, kid, is acting strange."

"What do you mean?" I asked.

"Well, I found some cans of fruit and pudding cups we had collected for the food drive hidden in his backpack. He normally brings his lunch from home. Yesterday, I decided to eat with the kids, and I sat next to him. His lunch consisted of 100% vegetable juice, a plain yogurt, some baby carrots, and a dry turkey breast sandwich on what looked like pita bread. He also had a bottle of water. He picked it up, opened it, and said, "I better finish my water. Mrs. Walker gets really mad when I don't eat all of my lunch and drink my water." Claire fixed her eyes on me. "It's weird, Jen. He steals food and shoves it in his backpack like he's deprived or something. We both know Mr. and Mrs. Walker are very well off. Anyone can tell by that huge house they live in. He does not look starved by any means. He looks very fit and healthy."

"Should we call home and talk to Mr. and Mrs. Walker about this?" Claire asked.

"And say what?" I answered. "You're keeping your kid too healthy. No, there's something weird going on, and it's a lot deeper than we think," I said.

"Claire, have you covered shelters in your classroom yet?"

"A little, yes, but we have not gone into depth about it."

"Okay. Today during social Studies class, ask the kids to share about their families. Let me know what David says. Leslie and Mike shared nothing about their home and family life. I also noticed the letter "B" on the bottom of Leslie's toe in marker or something. Keep me posted, please."

I turned and started down the hall.

"Where are you going?" I heard Claire ask. "I'm going to see Mr. Brooks. Maybe he can talk to the kids for us. He can bring a book about stealing and get the message to the kids in a gentle way. He's good at that."

I approached the counselor's office door and was just getting ready to knock when I noticed the door was open a few inches. Before I could push the door open, I heard Mr. Brooks' voice in a tone I had never heard before.

"Look, I have given you what you wanted, and I'm not going any further. You lied to me! Enough is enough! Go to hell! I don't give a damn what you do. I'm not losing my family because of you!"

He slammed the phone down so hard the whole room seemed to vibrate.

I could hear Mr. Brooks mumbling something, but I couldn't make out what it was. I decided I would wait to talk to him later or on another day when smoke was not blowing out of both ears. Something told me I was running out of time, but I was hopeful. I was hoping I had time. I could still hope, couldn't I?

Innocent Echoes

I walked back to my classroom to prepare some color cardstock signs I needed to post in the auditorium. I grabbed some fat black markers and sat at my reading table. All I needed were seven signs, Pink for Kindergarten, Green for 1st Grade, Blue for 2nd Grade, Yellow for 3rd Grade, and Purple for 4th Grade, White for 5th Grade, and Orange for Class Projects. I finished writing the signs and walked down the hall. Except for this time, I did not pause at Mr. Brooks' door. I headed straight to the auditorium before I ran late.

18

That afternoon, I picked up the kids from the cafeteria and walked them single file to the auditorium for a fifteen-minute recess. I noticed that Bill was wearing the same clothes two days in a row and they were looking very dirty. A white shirt on a first grader for two days is very easy to notice. If I had not noticed the stains, I would not have been able to ignore the stench of cigarette smoke and stale food that followed him like a cloud. I had my class sitting in a circle, preparing to play a game of duck duck goose. I looked over to see Claire doing the same with her class on the other side of the auditorium.

The game of Duck Duck Goose requires the first child to stand and walk around the outside of the circle while touching each child he passes on the head, saying, "Duck, duck, duck." When he says "Goose," the person whose head he touched last would get up and chase him. If he were tagged, he would have to sit in the middle of the circle, and the other child would then repeat the process. If the person tapping the kids on the head reached his space after running around once, he was safe. My kids had been playing this game for a few weeks now, so they had it down pat. Leo was walking around the outside of the circle, saying, "Duck, duck, goose," tapping Bill on the head.

Bill looked up and said, "Aww, I'm kind of tired. Can you tap someone else so I can rest?"

Leo complied and kept moving. He tapped Charlie, and they went running!

"Go! Go! Go!" the kids screamed, cheering Charlie on. He reached his place before Leo tagged him.

Leo started again, "Duck, duck, duck."

"Hey Claire, how is it going?" I asked cheerfully.

"Oh, things are moving right along," she replied.

I looked over at the circle of children playing and saw Claire's student, David, running. Boy, that kid was fast. There was no way he was ever getting tagged. The kids chanted, "Go, David! Go, David!"

"Claire, your student, is fast," I said in amazement.

After David reached his space, I called to him.

"Come here, little fella."

He stood and began running toward me. Ten feet before he reached me, he stepped on something that stung his foot.

"Ouch!" He hollered, and I reached to catch him before he fell to the floor. I gently sat him on the carpeted auditorium floor. "I think something cut my foot," David cried.

I removed his shoe and sock. He had stepped on a tack that went through the sole of his shoe but barely punctured his foot.

"Oh, you'll be okay," I said. "It's just a scratch. It must have been the sudden poke that shocked your little foot."

I looked at his toe, and to my horror, I saw the letters B.P. written on his big toe in blue ink about half an inch tall. He quickly pulled his foot back away from me and began to put on his socks and shoes. Pretending not to notice the print, I stood and sent him back to his group.

Claire blew the coach whistle she wore around her neck and lined up her students. She said she would send David to the nurse just in case the puncture was deeper than we thought. I waved my kids in, and they walked single file toward the classroom. The kids settled in their seats and began to get busy with the math work at their table. This week the kids were working on spatial reasoning problems using a tub of math manipulatives I had at each table. The kids love to work with geometric tiles. They get very creative and don't even know they are learning math. I turned on the Promethean board and began the lesson by introducing a game that detailed the math concept they would be learning this week. All went well. They played their math game, watched the video, and worked in pairs to complete their lessons after their guided practice. The students had moved ahead and were now working on their shelter drawings and family posters. They were to drawing their families and quietly discussing when Claire peeked in.

"Hey, Ms. Knoes," she said, waving her hand and gesturing for me to come to the door.

I walked over to where Claire stood.

"I just passed by Mr. Brooks' office, and he seems torn up about something. I guess it's his wife giving him hell. Rumor has it that he's on the brink of a divorce. Oh, remind me later that I have to tell you something important."

I could see a cloud of worry on her face.

"I know, Claire. I walked by earlier, and he had it out with her. Boy, he was sure letting her have it, though." I said in a whispering voice. Then I remembered, "Oh, Claire. Did you ask David about his family and shelter?" I asked.

"Yes. That's why I was going to see Mr. Brooks. David says he lives in a big house with his parents, two brothers, and one sister.

"That's pretty normal. We know that," I said.

"This is the strange part. He finished by saying that is not his stay-home." Claire looked at me, confused.

"That's strange. The forms Sam showed me don't say anything about them being foster kids. As far as the paperwork goes, Mr. and Mrs. Walker are their adoptive parents," I responded.

"I am a little concerned about our kids. I don't think we have time to wait on Mr. Brooks. Maybe someone else can help talk to the kids."

"We can ask Mrs. Flor, I said.

Mrs. Flor was in the classroom next to mine, and she was very wise when it came to approaching children.

"Why? He's just going through a tough divorce. He'll get over it." Claire said. "Besides, he's had so many professions and has so many friends; he'll probably bounce back quickly."

"You're right," I said. "After the bell rings and the kids are gone, let's stop by and cheer him up."

"Cheer him up with what? A jeans pass?" She said sarcastically.

Jeans Passes are routinely given to teachers as a reward for something well done. It allows the teacher with the pass to wear jeans to work any day of the week. The principal is the only one who has the authority to give the passes. We get them for having perfect attendance or for donating to a charitable cause. Last year I received ten passes for donating more than $100 dollars to the United Way Foundation.

"From the way, he sounded this morning; I would say he needs a Tony's Bar pass instead," I said.

Innocent Echoes

Claire looked at her watch, "Gotta go. I will talk to you later." She turned and started heading down the hall to her classroom.

I decided to go to the office and ask Sam to announce that all inventions should be taken to the auditorium no later than next Friday before winter break. Inventions should be displayed no later than 11:00 am. and have the proper forms attached, or the judges will not judge them.

"Hey Sam, can you announce this before school lets out?"

I handed her the piece of paper where I had written the information.

"Sure, Ms. Knoes. I can take care of that for you right now. Just give me a minute."

She turned and powered on her microphone to the intercom system.

"Teachers, please pardon this interruption. Students participating in this year's Invention Convention, please take your inventions to the auditorium and place them underneath the sign with your grade level. Grade level signs are posted on the auditorium walls. Inventions are due by next Friday before winter break, no later than 11:00 am. If you have any questions, please contact Ms. Knoes. Thank you."

She turned to me and winked.

19

Claire and I waited until all of our students had been picked up. We walked into the building and headed toward Mr. Brooks' office. We were both anxious to arrange a meeting between Mr. Brooks and my kids to see if he could find out what was going on at home and why David was hoarding food.

When Claire and I turned the corner, we saw Mr. Brooks with his leather satchel in one hand as he locked his office door with the other.

"Hello, ladies." He looked over at us and smiled his signature sideways smile. "I'm on my way to a meeting," he said in a professional tone as he turned the doorknob to make sure it was locked.

He turned in the direction of the front door and walked slowly at first. Claire and I walked with him.

"Mr. Brooks, we would like to arrange a meeting between you and some of our students," Claire said.

"Great! Not a problem. Let's talk more Monday," he said as he looked at his watch and increased his pace.

Claire and I stopped walking alongside him. It was apparent he was in a hurry wanted to shake us off his tail. We watched Mr. Brooks turn the corner of the building and disappear.

I sighed. "Well, Claire, what do you say we call it a day?" I said.

"I still have to prepare for Monday," Claire answered.

I decided I would work in my room, as well.

I cleaned up the desktops and organized my room. I was staring at my aquarium fish chasing each other before stopping to play what looked like a kissing game. I signed onto my computer, checked my e-mail for the last time, and filed my report. Claire came in just as I was completing the final section.

"I'm all done," I said in a victorious tone.

"Want to stop at Tony's for a cold drink?" she asked.

"Oooh yeah," I replied and grabbed my purse off the reading table where I usually worked.

It had been a long week, and we both deserved a Tony's Pina Colada. Tony's was the best.

"Okay. Let's just have one, then head to our empty apartments," Claire said.

We both laughed. We happened to like being able to call our own shots for now. We decided we would drive in our own cars and meet there. I climbed into my car and checked text messages on my phone before heading out.

The weather was colder now. Consequently, we were expecting freezing rain mixed with possible snow this evening. The weather was freezing yesterday as well, and a short drizzle caused plenty of accidents on the slippery roads. The weather in Texas can change as quickly and as often as a woman changes her shoes.

"If the weather is sunny one day and snowing the next, you're probably in Texas!" I heard the radio announcer say as he gave the weather forecast for the evening and tomorrow morning. Tony's was about a 10-minute drive. Traffic was unusually light for a Friday evening. Perhaps people were trying to stay in to avoid any accidents or getting stranded on the ice. I drove slow and watched out for the other cars.

It's incomprehensible why some drivers, even knowing the hazardous conditions, still drive at very high speeds. Some cars were snaking between lanes. Just ahead, I could see two fire trucks, two ambulances, and a slew of police cars. Emergency crews were scrambling to rescue people in a six-car pile-up on the opposite side of the highway. Lucky for me, the visibility was still reasonably clear. I kept driving silently, saying a short prayer for the victims and families involved as I went on my way. In my heart, I knew some children had died, and some adults were very hurt. I remained focused on the road. When I had passed the accident, and all was quiet, I drove slowly to meet Claire.

20

Tony's was a small but classy pub where not many teachers went. It rendered the privacy and quiet Claire, and I preferred after hours. The best part of meeting at Tony's was that it's only ten minutes from my house and ten minutes from Claire's place in the opposite direction.

The waitresses were pleasant and conservatively dressed in white shirts, black slacks, and pink bow ties. They all appeared to be tall and slim. Their makeup was perfect and clean. It was almost too perfect. It was kind of creepy in a way if you thought too much about it. You'd begin to think the Stepford wives were all employees here. The music for that night was country. It seemed someone had loaded the jukebox with quarters and had chosen a collection of sad, cheating, and bleeding heart country songs.

Claire had arrived first. She waved at me when I walked in. She sat in a small booth just big enough for two people. The booth was red and reminded me of the old sixties booths. It also had a mini jukebox in the middle. For a quarter, you could choose one song. For two quarters you could choose three songs.

I slid into the booth, and before I could say a word, Claire said, "I already ordered our drinks and paid for them since we are just having one. It's my treat."

"Thanks. I'll cover your morning duty next week," I said.

She laughed. We don't have morning duty in our building.

We quietly started to discuss what we would be doing on our two whole weeks off.

"I think I'm going to hang with my big sister," Claire said. "What about you?"

"Jack and I are planning a brief getaway."

"Are you and Jack serious? Claire asked with a hint of concern.

Before I could reply, the waitress showed up with two Piña Coladas.

"What a beautiful sight," I said as I reached to take mine.

Claire reached for hers and took one large sip.

"Mmmm! These are like heaven," she said as she leaned back in her booth, holding her drink in her hands.

Claire took the cherry off the top of her drink and was about to pop it in her mouth when she stopped, put it down on her napkin on the table, and said, "There's something I have to tell you." I leaned in with my drink in one hand while my other elbow rested on the table.

"Tell me," I encouraged her.

"Last week, I went to visit my sister at the Halston Hotel. She is the night manager there. It was her birthday, so I dropped in at around 8:00 pm. As I walked down the long hall, I passed the dining room."

Claire stopped and looked at me sadly.

"What are you trying to tell me, Claire?"

"I stopped and looked into the dining area because I heard a familiar voice."

"What voice, Claire?" I asked.

"It was from Jack. He was having dinner with a brunette I have never seen. It seems they were engaged in light conversation."

Claire had only seen Jack a couple of times when he showed up at school to bring me lunch. Perhaps she was mistaken.

"Are you and Jack having problems, Jen?"

I felt my face flush, but inside, I was sure it probably was not Jack. Perhaps it was someone that resembled him. Hotel dining rooms are dim, and sometimes lighting can be deceiving.

"No, we are not having any problems. I am sure that if it was Jack, he had a good reason".

I put on my confident face and started to change the subject. I glanced at Claire.

"Okay," I said.

Claire was still and did not respond. She was looking in the direction of a dim, far corner of the bar.

"Look over there," she whispered.

I followed her eyes to the same spot. There, in the corner booth, was a man that had already had way too much to drink, summoning the waitress to bring him another shot of whatever he was drinking. The waitress politely ignored him.

"Whoa, that's Mr. Brooks. What's he doing here?" I whispered.

Claire said, "That wife of his must be putting him through some serious hell."

Claire reached for the cherry she had placed on her napkin and plopped it in her mouth. After 45 minutes of discussing how fast the year was going and our plans for Christmas break, we finished our drinks, grabbed our purses, and started to head out the door. Mr. Brooks was passed out in his booth.

"Well, at least we don't have school tomorrow. He's going to need that time to recover from his hangover," Claire said as we exited the bar.

"It must have been a bad meeting for him to be this desperate to forget," Claire said as we both walked out into the dark night. "Or, maybe this was his meeting," I thought to myself.

Claire had parked right up front, and I had managed to get parking next to hers. I drove a gray Lexus, courtesy of Jack. Claire drove her red convertible. We both had our keys in our hands. Claire turned to me.

"See you on Monday."

She leaned over and hugged me. I told Claire to go straight home.

"Yes, ma'am," she said sarcastically with a military salute.

She smiled and climbed into her car. I waited until she was buckled and ready to leave before I began to drive towards home. Claire and I live on opposite poles, but that never seems to get in the way of what we have planned together.

I drove home without the radio. I needed quiet time to think and sort through what Claire had said. Claire and I had stuck together through thick and thin. She was the first friend I made when I started working at Coronado Elementary. Claire knew almost everything about me, except that I could sometimes read her thoughts as if she were talking aloud. I do my best to stay focused when that happens. Perhaps someday, I would have to come clean and let her know more about me. For now, I had kids and a Mr. and Mrs. Walker I was determined to figure out.

I arrived home to be greeted by my two cats in the foyer. No doubt, they were expecting dinner. I placed my keys in the crystal bowl and bags beside the entryway table. It was a long day. I showered and climbed into bed. I wished to sleep peacefully and hoped I would not dream.

My dreams are always about or with people I do not know. Once during one of my dreams, I sat with a male artist who was instructing me on how to best duplicate the Mona Lisa painting I had sitting on my easel in my art room. He gave me advice, pointers, and encouragement. The next day, I knew how to layer the oil paints so that they would not smear, and I completed my painting in record time. Another time, I was preparing to paint a picture of Jesus praying on a large rock. In my sleep, I was assured that all would be well if I just had faith in my God-given talent. God must have given it to me because I have never taken an art class in my life, nor have I studied art or how to oil paint in any form. I just pick up the brush and do what I want. The next day I set up my picture of Jesus praying on the rock, and I began to paint. As promised, my brush moved swiftly and quickly as if someone was guiding my hand. The results were beautiful.

Sometimes, my dreams are weeks or months long. A weekend for me could feel like months. I dread long weekends off from work because I sometimes forget by Monday what I was trained to do on the previous Thursday. To me, it feels like I have been away for months or weeks, not just two or three days. For this reason, I have to re-read notes and keep a notebook with my school passwords. I have become accustomed to re-learning. I also have to pay attention during meetings so I will remember what I have learned just in case I go on a 3-month dream that night. I have accustomed myself to sleeping only 3 to 4 hours a night in hopes of avoiding those dreams. Some nights I don't sleep at all.

21

Monday morning, my alarm went off at 6:00 am. I reached over to turn it off and climbed out of bed wearing my nightly pajamas, which consisted of a muscle top and panties. I grabbed a clean towel from the cabinet outside the bathroom and took my morning shower. I had some answers, bad ones. It is normal for me to wake up knowing things and places I have never visited. Once I dined in a quaint French café with a friend. I remember the delicious aroma of fresh pastries and rich coffees. I remember the smell of the air that early morning I visited the café and the sounds around me. Months later, while scanning a Travel Magazine left in the teacher's lounge, I came across a picture of the café and the waiter who served me.

Often I have answers to problems I have been thinking about. Katy will sometimes ask me questions like, "Do you think I should change my job? Or I'm thinking of moving to this area, what do you think?" I usually tell her I will have to think about it. The next day, I will confidently tell her a job change would be a bad idea since she is in for a raise. I might tell her that the area she wants to move to is not safe for her. Sometimes, I wake up knowing things I can't explain or prove. Last month, I woke up with the knowledge that there is not one but three more galaxies besides our own out there in the mysterious place we call Space. I also woke up with the knowledge that there are 12 planets in our solar system that can inhabit life, not the number we presume to be correct. I have learned to keep these things to myself. I play it safe by asking questions and not jumping to conclusions. In the end, I appear to be just a good guesser.

My biggest fear is to be classified as a freak, or worse, killed because someone might think I know too much. I like my life and don't want people to be afraid of me. That would make my job as a teacher scary for some parents, I guess. What I fail to understand is how wizards, werewolves, vampires, and superhero kids have become a part of the everyday sitcoms on television, and no one flinches. Put a teacher in a classroom that can know things in advance, and the neighborhood watch would gather their torches, now known as media coverage, and destroy her, her, meaning me. No thanks, I'm out. My point is I don't want the attention of believers attempting to use me. The skeptics who will constantly plot to prove me wrong. The eager beaver psychiatrists who will want to hypnotize me for their benefit or turn me into some experimental monkey or a sideshow freak. I don't want to become a victim of some reality show wanting to increase their ratings at my psychological expense.

I like being low key. All I want is to be left alone to live my unique life as fully as I can, as happy as I can. For this reason, I do not have many friends I relate to personally. I keep business at work and my personal life at home. My family of brothers and sisters is my sanctuary.

This morning something told me to lay off Mr. and Mrs. Walker and focus on Jack. Why? That didn't make sense. Was something going to happen to Jack? I headed for the shower. I dried up and slipped into a crisp white shirt, some camel-colored slacks, and my brown ladies' wingtip shoes. I dried and styled my hair loosely. I applied just a touch of bronze eye shadow and mauve lipstick. On my way out of my apartment, I filled the cat's food bowls. I blew kisses at Kayla and Chloe, who had sprawled themselves in the center of the corridor. I grabbed my bags, keys, and locked my apartment door. Two steps outside the door, my phone rang.

"Good morning to you, Katy!" I said, expecting a question to follow. I was not disappointed. "Hey Jen, a nurse here at work said she had her rent money in her hand, and somewhere between clipping her hair and grabbing her purse to leave to the manager's office, she lost it! She can't remember what she could have done with her ten, one hundred dollar bills."

"Katy, I am heading to work, and I don't like to drive and talk on the phone, so pay attention. The bills are folded in four. I figure they are behind a brown bottle on the third shelf of some cabinet. She was distracted by something and decided to put them there. Repeat what I just said, and she will know where to look. I think that's it."

"Thanks, Jen!"

"You're welcome. Bye." I said and tossed the phone in my purse. I climbed into my car, locked the doors, and buckled in.

After the windows had cleared up, I headed off to school. I know I gave Katy the correct information, but I don't understand where it comes from. Often, I say things that will help me in some way or put a person in their place. I never know what the information is until it spills out of my mouth. The good part is that it is always fluid and flawless, hence making me convincing of what I am saying. The bad part is that I don't have proof of what I am saying. It is for this reason that I keep my thoughts to myself and control what I share with friends and family.

22

I arrived at school on time and walked in the main entrance with the load of homework I rarely touch. I've lost count of the times I give my work a free ride to and from school. As soon as I stepped into the building, I heard Claire calling my name. She was hurrying down the hall toward me, carrying her load of homework.

"What's up?" I asked.

"I was wondering if you wanted to join me in talking to Mr. Brooks about our kids," she asked, catching her breath.

"Sure, why not?" I answered, but I knew we would not be talking to Mr. Brooks anymore.

I could feel my stomach turning and my head feeling numb. What I get are not headaches that are painful; it's more like head tingling. We approached the counselor's office and found the door locked.

"I hope he is not late," Claire said.

With the look of disappointment on her face, she made an "Aaaaa" sound. She glanced at her watch, frowned, and looked at me.

"Well, let's start our day. We will run into him sometime during the day, I'm sure," Claire said. Mr. Brooks was absent that morning, and I knew why.

Claire headed to her room, and I decided to check the lounge for fresh coffee. I was pleasantly surprised to find a full pot. I took a foam cup from the stack of cups next to the coffee pot and poured myself a cup when Nicole came in to make copies for a teacher.

"Good morning, Nicole. You're here early. Do you have PTA activities going on?" I asked. She had been looking at her stack of papers and now looked up at me. She approached the copier and began pushing buttons.

"All of the time. Busy, busy, busy." She answered.

I smiled. "Well, it's good to have a dedicated PTA staff."

I took my coffee and headed toward the door. I stopped and looked back at Nicole.

"Nicole, have you been in my classroom?"

She appeared surprised at the question.

"No. Why would you ask that?" she asked in a curious tone.

"I know that sometimes teachers need materials and such. Since I do have a reputation for always buying my own supplies, I was wondering if you had stopped by when I wasn't available."

"No, I did not stop by," she answered.

"Okay, you have a good one," I said

I exited the lounge as other teachers were coming in with their own papers to copy. I haven't a clue why I asked her if she had been in my room, but I am sure it will fall into place later.

I walked on to my classroom to find my door was locked. Delmon and I had made a deal the first week of school. I promised to keep my room as clean as possible so it would not be difficult for him to clean it after hours if he promised to unlock my room every morning when he arrived at school.

"Oh, snap!" I said out loud as I took my badge and key from my pocket and unlocked my classroom door.

I brought in the breakfast bags and turned on my Promethean board so that it would be ready for today's lessons. I watched as the children trickled in and greeted them warmly.

The day was rigorous and pleasant. I was very excited that the children were learning so much so fast. That afternoon, once the children were gone, I returned to my room and signed on to my computer to follow-up on a Child Protective Services report I completed weeks earlier. It is my duty as a teacher to file a report if I suspect the neglect or abuse of a child. The law gives me 48 hours to file after I discover a child might be at risk of abuse or neglect. I hate filing CPS reports, but it seems every year I have at least two children who are being severely neglected or battered. The worse cases are the ones where I don't have proof, only what I know to be true. With just that knowledge, I could end up in a lunatic box or lose my certification and credibility as a professional.

Two years ago, I had a young girl in my classroom that was being sexually molested by her grandmother and stepfather. She was the neatest child in the classroom and very polite. Her hair was always perfectly braided or curled, and her dresses were always neatly pressed and clean. Her lunchbox was always nicely packed with a wholesome lunch. Her grandmother showed up to pick her up every afternoon, displaying all the affection in the world for that child. There was nothing I could do. The child was unaware that anything wrong was happening. I hurried through my e-mail and spam but did not find a reply from CPS regarding the case. When I finished searching for a response, I was mentally exhausted and broken-hearted for my little boy. The tears welled up in my eyes. First, one streaming down my cheek, then another, and I wept.

After a few minutes, I touched up my makeup and quickly cleaned my classroom before heading out. I went to Claire's room to say goodbye, but she was already gone for the day. I was meeting with Rachel that evening for the first time in years. I was anxious to see her again and hopeful that we could reconnect.

23

I was at Tony's sitting in the booth that has become a regular for Claire and me. The cute waitress, wearing a ponytail and a well-tailored uniform that enhanced her tall, curvy body, took my order.

"Two Bud Lights and a club sandwich basket with chips and pickle slices."

I looked up at the door to see Rachel walking in.

"There's the person I was waiting for," I told the waitress. "Will you come back for the second order in a few minutes, please?"

The waitress, in her white top, pink bow-tie, and black slacks, looked over at Rachel and smiled.

"Yes, take your time," she said and slid my menu, which I no longer needed, to Rachel's side of the table.

Rachel appeared to have grown about 4 inches taller. She still wore her long, curly hair in a rolled tight bun. It made her hair look like a donut on top of her head. That never stopped the male gender from gawking at her. Her smooth, pearly pale skin made her big brown eyes look mesmerizing. She had a perfect pearly white smile, the kind you see in close up toothpaste commercials. Her bright pink lipstick appeared to be the very same shade she wore in school. It suited her features very well. She walked up to the table, and I naturally stood to give her a huge hug. It felt so good to have my partner in crime back. I could tell she was also glad to have me back in her life. She was not in uniform. To the people in the restaurant, we were just two girlfriends meeting for dinner and a drink.

Rachel slid into her side of the booth and asked,

"Did you order some food for me? I'm starving."

"No, girl. I haven't seen you in over ten years; I didn't know what to order! For all I know, you could be a Vegetarian or one of those strange alien people that don't eat anything but rabbit food."

She laughed and took a look at the menu, smiling. I was still talking.

"What do you call them, Vegans? You know, those people don't even eat animal bi-products like ice cream or cheese. That's just crazy! I would die of depression if I were placed on a rabbit food diet." I finished.

"The sad thing is, those are the people that will outlive us all! Life just isn't fair. Now that I think of it, I might consider giving up some of the garbage I am putting in my body," Rachel said.

She raised her index finger to get the waitresses' attention.

When she arrived at our table, Rachel said, "I will have whatever she ordered," nodding to me.

"To drink, I would like…"

"…a cold Bud Light," I interrupted. "I already ordered our drinks."

"That's right," she said. "Two Bud Lights are coming up."

The waitress took the menu from the table and headed to the bar.

Rachel and I were a lot alike in some ways and very different in others. One thing's for sure; we took care of one another.

I looked at Rachel and asked, "How is that investigation coming along?"

"They called it a robbery gone wrong, but it wasn't. I believe it was a murder made out to look like a robbery," she said. "For one thing, most robberies that have gone wrong consist of a scuffle where the victim tried to disarm the robber. Or the victim tries to get away upon finding someone in their home. In many cases, the victim is caught by surprise, leaving some kind of tell-tale sign like a broken dish or a spilled drink, or items left on the stove. In cases like this, the shots are fired at close range and usually to the body. Mr. and Mrs. Whitman were both shot in the head. The forensics report states it was most likely from a 5 to 6-foot distance. I believe what we are looking for is a professional hit."

"You're right," I replied. "That individual is linked to one bigger fish. You have to catch that one, and it won't be easy."

"And you say this because…" Rachel asked as she looked at me, attentively.

"I say this because I know it to be true. I just know." I said.

"Two Bud Lights and two Club Sandwiches with pickle spears and chips," I heard the waitress say as she arrived at our booth and placed our sandwich baskets in front of us.

"Yum! Thanks." I said and waited for her to leave before I spoke again.

"Rachel, remember all the times in school when I knew what teachers would be running late or what assignments we could skip because they would not be on our exams? Remember we freaked out Mr. Morales when we sent him a get well card in the mail that arrived on the same morning he called in sick?" I laughed.

"I was sure glad we didn't sign our names on that card. Mr. Morales was on a witch-hunt all year after that."

I took my pickle spear and took a bite.

"You and I would have been labeled as freaks. Well, mostly me since it was my clever idea," I laughed again.

Rachel's eyes were still fixed on me.

"Jennifer, I can't discuss much of the case because we are not supposed to divulge certain findings."

I didn't argue; I just looked at her and smiled. I picked up my sandwich and took a bite. Rachel took a swig of her beer.

"I hate you," she said and began talking. "Jennifer, we found no prints. There was no trace evidence. Not a damn thing. No one heard anything. No one saw anything. We are at zero at this point. With the little we know, those murders could have been a setup. I am guessing contract kills. The reporters claimed they were model citizens liked by everyone, including their neighbors who claim to have seen or heard nothing."

"That's because they used a silencer," I said. "You can't hear gunfire with one of those, even if you are in the next room."

"How the hell do you know they used a silencer?" Rachel asked.

"Well, I am taking a good guess. That's the only way no one could have heard anything. Also, it was not a stranger contract kill. The couple knew the killer because they let him in, right?" Rachel flexed her neck as if trying to smooth out a kink that was too stubborn to budge. Then I heard her neck make a popping noise.

"Ah, that's much better." She straightened her head and said, "Yes, they probably used a silencer. Good guess"

We ate our sandwiches and tried to make heads or tails of things. I changed the subject to the situation with the kids and the letters on their toes.

"All of these kids have been adopted by Mr. Ted and Mrs. Erica Walker. I sense something horrible when I think of the kids.

I looked at Rachel and waited for a response.

"You know that sensing of yours is scary sometimes, Jen. I can see if we have had any previous cases where letters were printed on the body. Maybe I can help you with that," Rachel said.

She took another swig of her beer.

"So, how do you like Lake Worth?"

She smiled and welcomed the change of subject.

"I like it. Our workload is lighter than in D.C., and the crimes here are not so horrendous. I'm actually bored sometimes," she laughed. "I haven't been spit on, threatened, insulted, or assaulted by a civilian yet. That was almost a weekly thing in D.C."

"Well, you said you've only been here for a couple of weeks. It might be the calm before the storm."

Rachel gave me a concerned look.

"Here," I said, handing her my cell phone. "Give me your contact information so I can get ahold of you. If I find something you can use, I will notify you ASAP."

Rachel typed her information in my phone and looked up at me midway.

"You can't tell anyone I am giving you information," she said, using her signature stern look.

"Not a problem. What I hear, I won't repeat. I have mastered that skill," I said with a sly smile.

I gave her my information as well as my work number in case my cell was off when she was trying to reach me. We finished our beers. The waitress placed our ticket on the table when she saw we were ready to leave. I tossed a $10.00 bill for my meal, and Rachel added $20.00. That was more than enough. She covered her dinner and a nice tip. It was understood that the next time we meet for a meal, she would lay the $10.00 and I will lay the $20.00. I think the reason Rachel and I got along so well in the past was that things were understood, and responsibility and loyalty never change. Even when we did not speak, we communicated clearly.

We walked out to our cars. I hugged Rachel. The part of me that was safe only when Rachel was at my side did not want to let go, but I did.

"Stay out of trouble," she said in her authoritative voice, smiling and turning to walk to her black Ford Ranger.

She stopped and turned after a few steps and said, "You better call me if you need me."

"I most definitely will," I responded.

"It's good to see you again, Jen." she smiled. "Good night."

She raised her hand in a wave and turned toward her vehicle. I smiled and headed for mine. It was dark now, and the weather was cold and drizzly. I climbed in and started the heater and window defroster. When the windows were clear enough to see through, I exited the restaurant parking and headed home.

24

At 7:15 Tuesday morning, I went into the office to check my mail. The office's left wall consists of built-in wooden cubbies, each the size of a large shoebox, with a teacher's name on it. After noticing I did not have mail, I decided to return to my classroom. On my way back, I encountered Ms. Bernadette outside of the library, putting up a wall display. She was neatly hanging vines made out of green construction paper and some monkeys with a catchy slogan encouraging kids to read more. "Don't Monkey Around! Grab a Book!" Next to that colorful display was the list of Bluebonnet Award books. Ms. Bernadette was busy at work. I almost mistook her for a student, which was a frequent occurrence with her. She was slim and petite with big sea blue eyes. Her wavy wheat-colored hair framed her face beautifully.

"Hey Ms. Bernadette, have you heard the good news?" I said enthusiastically.

"What news?" She asked curiously, looking away from her display.

"I heard Mrs. Phillips talking, and I believe she said you were getting an assistant."

"What? Shut up, an assistant, finally! Oh, happy day!"

She finished up and collected her strips of construction paper that had fallen on the floor.

Ms. B. held her hands in a prayer position and said, "They do work!"

"Why don't you check your mail? You might have something there," I said with a smile.

"I will right now," she said as she hurried to her computer.

I felt confident telling her the news since I knew that an e-mail of the news had been sent this morning. Apparently, she hadn't had time to check her e-mail yet. Delmon Black, our friendly custodian, was in the hallway walking the opposite way from me, making his daily rounds. He smiled and kept walking. Then I heard him holler at the librarian.

"Hey Chula, your wall is looking good!"

Delmon was always flirting with the teachers, but especially with Ms. Bernadette. One of these days, I thought to myself, he is going to find the right one. Ms. Bernadette was not her, though.

I arrived at my room to find it unlocked. Delmon had followed through with our deal once again. Thus far, he had only failed me once. I began the morning routine of placing the breakfast bags on the table so that the students could grab their breakfast after putting up their backpacks and turning in their homework in the homework basket. Every student ate at his or her table. They cleaned their area and proceeded to complete the seatwork provided.

Bill came in, took his breakfast, and quickly ate. His breakfast consisted of a sausage biscuit, a container of milk, and a small bag of sliced apples. Two minutes later, he was fast asleep with his head on the table.

"Ms. Knoes, should I wake Bill up?" Leslie asked.

"No, just let him rest."

I prepared a sleeping mat and blanket in the quiet area of my classroom. I picked up little Bill from his seat and laid him down to sleep.

His parents fought most of the night, and his mother had been arrested. I was aware that he possibly had only one hour of sleep the night before. How I was mindful of this, I can't explain. I would tell you that I see visions, but that is not always the case. Sometimes, I just know.

The students finished eating their breakfast and cleaned their area. They sat at their chairs and listened to the morning announcements. After announcements, they came to the carpet for the morning message and read aloud. The morning went smoothly as the children worked in their centers. I was pulling groups of four to work with them on their weekly vocabulary. Mike and Leslie were engaged in a game of word matching that they enjoyed playing. I rotated the groups and was able to meet with all of my students requiring intervention. It's imperative that I meet with them daily.

I rang the school bell that I kept on my reading table to get their attention.

Innocent Echoes

"Okay, students, it's time to clean up your centers and prepare for lunch," I said.

I woke Bill up gently and sent him to get a drink of water at the water fountain right outside my classroom door. He came right back in and sat sluggishly. The students that brought lunches stood to retrieve their lunch boxes from the shelf where they placed them every morning. The rest of the students lined up quietly. Bill rubbed his eyes.

"It's lunchtime already?" he asked happily and joined the group in line.

I escorted them down the hall to the water trough where each student was given soft soap and allowed to wash their hands before lunch and then quietly into the cafeteria. Once they had all passed through the line and were seated, I headed to my classroom.

I was sitting at my reading table, eating my peanut butter and jelly sandwich when my phone rang.

"Hey honey, I set up a Colorado getaway during your Christmas break, so don't make any plans." Jack enthusiastically announced.

"Okay," I replied cheerfully. "I will definitely need some time away by then."

"And I will provide all the TLC you need," Jack said in a low sexy tone.

I hung up the phone to find I was out of lunchtime and the other half of my sandwich would have to wait until 3:00 when class was dismissed. I walked briskly to the cafeteria to collect my students.

The afternoon went smoothly, and before I knew it, the kids were gone, and I was sitting at my reading table, finishing my PB&J sandwich and grading student's work for that day. Then I remembered Mr. Brooks. God, please let me be wrong. I put my sandwich wrapping in the trash as I hurried out. I went straight to the administrative office.

"Hey Sam, have we heard from Mr. Brooks? I was scheduled to meet with him. Do we know when he's coming back? Is he sick or something?"

Sam just looked at me and then looked towards the principal's office.

"She'll talk to everyone soon. No need to worry, Ms. Knoes."

My heart sank. They knew. I turned to go back to my classroom. I could feel the loss of a good friend as I walked down the same hallway where Mr. Brooks had given me that last high-five.

You see, I don't stop things from happening. I am not God, and it's not my place to change God's plans. I also cannot make things happen. If I was at the circus, I could not make the trapeze flyer fall just for fun, knowing that there is a net for safety. I can't keep things from happening. Although I have removed or convinced someone not to attend a place where I know things will go bad. It's very difficult knowing things, watching friends suffer, sometimes knowing what others are thinking. I struggle with this daily and have to maintain my focus on my work. My friend Katy says I should help people. What Katy fails to understand is that the average person lives in a concrete world where evidence and logic rule. Those two things are not always present in my world.

When I was eighteen years old, I tried to help my aunt, who had gone blind due to glaucoma complications. I figured I could live with her and help her out with chores around the house. I was working at a department store blocks from her home, so it was helpful to me to be able to walk to work since I did not own a car at the time. Because my aunt was legally blind, the city had appointed a caregiver that would visit her every day for about four hours. I am not one to snoop into people's mail or belongings, but for some reason, I decided to open her mail. It was a credit card bill for $5,150.00. I found a second bill for another credit card mixed in with the same pile. She had credit cards being used for items that she could not have purchased, like gas for a vehicle, clothes from an expensive young ladies store, and a stereo system.

She had complained about stomach cramps the week before. It took me two minutes to know what was happening. I knew she had been poisoned. I took the credit card bills and called the companies informing them that these purchases were not made by my aunt. I then called the police and gave them the information. I was 18 years old at the time. I told them she had been poisoned. I told them to check her coffee cups because that's where it was put. I showed them the mail my aunt was getting showing all the credit card debt. I told them it was the caregiver going shopping at my aunt's expense, and now she was going to kill her so the credit companies would have to dismiss the debt. The female police officer heard everything I had to say. She said she would file the report and stay in touch with me.

The next day, two police officers came to my aunt's house and knocked on the door. They said they wanted me to go with them for questioning. They were prepared to arrest me for the crimes being committed against my aunt. Listening to their accusations made my stomach turn, my head pound, and my eyes start filling with tears. I told them I did not want to go, that I was sorry I had said anything. I asked them why they would think I was involved. One police officer said there was no way I could have known all the details without being involved. I pleaded and told them how I knew things. I cried for hours, and I threw up in the kitchen sink when they started asking me question after question. I was petrified. They finally relented and decided to investigate the caregiver. I guess they were finally convinced that I was innocent. It was then that I decided to keep things to myself.

25

The confirmation of the news I dreaded came the following morning. I was getting ready to start the day, setting the student's breakfast on the table and putting out their morning work. I had just sat down at my small desk to check my e-mail and turn on my Promethean Board when I heard Mrs. Phillips make her announcement via school intercom.

"Please pardon the interruption. I would like for all staff to please meet in the library for a quick announcement."

I took a deep breath and shivered as I stood and checked that I had my classroom key and name badge on my neck. I locked my room and headed to the library. I had only taken a couple of steps in the direction of the library when I heard, "Hey Jen, wait up."

I looked to see Claire walking fast to catch up to me.

"I wonder what now," she said in an agitated tone. "I did not even have a chance to start on my morning routine," she whined.

Claire gets upset when she doesn't have time to meditate before her day starts. She also hates being rushed in the mornings.

When we reached the library, I could see Mrs. Phillips in the book check-out area waiting patiently for everyone to arrive. As soon as we were all present, she began.

"I am sure some of you have noticed that Mr. Brooks has been absent for a couple of days. Unfortunately, Mr. Brooks has passed away. His office will remain locked until Delmon packs and organizes all of his belongings. Please change your calendars accordingly. I will not begin to look for another counselor until a few days after we return from Christmas break," she said solemnly. The group of teachers who worked closely with Mr. Brooks gasped.

"What? How? When?" they asked, sadden by the news.

"I am not at liberty to discuss things further. I will notify you by e-mail when funeral services will take place," Mrs. Phillips assured the group.

I could see some teachers were crying quietly. I noticed Nicole and Ms. Gomez listening to the announcement expressionless. Claire stood next to me in utter shock. I could see Ms. Bernadette at the side door just arriving. She went into her office and put up her bags and lunch tote. She quietly walked into the library with a smile that instantly faded when she heard the news. She was the hospitality chair, so she would have us all sign a sympathy card delivered with flowers to the Brooks' residence, probably tomorrow. She would also purchase a small St. Peter rosary to be delivered with the flower arrangement to the church where Mr. Brooks' funeral service will be held. I looked over at the librarian's check-out counter and noticed a handsome male with a pearly smile: her new assistant, no doubt. I smiled.

"Jennifer, do you think he had a heart attack?" Claire whispered. "Maybe that witch wife of his finally got to him. He had all that stress and no one to talk to. That's probably why he was drinking that night at Tony's," she said.

When Mrs. Phillips finished relaying the information, she dismissed us to our classrooms. We all left the library in silence and headed to our classrooms.

I walked listening to Claire, but I knew Mr. Brooks had taken his own life. I knew he had used the 38 Special caliber handgun he kept in his desk drawer at home. Mr. Brooks knew he was too drunk to hold a gun straight at his temple, so he did the next best thing. He held the gun barrel in his mouth and shot off the top of his head. Something he could not live with would no longer haunt him. The saddest thing is that he left behind two daughters and a wife whose lives he has changed forever and who will miss him dearly.

26

It was finally Wednesday. Field Trip Day! I could tell that the children were anxious about their trip to the Casa Manana Theatre to watch *The Polar Express*. They trickled in and took their breakfast from the red insulated bags and sat at their tables to eat. As they came in, I placed a bright pink bandana around their collar. While they were eating, I walked around and clipped their name tag on their collars. I have never lost a child while on a field trip, and I'm not going to start now. The bright colored bandanas can be spotted a mile away. With these aids, as soon as I notice anyone straying or not keeping up, I manage to intercept the problem of a lost child. The bus would arrive at 9:30 am, so we had time for our morning songs and reviewed our field trip rules.

The children enthusiastically participated in our morning songs, and we discussed the rules of conduct at the theatre and on the bus. We still had a few minutes before the bus would be arriving. I decided to give them time to draw a picture of what they liked most about Christmas in their journals. The journals they use have a box on the top half of the page and a few lines underneath. I asked them to first draw their picture. I reminded them that we did not have time to write this morning, but we would have time this afternoon. "Right now, I just want you to focus on drawing the picture in the box," I instructed. At 9:20 a.m. I heard a call from Sam via intercom.

"Mrs. Knoes, your bus has arrived. It is waiting in front of the school."

"Thank you," I replied.

I lined up the children after pairing them up.

"Okay, each of you has a partner. You are not to leave your partner's side without letting me know. Understood?"

"Yes, ma'am," they answered in unison.

The show was spectacular. I had invited two adult chaperones, one male and one female, for the kids that would get restless and began to want to go to the restroom in the middle of the presentation. To my complete surprise, not one child moved from their seat once the show began. They were so enthralled in the production, laughing and listening attentively. The bus ride back was filled with buzzing sounds of the kids discussing the train and Santa Clause.

When we returned to school at 2:30 pm, the children were tired and hungry. I decided to give them some time to free draw since most of my students like to draw. I let them know that tomorrow, I would be handing out their journals so they could complete the sentences to go with what they enjoyed most about Christmas. I walked around and handed them a large piece of Manila paper and a small cup of animal crackers as a snack. Leslie passed out the crayons. The students diligently drew colorful pictures making sounds of approval. I could see Bill drawing a Christmas tree without lights, tinsel, or anything that would reflect joy. The little house next to the tree was a simple square and roof. There were no lights and no wreath on the door. At the window, there was a stick figure with a sad face. I walked around and encouraged them to do their best work, feeling sadness for those I knew were drawing what they knew or experienced every Christmas.

Little Leo drew a big house with a snowman on the lawn. Around his house were lights that extended down the sidewalk. Mike came up to me and handed me a picture of a green Christmas tree, balloons, and Winnie the Pooh bears with a rainbow right in the middle that he had traced out of a book from the reading center.

"This is for you. You're the best teacher I've ever had!" he said, hugging my legs.

"Thanks, Mike. That's very sweet." I said as I smiled appreciatively.

I took the picture and tacked it to my bulletin board, which hung next to the door. It was a place I made for special artwork from my students. In bold lettering on the top were the words

. *Very Special Art Made by Little Angels.* The kids loved seeing me post their work on my board. Their eyes lit up every time I hung one of their pictures there for all to see. When I turned, I noticed Mike had followed me.

"I'm going to miss you," he said.

"Well, your next grade is across the hall. You'll be able to drop by some days to let me know how you and your sister are doing." I reassured him.

He looked at me with a sad expression.

"Yeah, but when I leave this school, and I pass to the 6th grade, I go back to Mexico. My sister Maria is there, but I don't know where. I haven't seen her since she was sent back last summer," he said.

I glanced up at the clock. It was ten minutes before 3:00 pm, and I had to get the students ready for dismissal. I kneeled at his level.

"Can you tell me about that tomorrow? It's time for you to go home now."

"Okay," he said and hugged me.

I lined them up, made sure they all had their homework, and exited the room out into the dismissal area. Mike and Leslie were picked up by the lady in the white van. She rarely made eye contact and routinely drove up and sped off. It was 15 minutes after 3:00 pm before all of the students had been picked up. I remembered what Mike had said about not seeing his sister. I headed to the office and hoped Sam had not left for the day. She was still sitting behind her desk.

"Hey! Sam," I called out.

Sam looked up from her computer screen.

"Yes, what can I do for you?" she asked in her professional, friendly tone.

"Well, my student says he has a sister that left here after finishing fifth grade, and he has not heard from her. I thought it would be nice for him to send her a card for Christmas. Can you help me with getting a forwarding address?"

"Sure thing," she replied, "I will place the info in your box before I leave."

"Thanks, Sam. You're the greatest."

I turned to exit the office when I heard her say in a low tone, "That I am."

I returned to my classroom to prepare for the next day. I cleaned up and reviewed my plans.

I always check my school e-mail before I headed home, and today was no different. As promised, we received notice regarding Mr. Brooks' funeral arrangements from Mrs. Phillips.

His Rosary was going to be that Friday evening, our last day of school before the break. A short Mass would occur at the burial site the following day, Saturday, at 9:00 am. The burial site was less than 100 yards from the church. There would be no long procession line to the burial site. After the mass, the coffin would be placed in the ground. I was determined to attend Friday's service to pay my respects and also because I was sure that some answers awaited me there.

The e-mail that followed the one sent by Mrs. Phillips caught my attention. It came from Sam, and it was marked as a high priority. The subject was "Vanished" and read:

Mrs. Knoes,

The student, Maria Cardenas, which left here and supposedly returned to Mexico, is nowhere to be found. The forwarding address does not exist. I also found five other children that have come and gone that were also adopted by Mr. and Mrs. Walker. The children seem to have disappeared.

I felt a rush of chills and my stomach turning as I read the last sentence in disbelief. I stared at the mail as my brain searched for answers. I replied:

Sam,

Is there any way to find a legitimate excuse to contact Mr. and Mrs. Walker and ask that they give an address for Maria? What rights does the district have in locating children that have left our school? Please send me the names of the other children. I sat quietly, took a deep breath, and sent the e-mail.

I finished in my classroom and headed for the door. My phone rang right as I was getting ready to leave.

"Hi Jennifer, I have a question," I heard Katy say. "What colors should I wear when I run into Mr. Right?"

It was questions like these that sometimes made me want to scream.

"Wear blues or something green. Those are his favorite colors," I replied.

It had been months since Katy had even asked how I was doing or how things were going at home. To her, I was becoming more and more like a crystal ball and not a friend. Still, I cared about her, so I ignored the selfish attitude. Katy gave me cheerful thanks and hung up the phone. I had already reached my car when it hit me. Katy could help! She frequented Mexico to visit family. She also knew people there that were very wealthy. During the summer, she worked as a housekeeper for a dozen rich families in Mexico. Sometimes, she made jokes telling me she made more money in those three months than she made all year working as the coordinator for the medical clinic. I called her cell phone.

"Hey Katy, are you going to Mexico this Christmas break?"

"Yes, why?" she asked.

I told her I was interested in touching base with some of my old students that had moved back to Mexico. Maybe she knew someone who knew them.

"Okay, sure. Give me some pictures of them and their addresses. I'll see what I can do."

"Okay, thanks. You'll hear from me soon. Bye." I clicked off the phone.

I hurried home and entered my apartment, startling my two cats that were sleeping in the corridor. Without even stopping to greet them or pick one up and pet it, I rushed into my study and began looking through the yearbooks sitting on the built-in shelves. I started to pull out the yearbooks and locate pictures of the students with the last name of Cardenas that had left Coronado Elementary last year and the year before. I found five who may have been adopted by Mr. and Mrs. Walker.

I made enlarged copies of the photos and wrote the full names of each student on the bottom of each print. I placed the images in an envelope and prepared them for delivery. I opened my school e-mail to find that Sam had responded with the exact names I had located in the yearbooks. Tomorrow morning I will drive by the clinic and leave it for Katy. It was late, so I showered and fell asleep. That night I dreamt.

27

I was inside a beautiful home with high ceilings and crystal chandeliers. I was standing at the bottom of two staircases that extended from the second floor. They extended down like arms welcoming an embrace. The rails were of solid heavy wood with carved elegant designs of spirals and paisley. On the bottom of the stairs was a large Ming burgundy rug. Antique furniture furnished the corridor and the large living area. I went up the stairs to find a middle-aged man standing on a balcony looking out at the blue ocean and smoking a cigar. Next to him sat a young boy who was quietly enjoying the peaceful view.

With every breeze, I could smell the scent of tobacco mixed with sweet cherries. A tall, thin-faced man that looked familiar came into the room and announced in a low but firm tone,

"It's time."

Then he departed as quickly and silently as he had entered. The man on the balcony never turned around but continued to look at the clear blue ocean view. The young boy arose from his chair and walked in the direction of a room that appeared more like a piece of a hospital inserted into this elegant mansion. As the boy approaches the door, I realize he is praying. I could not tell what he was saying, only that it was a prayer in broken English words.

His facial expression was no longer peaceful and what I did understand about his prayer was that they were words of dread and despair. He entered the room slowly, and the tall, thin-faced man closed the door behind him. I could see the inside of the room. It mirrored a hospital room with a small bed, lights, and surgical trays. Had I not entered through the door, I would have sworn I was standing in an actual hospital operating room.

Against the back wall sat several small ice chests, the kind someone would take to a picnic for two. I looked at the boy, but his face was blurred, and I couldn't identify him. A young female nurse came to him and said, "Hey, do you want to smell something that smells like bubble gum?"

She was pulling what looked like an oxygen tank on a small roller.

"Sure," the little boy said as he took her hand and climbed up on the bed.

It was covered with cute animal print fabric. The pillow was fluffy and light blue.

"I like bubble gum," he said.

The young nurse turned some knobs on the machine and held a small oxygen mask to his face as she watched him fade into a deep sleep. She straightened him on to the bed and gently stroked his angelic face for a few minutes before turning away.

I walked over to a small window in the surgical room that presented a view of horse stables and a dozen horses at pasture. I could see large patches of beautiful purple wildflowers. The trees swayed with the wind, but I felt a chill and a sense of loss and dread instead of peacefulness.

Beep, beep, beep!

It was 6:00 am, and my alarm was blaring. I awoke a little startled. I almost never remember specifics about the dreams; I only know that I always dream of people I do not know. When I do know them, I can never see their faces, so I can't be sure. The strange thing is, although I can never remember what they look like when I wake up, I remember things like their character and some of their distinct features like tattoos, scars, hair color, or voice tone. I can even remember scents. The interesting part about dreams is that I almost always know who to trust when I come across those people in my waking world because something tells me I have met them before. I know who the jerks are and who to stay away from before they even say a word. That always comes in handy.

I remember having a discussion about not knowing the people I dream about with my sister Estel once.

"Oh, that's just creepy! That would stress me out," she said.

I disagreed.

"In my opinion, dreaming about people you know is creepier. For example, what if you dreamt you were having sex with your boss, whom you secretly thought was hot? Or your married neighbor whom you disliked? Then you have to face them when you wake up. Now that is awkward!" I said.

My dream world is nothing like Sigmund Freud described. My dreams are not feelings bottled up inside me. They never resemble things I am trying to sort out in my waking life, and they definitely don't fit in the symbolic book of dreams category. I take my dreams more as sneak peeks of what is to come. Sometimes they are sneak peeks of the past. The worse part of my dreams is, not knowing if what I'm looking at is past, present, future, or some meaningless brain wave.

28

Thursday was our Christmas program in which the 3rd and 4th-grade classes were going to sing and dance to a variety of classic Christmas songs. It was the last Thursday before Christmas break. Last week, an e-mail was sent out to all teachers from Ms. Gomez requesting volunteers for the night of the program. I had already volunteered.

The day's lessons went as planned, considering all the interruptions and the kids being anxious about the program. In the art center, they were making clay using salt, flour, and warm water. They enjoyed patting the clay down and cutting out a snowman with a giant cookie cutter. I had the three ingredients separated for them. On a round tray were single cups of water, snack bags of salt, and snack bags of flour. Next to that was a stack of small yellow mixing bowls.

The morning went well, with learning still taking place. After 25 minutes in their first center, I asked the students to clean up and prepare to rotate to their next center. The children laughed and focused on cleaning up. Minutes later, they were engaged in their new center. Time moved swiftly, and they were soon walking toward the cafeteria for lunch. I escorted the group in and waited for them to be seated with their lunch before I left the cafeteria. I returned to my classroom to check my e-mail. I found nothing important.

I picked the students up from lunch and decided to show a movie. I chose a Christmas cartoon about a snowman that comes to life. The kids enjoyed it so much that they attempted to sing with the film as they danced around the room. One of the beauties of teaching 1st grade is that much of the learning occurs with movement, games, and interaction. Although they appeared just to be enjoying a movie, they are learning about character traits.

After the movie, we dove into the math lesson for the day. I was teaching addition and subtraction. We started every math lesson with a short video clip introducing our math concept and vocabulary for the day on my Promethean board. I asked the students to follow along with it and raise their hand if they needed clarification. I completed the guided lesson with the help of the students. I gathered the math game sheets that came with the unit and guided the students in a game of addition where they would have to spin a wheel and move that many spaces forward. The one reaching the finish line was the winner. After I finished explaining the game, the students found their math partner and proceeded to the floor to play in pairs.

After the game, they knew that it was their responsibility to complete the independent practice sheets placed neatly on the reading table. Two by two, they took a pencil from the pencil cup sitting beside the math sheets and took their math work. They were all at their desks, working diligently. I played some classical music as they worked.

Tap, tap, tap!

I looked over to the door to see Claire motioning to me and touching her watch. Oh, snap, it was time for specials. I had lost track of time. The kids had P.E. today, and Coach hates it when we are late. He does not say anything, but he is easy to read. I quickly lined them up and escorted them to the Gym. Claire walked next to me.

"There's a stack of papers in your box that must go home today. Samantha asked that I let you know."

"Okay, I'll get it on my way back to the classroom," I assured.

"Oh, and David traced pictures of horses in green pastures and said this one was for you."

She handed me a picture drawn on a white sheet. I saw beautiful brown and black horses in green pastures. On the bottom, right-hand corner were small purple flowers.

"Thank you! Tell him I will post it on my bulletin board," I said, staring at the picture I had seen the night before.

I arrived at the administrative office and noticed several forms in my box. I grabbed the stack and headed to my classroom. I looked through the papers to make sure I sent home all important notices in their folders. One was a reminder that Friday was the last day of school until January 3rd. The next one was a list of titles students could read during their break. The third one was a karate flyer to a karate dojo just down the street from Coronado Elementary. By the time I was finished with the papers to go home, it was time to collect the students from P.E class.

On my way to the Gym, I heard Rene, our 4th-grade volunteer, calling my name.

"Ms. Knoes! Ms. Knoes!"

I stopped and turned to see him walking toward me. Before reaching me, he turned to see if anyone was looking and made his last six steps a hip display any runway diva or Victoria Secret model would envy. Rene was, how should I put it, eccentric. His face was a cross between a young Matthew McConaughey and David Bowie. His innocent character made anyone who met him instantly liked him.

"Hey, this envelope was on the floor in the office. You must have dropped it when you collected your mail. It has your name on it." He extended his hand. "It feels empty," he said as he swayed it side to side and gave me the envelope.

Rene had become a volunteer at our school after realizing his two nephews were struggling in literacy. He began tutoring writing and then moved on to reading comprehension. His nephews succeeded in passing their exams and had moved on to middle school. Rene, however, continued tutoring struggling students and became part of the Coronado Elementary family.

"Thanks," I said, smiling and taking the envelope.

"If it's a winning lotto ticket, I want half," he said.

"Sure thing," I said and continued to the Gym.

I did not want to be late for collecting my kids. Before reaching the door that takes me outside to the Gym, I came across Mrs. Phillips as she was coming out of the science lab.

"Hello, Ms. Knoes. How are you doing?"

"Terrific," I answered.

We walked down the hall and she asked me if I was doing anything special during our Winter break. I very cheerfully let her know that my boyfriend and I decided to go on a skiing trip.

"I was thinking this time away would be good for the soul," I said.

She nodded and smiled, not saying a word. Mrs. Phillips was an excellent principal. It never mattered how challenging her principal demands were; she always placed the children first and worked late to connect with parents. We walked side by side until we reached the door to the outside area close to the gymnasium.

She smiled and said, "Have a good rest of the day, Ms. Knoes."

"Absolutely," I replied.

I smiled and continued to get the kids from gym class.

I collected the kids and proceeded to my classroom. To my surprise, standing at the door waiting for us to arrive was the lady from the van. She stood expressionless and waited for me to reach our classroom door.

"Okay, children, please go to your desks and read your library books. I will need a minute."

I turned to the van driver as soon as all of the children had entered the classroom.

"Well, hello," I said as I extended my hand to greet her.

She smiled faintly and presented an early dismissal form for both Mike and Leslie.

"The school winter program is tonight. Will they be able to attend and show their support?" I asked.

"Mrs. Walker is not feeling well. I'm afraid they won't be able to attend this time," she said in a cold disconnected tone.

Mike and Leslie collected their mail from the student's mailbox and placed it in their backpacks. "Will they be coming to school tomorrow?" I asked.

"No, they will be visiting family in Mexico," she replied.

"Will Mike be visiting with his sister? He said he has a sister in middle school in Mexico. What school does she attend, do you know?" I asked, concerned.

Her face went white as she quickly turned to the two children who were now standing at her side.

"We are running late, please excuse me," she said coldly and escorted the children out of the classroom.

She didn't say thank you, and none of the three looked back to say goodbye. I watched them turn the corner as I turned to close the door to my classroom. I stopped when I heard Mike running back down the hall. He clung to me, and in a low cracked voice, he said, "You're the best teacher in the world."

I hugged him back, and tears welled up in my eyes. Mike's little hands felt cold. My heart began to break.

29

All of the inventions had been moved to the library due to the Christmas show being in the auditorium. I was placing a clipboard and pen with a blank rating sheet next to each invention. Meanwhile, Ms. Bernadette was methodically checking in the books that had been returned during the day.

"Hey Ms. Bernadette," I called, "Thanks for letting me throw these inventions in here while the Christmas program goes on."

She looked up at me and gave me a thumbs up and a warm smile.

"Not a problem. Since they were in here, I took the liberty of checking them out. I'm very impressed. This year's inventions are very cool. Talk about creativity! It's going to be hard to come up with just one winner per grade level. Check out 4th grade! That vest is awesome. I would have never thought of that one!" she said as she rolled her book cart to the far end of the library and began to file books back onto the shelves.

I walked over to the 4th-grade section and felt my jaw drop. A 4th-grade student had invented what she titled Styling Safety Vest. I was tickled to see the actual model that appeared to have been put together with large stitching and a glue gun. It was a Kevlar vest that had been bedazzled with sequins. It was very stylish with paisley patterns. Another invention that caught my attention was under the 1st-grade sign. Mike Cardenas, my student, had put together his own invention. It was quite impressive considering his age. His invention was titled Sock Pockets. It displayed a pair of gym socks with pockets. A page next to the socks mentioned the usage.

"With Sock Pockets, you can store a key, your money, jewelry, or an I.D. card that you don't want to lose."

The socks were very cute and well displayed on the trifold board. The next invention that caught my attention was titled Purse Boots! Now you can drop your phone, lipstick, or small notebook in your pocket and not fear that the item would fall all the way down into your boot. Just reach in and grab!

"Wow," I thought to myself, but I must have said it out loud.

"I told you," Ms. Bernadette responded.

I walked over to where she was still filing some books.

"Ms. B, the judges will be coming in to judge the inventions tomorrow morning from 9:00 to 11:00, so I will have them out of here by this evening after the show."

She stopped to glance at me.

"Oh, it's not a problem. You can even move them tomorrow morning if you want. I will be glad to help you move them now that I have an assistant helping me in the library." she said.

"Thank you. I appreciate you letting me take up your library space for one day. I want them set up in the auditorium tonight so judges can come in at their leisure tomorrow and judge them. After that, all I have to do is check the rating sheets and apply the ribbons to each board."

"Okay," she responded, now at the far back end of the nonfiction book row.

There were trifold boards filling the entire carpet reading area. I took a last look at the boards cluttering the library. This was my first year taking over the Invention Convention, and I wanted it to be a fun adventure for the students. We were off to a good start. Just enough students participated in making it challenging for the judges.

I am aware that the upper grades are continually testing and preparing for the State Standardized Testing. I did not expect much from those grade levels, but they never cease to amaze me. The teachers here are great, and I really appreciate how these teachers support one another, in this case, me. Invention Convention is not a school priority. If too few students participate, the principal has the option of scratching it off our school activities list. I would hate for that to happen. I am so very grateful to the teachers that encourage their students to participate. "I love these teachers!" I whispered to myself as I stared at the sea of inventions cluttering Ms. B's library. Then I heard a voice beside me. It was Mrs. Flor, my neighboring classroom teacher. She looked at me up and down.

"Wow, Jen. You really made yourself beautiful for the show."

I laughed. "Thank you Flor."

"I brought a change of clothes so that I could look professional volunteering, not beautiful."

"Well, you look very nice," she said.

"Thank you," I repeated and exited the library.

I like Mrs. Flor. She is always so cordial.

30

Since the program would begin in a short while, I decided to have a snack in my classroom and get some work done. Perhaps I would arrange my supply closet that currently looked like a hoarder's closet of school supplies, puzzles, and educational tools and games. In other words, my supply closet was indeed a nightmare. The Teacher before me had zero organizational skills. I had made a conscious note when I moved into this room to organize it a small section at a time. I decided to save the closet for later and not ruin my red silk dress. Instead, I planned on grading papers that I had stacked in my *To Grade* tray.

I left my classroom door open, and I locked my closet, which was visible to anyone walking down the hall. I looked up when I heard Ms. Esperanza Gomez's voice.

"Well, Ms. Knoes. Are you ready for a spectacular show?"

"What other kind is there?" I asked in a playful tone.

"I have meant to touch base with you, but the last time I saw you, you were racing for the toilet. Claire told me you were very sick. I can see you are all better now."

She came closer.

"Oh my goodness, don't you look ravishing! That's a beautiful dress!"

"Thank you," I answered, sitting at my reading table.

I wanted her to leave, but I figured she had news about the show tonight or something.

Not too much to my surprise, she said, "You are interesting."

I picked up my pen to begin grading papers; she did not get the hint. I put my pen down and looked up at her, trying not to show my agitation.

"How so?" I asked.

Something about her gave me the creeps big time, but somehow I managed to smile. I looked at her curiously, waiting for her reply. Then it came.

"Well, for starters, I understand you have been here for a few years now, but from talking to other teachers, even the principal, no one really knows you. You never come to our gatherings outside of school, and your palms are strange."

"Excuse me?" I asked, trying not to sound offended.

"I can read palms, you know," she said, tilting her head to the side, glancing at mine. Most palms are transparent, easy to read. I have become pretty good at reading them," she said proudly.

I had often noticed her staring at my hands when we sat at staff meetings. I figured she was just fond of my nail polish. She continued on.

"The left hand is your past, and the right hand is your future."

I was not expecting her to reach for my hands, so I did not have the opportunity to retrieve them off the table.

"Oh my, your hands are cold," she said, turning my hands to see my palms.

She held them in front of her face as she studied them with amazement. She began speaking.

"See, your left hand, your past, does not match your right hand. It's almost as if your past was another person. Your present palm lines are completely different, and no one changes that much"

"Well, I would imagine it's because I am an adult now, and my choices are smarter."

"Uh, excuse me!" I said as I took my hands away from her and squirted some sanitizer from a small bottle I keep on my table.

After my brief cleaning ritual, I began sorting my papers and pretended she was gone. She smiled, oblivious to my discomfort.

"Still, I think you're interesting."

She stood and pushed her tiny chair in and looked at her watch.

"Oh shoot, I better go. I'll see you in a bit."

She adjusted her pink pantsuit jacket and exited my classroom.

"What in the hell is wrong with that idiot?" I whispered to myself.

If she is so good at reading palms, why couldn't she see the invisible *"fuck you"* finger I was showing her. I grinned, sighed, and finished my grading and sorting just in time to get to the cafeteria for my evening duty.

At 6:30 pm. family members and children started pouring into the building through the front double doors. Charles, our kindergarten teacher, was standing at the entrance of the building ushering parents into the auditorium. He was wearing pressed khaki slacks and a black shirt that made him look very handsome and professional. He winked at me, staring me up and down.

"Hot, very hot!"

"Thanks, Charles," I laughed and continued into the cafeteria.

I could hear Mrs. Phillips announcing to the crowd that parents with strollers and small children were to sit where they would have easy access to the exit in case of a fussy child. This arrangement allowed parents to exit and re-enter the auditorium without disturbing the other individuals enjoying the show.

The Christmas program was only forty-five minutes long. As each grade level finished their performance, parents were encouraged to collect their child from the cafeteria and return to the auditorium. If parents weren't ready to collect their child right away from the cafeteria, the children were to sit with their classmates and wait. The tables were labeled by grade level to keep the children sorted and make dismissal safe and easy. My duties were to monitor the students who were due to line up for their performance. My other responsibility was to keep track of the classes that had finished performing and were coming into the cafeteria. Rene took his position outside the cafeteria and was ushering in the students who had just finished performing. Once they were in the cafeteria, I asked them to sit at their designated table. After they were seated, they were offered crayons and activity books to work on until a parent or guardian arrived to collect them.

Bringing in a group of 3rd graders, Rene looked over at me and waved, flashing his pearly white smile. I did not see any of the Cardenas kids, nor was there any sign of Mr. or Mrs. Walker. Nicole, the PTA president, was also in the hallway, ushering students into the cafeteria.

"Parents, please wait until your child has entered the cafeteria and been released by Ms. Knoes before you take them."

Even though Nicole insisted that parents collect their children in the cafeteria in a pleading tone, some parents pretended not to hear her or just plainly ignored her and attempted to pull their child out of the line before entering the cafeteria. Rene politely intercepted.

"No, please wait until your child has entered the cafeteria."

He stood between the parents and the children forming a barrier with his body . "For your child's safety, parents, please be patient. Please remain on that side of the hall," he said calmly.

It reminded me of the friendly stewardess on airplane flights giving seatbelt instructions. He was such a cutie that they complied. For safety reasons, we always kept tabs on who was being picked up by what family member. Between Charles managing the auditorium, Rene the hallway to the cafeteria, and me carefully releasing the children to their guardians, all went perfectly well. Where was Ms. Gomez, I wondered? She sent the teachers an email last week desperate for volunteers, and she was nowhere to be found. I was sure she was in the building, though. Then it hit me; the bitch was in my classroom. But why would she go back to my room? Did she leave something on my table when she was there earlier?

31

The program was over by 7:45 pm, and by 8:00 pm, all of the parents had collected their children and exited the school. As soon as the auditorium was empty, Delmon began to stack chairs along the wall to make room for the inventions. I decided to go to the library and begin setting up the inventions in the auditorium. This year I had just the right amount of entries, and they were all very creative. I placed all of the inventions by grade level, beginning with 1st grade to 5th grade. Then I placed a cardstock sign over each grade level. Tomorrow the judges would come in, take the clipboard from each invention and rate it accordingly.

I was moving the last invention when I heard Rene come into the auditorium.

"These kids have a wild imagination. I like those earrings that don't require ear piercings," he laughed.

"I agree! Those are pretty clever, and they even look classy. Think they would enhance your weekend wardrobe?" I asked sarcastically.

He replied, "Yes, yes, they would. OMG, I even like the color! Who came up with this invention? I will bet it's a boy who's family if you know what I mean. Oh, very nice." Rene was about to start admiring the other displays when he stopped and said, "You know that dress you're wearing looks really nice. I'll bet I can make it look gorgeous," he smiled.

"You can't have my dress," I hesitated, "but you can borrow it," I laughed.

Rene hides the fact that he is gay from everyone except Claire and me. He looks handsome and straight when he wears his man clothes. Rene walked around, admiring the inventions.

"These look fun. You did good Jen."

He stood by the door now, looking at the tri-fold boards with his hands at his hips.

"I am heading out. I'm tired, and I need a Martini. You should do the same." He insisted.

I looked over at Rene after setting up the last invention.

"All finished. I am right at your heels, no pun intended." I said.

He smiled.

"See you in two weeks; I'm not volunteering tomorrow. Have a Merry Christmas and a Happy New Year! If you get bored over the holidays, you know where I am," he said in a kind of musical tone.

Rene was right. I knew exactly where to find him.

He waved and walked out the door. I took one last look at the inventions and was returning to my classroom when I heard a voice behind me.

"Well, it went really smooth, and I am glad it's over!"

I turned to find Nicole.

"Hey, what are you still doing here? I asked.

I let her catch up to me as I walked to my room.

"I thought I was the only one here besides the custodians."

"I was going to leave a few minutes ago. I am waiting for Ms. Gomez. She's putting away the costumes and instruments we used tonight. Once we leave the school, we will be locked out, and she wants to leave everything secured."

Nicole looked in the direction of my room and stopped. I really wanted to bust Ms. Gomez if she was in my classroom.

"Nicole, I really would like to chat, but I'm tired, and I have to get my purse and stuff from my room so I can go home." I smiled. "Have a Merry Christmas and Happy New Year," I said.

I turned and started walking away. I entered my room to find no one there. I went straight to my aquarium to feed my tropical fish of many colors. I tossed in five-weekend feeders to sustain them for the two weeks that the school would be closed. Weekend feeders are small and round white pressed fish food. They come in the shapes of different shells. If it weren't for those ingenious inventions, I would have already lost a dozen fish to starvation. I turned off the aquarium light and opened my storage closet to get my purse. Oh, snap! It had tipped over off the shelf, and my stuff was scattered on the closet floor. I quickly threw everything

Innocent Echoes

back in my purse and grabbed my coat from the coat hook behind my closet door. I turned off the closet light, locked my classroom door, and headed home.

32

Friday morning started with children bringing the items they had volunteered to get for the afternoon's party. By the time the morning bell sounded, and the children were having their breakfast at their table, my reading table was overflowing with an assortment of cookies, small cases of juice boxes, large bags of chips, and brightly decorated cupcakes. I managed to organize the items inside a large storage cabinet in the far corner of the room. If the children can't see the party goodies, perhaps they would concentrate on today's lessons. I usually purchased a small gift for each student. Some years it's a diary or photo album, other times it's an activity book or a puzzle. This year it was a diary.

I did my best to manage the morning as close to a regular morning as possible. The students completed painting their salt clay ornaments. As soon as they were dry, my assistant took them, made a small hole on their hats, and ran a red piece of yarn through it. In minutes they were all ready to take home and hang on their trees. Today we were learning how to recall the sequencing of events. I brought some sequencing cards from home to engage the students in a sequencing game. I passed out four cards to each student. They were to put the events in the cards in the correct order. I had them sit in pairs in a large circle on the floor. The kids quickly sat and waited for instructions. I assigned a timekeeper, and each pair of students had 60 seconds to put their cards in order. After 60 seconds, the timekeeper would say switch and hand their cards to the pair on their right and begin again. The classroom was instantly filled with laughter. Some students hollered out, "No! Not that one! That does not go next!" They were having a blast.

I sat at my reading table, clearing off and placing in my cabinet the last of the bags of chips. I opened my book bag to retrieve my grade book to record the grades for the day, and I noticed the letter Rene handed me the day before. I had forgotten all about it. I placed it on my table and quickly began recording grades in my grade book.

Ten minutes later, I called the children to the carpet for their Christmas read-aloud. Today it was <u>The Longest Christmas List Ever!</u> They all listened attentively as I read and showed them the pictures. When I was finished, the children clapped.

I heard Andy say, "That was a funny book, but I know it's not possible to make a list go all the way out the door!"

The children laughed.

"What was the lesson learned in this story?" Bill raised his hand.

"To not ask for too much 'cause then you might not get anything!" Bill said. "Sometimes, I only ask for one stupid toy. For three years, and all my life, I have only asked for a dump truck, and I don't even get that! Santa is stupid," he said in a sad tone.

My heart broke, knowing that his mother, a single parent, had been too drunk or too high on drugs to even worry about what day it was for the last three years.

The children were talking together about what they wanted Santa to bring them this year when Luisa, a tiny framed child with long brown hair and big brown eyes, came to where I sat in front of the group and very politely asked, "Ms. Knoes is it almost lunchtime?"

I sprang from the table.

"Yes, yes, it is, and we are right on schedule."

I hurried to line them up and get them to the cafeteria on time. I looked at Luisa, who was my line leader, and winked.

"Thanks," I said.

I escorted the children to the cafeteria. As they filed into and through the serving line, I turned to head to my room. Teachers are only allowed a 30-minute lunch. By the time I escort them to the cafeteria and watch them go through the line, I usually have 15 minutes left. I kept a variety of Cup of Noodle soups in my classroom cabinet. Those require 3 minutes to fix. I had 10 minutes left to eat since I had to pick my students up from lunch on time, and the walk from my classroom to the cafeteria was about two minutes.

I sat at my reading table with my soup, crackers, and a container of milk I purchased from the cafeteria. I remembered the envelope. I took it from my table and reached for my letter opener.

"Hey, Jennifer."

I looked up to see Claire peeking in my room.

"If you're going to Mr. Brooks' rosary this evening, can I follow you?"

"Sure," I answered.

"Okay, thanks," she said and walked back to her classroom.

Holding the envelope, I tore the flap and took out a sticky note shaped like a red apple. At first, I did not notice anything on it. I flipped it, and the back of the paper was blank. Upon taking a second look, I saw three small letters, ABN, on the right bottom corner. Nothing about what the letters meant, just the three letters. I folded the paper and put it back in the envelope. I placed it in my bookbag. I would look at it later and try to figure what it meant if anything at all. The only thing that came to mind for ABN was the word abnormal. Abnormal what? It was a message that would need more time to figure out. Who would give me this anyway? It did not have a name. For now, it was time to pick up the kids from lunch.

I arrived at the cafeteria and walked my students down the halls quietly. In the classroom, they all sat on the carpet to view a science video. I found a really good video that explained the difference between wants and needs very clearly. After that, each child would be working on their wants and needs flipbook.

At 1:15 pm, I escorted the students to music class. When we arrived, Ms. Gomez was getting a video ready for the kids to enjoy.

"Okay, sit where you are supposed to sit," Ms. Gomez addressed the students with her back turned to them as she pushed the play button on her DVD player.

"Hey Ms. Knoes, thank you very much for the help yesterday. You're my last class today, so if you need help with your party or managing the kids, I will be happy to help you."

"Oh, thanks," I said. "No, I'm fine, I can manage."

In my mind, I saw Ms. Gomez rummaging through my purse the night of the Christmas program. I smiled and closed her room door behind me. I hurried to my room and prepared for their Christmas party. I quickly set up the serving table with the cupcakes, cookies, drinks, and a candy goodie bag. The tables were labeled with each student's name. Next to each name, I placed their gift from me and an empty plate with a napkin and fork.

Innocent Echoes

At two o'clock, I was walking down the hall with my little ones. They walked with their finger at their lip as if to say, "Shhhh." They knew the halls should remain quiet as not to disturb the other classrooms. They all went to their seats and started grabbing their gift and plate.

"Okay, listen up," I said while ringing the bell I kept by my computer. They knew that the sound of that bell meant I wanted quiet.

I informed the children that I was going to play a Christmas story for them. While it was playing, I would call them by table color to take what they wanted from the party table.

"Please only take what you will eat. I don't want you throwing food away another child could have had."

"Yes, Ms. Knoes," they replied in unison.

By the time everyone had served themselves, there was a low roar of children talking, some singing Rudolph the Red-Nosed Reindeer and others just eating quietly, enjoying every morsel of cupcake or cookie in their mouth.

All went well. The kids enjoyed their party snacks as they danced and jumped around to music coming from their Christmas story. I tried to be cheerful, but the thought of Mr. Brooks being dead kept me wanting to find the answers. I was going to the Rosary to say my farewell to Mr. Brooks, who had often gone out of his way to help my students in need.

I wasn't sad because he was dead. Death is not the end. People believe that when a person dies, they live forever in heaven or hell. My friend that comes by on Sundays claims that when a person dies, they are gone. That's it, the end. When the big book of wisdom speaks of eternal life, I believe it means you keep coming back but as someone else.

Death is the opportunity to be new again. Hence one can live forever as many people. I don't think death is the Grim Reaper touching people. I have heard people say, "His number was up" or "His death was meant to be." I disagree. I believe that the event is meant to be. For example, the plane is going to crash, or the ship is going to sink, but the people that are to die are not numbered. In other words, if you choose not to take that flight that is destined to crash, you have extended your life. Death will not feel cheated and come after you like it does in that *Final Destination* movie. Still, when I lose someone I care about, I often weep.

"Ms. Knoes, can I have another cupcake?"

I snapped out of my trance to find Leo, my smartest student, looking up at me, wearing a chocolate ring around his lips. There were six cupcakes left.

"Sure," I told him.

He quickly turned and grabbed the last chocolate cupcake and left behind five vanilla ones.

At twenty minutes before the bell, Claire brought her students into my classroom to manage all kids while I took care of the Invention Convention entries in the auditorium. Since I had placed all of the inventions by grade level, it was easy to apply the ribbons. I took a glance at the projects then went to check the judging sheets. I placed 1st, 2nd, and 3rd place ribbons on the winner's boards and participation ribbons on those who did not place. I completed a list for Sam to announce the winners. I gathered my clipboard with judging sheets and headed to the office with the winner's information for Sam to announce before the 3:00 oclock bell.

It was almost time to dismiss the class, so I hurried back to my classroom. Claire lined up her students, who had arrived with their backpacks ready to go, and walked them into the hallway. I called my students by table color to collect their backpacks and jackets. I noticed some students had not finished with their snacks.

"If you have snacks to take home, please take a zip lock bag from the basket on the table and put your snacks in it. Be sure to close it so it won't make a mess in your backpack."

Bill came up to me and gestured for me to kneel so he could whisper in my ear.

"Teacher, can I take those cupcakes home for my sister?"

"Sure," I whispered back. I placed the five remaining cupcakes in a small container that had been filled with cookies earlier.

I was well aware he did not have a little sister. He wanted food for the evening. He quickly hugged me and took a container from the table. He was smiling the biggest smile I had seen yet. The children were all lined up with their jackets on and backpacks ready.

"Okay, kids, let's head outside. I will see all of you in two weeks. Please stay safe while you're enjoying your Christmas break."

"Ms. Knoes, you won't see Mike or Leslie after the break. They won't be coming back," I heard a voice saying. I turned to see Louisa.

"Who told you they would not be coming back?"

"They did," she said. "Leslie said they were going to Mexico."

I escorted the children out to the pickup area to be collected by parents, grandparents, or older siblings. By 3:15 pm, all of my students had gone home.

I returned to my classroom and started gathering some center ideas from an internet site. It would give me something to work on if Jack and I returned from our trip early. I was exhausted, and I felt like I was moving in slow motion.

"Hey," I heard Claire holler from the door of my classroom.

She came over to my reading table and sat.

"You know, Jen; I'm well aware that we don't have solid evidence of any kind, but I believe you when you say something isn't right. For example, that van lady withdrew David early this afternoon."

"You mean early dismissal?" I asked.

"No, she gave Sam a 24-hour notice and withdrew him. The Walkers completed all the paperwork this morning," she said in a concerned voice. "The folder was in my box to complete and return to Sam before I leave today."

"Did they say why?" I asked.

"No, just that he was going back to Mexico."

She stood up and sighed.

"I don't know Jen, I'm worried."

Claire looked down at her watch.

"I better clean up the room before we leave. The church is not far, so we have time. I will be back in a flash. I just need to get my bags."

She turned and walked back to her classroom.

"Okay. I'm going to bring the inventions that might make district to my room before I leave so no one messes with them while we are gone," I said.

This year I was showered with plenty of gifts from my parents. I had three large bags to take home. I began to load my car, which was parked beside the school close to our exit doors. Mrs. Flor was doing the exact same thing I was doing.

"Great minds think alike," she said as she passed me carrying bags in each hand.

She held the door open for me with her body.

"Jen, are you okay? You look sick."

I went to my classroom for the last box, and Mrs. Flor followed me in.

"Come here," she said, and she placed her hand on my forehead. "Baby girl, you are running a very high fever! Have you been running a fever all day?"

I smiled, "Since I woke up this morning. I thought it would go away with medicine, but apparently, it hasn't."

"Do you have any other symptoms? Stomach ache, vomiting, cough?" she asked with concern. I told Mrs. Flor I had nothing, just an unexplainable fever.

"Oh no," Mrs. Flor said. "You have Ojo. I bet someone really liked you in that red dress last night."

I sighed, "What's Ojo?"

She explained that some cultures like hers believe in the eye of envy. If someone envies you too much and they don't get to touch what they envy, they can make a person sick with fever and weakness. She went on to say that the only way to cure it is to use an egg and perform a short ritual. I looked at Mrs. Flor, "Okay, I will think about that, thanks," I said, trying not to look like I thought she was off her rocker. "Okay, you think I'm crazy, but I am very serious. Let me know if you want my help". She hugged me and walked to her classroom to probably finish up a few things. By the time I was finished and returned to grab my purse from my classroom, Mrs. Flor had left for the day. Claire was already walking down the hall in my direction.

We walked down the hall silently, both sad about Mr. Brooks.

33

The sun was setting, and the sky was a hue of blue and orange light. The large parking lot at the church was almost full. After driving down several lanes, we managed to find two spaces close to each other on the last row farthest from the church. The Gothic structured church was not extremely large, but it was beautiful. It had sculptures of angels by the front doors and large windows decorated with beautiful stained glass art of saints and Jesus. In front of the church stood two majestic doors of dark wood with engraved designs that may have been fig leaves. As we entered the church, we saw statues of saints and a large crucifix in the center wall directly behind the podium. The mass had not started, and the church was almost reaching full capacity. Claire looked over at me.

"Hey, there's a space. Let's grab it before its standing room only."

The space was just big enough to suit the two of us comfortably.

It took only a few minutes to realize why that space had been left vacant. We were sitting between a lady wearing too much Channel No. 5 and a senior-aged man with what looked like a severe case of the flu. Just minutes after we sat, he began coughing and hacking. We could hear the phlegm spewing out of his mouth into the handkerchief he held to his face. We immediately took a tissue from our purses and pretended to wipe our eyes as we attempted to keep our mouths from breathing in every time the older man started hacking.

Music was playing. I could hear people whispering about how Mr. Brooks had always been so kind. How he was going to be missed and how he helped even those he did not know. We had arrived just minutes before the service was to begin.

The tall and lean Pastor, dressed in a white vestment with a lilac stole, approached the podium. He began by acknowledging those present and then read the beautiful poem, which was inscribed on the back of the memorial cards. A quiet silence filled the room. I heard soft crying then, upon the balcony, we heard a young woman with the most beautiful voice begin to sing Amazing Grace. I looked over to the family side of the church.

I could see Mrs. Brooks weeping. Beside her were their two daughters, appearing very broken-hearted by the loss of their father. The man sitting behind the daughters caught my attention. Was it Mr. Walker? I had only seen him twice this school year. What was he doing here? He sat on the pew like a statue. No emotion that I could see. After the Rosary, the Pastor asked that individuals form a line to give their condolences to the family.

"Come on, Claire, let's get in line," I insisted.

"Why?" she replied. "I don't wish her anything. She drove poor Mr. Brooks to the grave."

"No Claire, Mrs. Brooks loved Mr. Brooks. There's more to this than we know. I just don't understand what it could be." I whispered.

We followed the line until I came to Mrs. Brooks.

"My condolences to you and your loved ones," I said, and I took her hand. I could feel her heartbreak and her sorrow. I did the same to the daughters. I glanced over at Mr. Walker, who remained stoic. I had seen him at school, but he had never addressed me face to face. It was usually his wife or the driver of the van.

Claire and I returned to the bench where we were sitting, but we did not sit down.

"Excuse my French Claire, but there is no way in hell I'm sitting down between those two characters."

I looked over at Claire.

"It's over knucklehead; we can leave. No need to hang around here," she said.

I looked over at the line of people giving condolences and saw some of the teachers from school and Mrs. Phillips approaching the bench where the family sat. Further toward the back, I noticed Nicole chatting with Ms. Gomez. Now my head was spinning, and my heart hurt.

"What's wrong? Are you okay, Jen?"

I looked at Claire and said, "Yes, I'm fine. I'm just choked up a little."

"Are you going to be okay driving home? I can follow you if you want," she asked in a gentle voice.

"No, I'm fine," I assured her.

We walked quietly to our cars. She followed me to my side of the car and hugged me.

"Go home and start your vacation. Send me pictures."

She hugged me again, then headed to her car. We both drove to the exit of the parking and turned in opposite directions.

34

I drove home with the radio off, still trying to make sense of things. My phone rang.

"Hey sweetheart, don't forget we start a stress-free vacation tomorrow. Get home and pack!"

"Hi, baby, I can't wait. I'm heading home from Mr. Brooks' Rosary. I should be home in about 30 minutes," I answered.

"Okay," Jack said.

"I love you," I said and hung up the phone.

Traffic was heavy people were rushing in and out of their driving lanes. I concluded that most of these drivers were on their way to a shopping mall or strip. Perhaps some were on their way to a glorious vacation, as I would be very soon. I sighed and smiled. I remembered that the inventions had to be transported to Dean Ike Elementary tomorrow, Saturday. I called Flor and asked if she could pick up the inventions from my classroom and deliver them for me.

"Sure," she said, but be sure, and please let the custodians know so they will let me in the building."

"Will do, Thanks Flor"

I hung up the phone and drove in silence.

I kept remembering the letters ABN, but couldn't come up with answers. For now, what was going through my mind was what I had to pack for my vacation and to prepare the feeding bowls for my two feline friends. Perhaps getting away from all this mess for a while would be good for me. I drove up to the driveway and backed in so that I could easily toss my bags in the trunk of my car the following morning. I walked into my apartment carrying the two bags of Christmas gifts I had received from my parents. I glanced at my phone to find the message light on my answering machine blinking.

I put my bags down by the table near the door and tossed my keys in a round crystal bowl I kept on the entryway table. I pushed the play button and listened. My first message was Jack.

"I'll see you at 8:00 am. beautiful. I love you."

The next message played.

"Hey Jen, it's me, Katy. Those kid's names and pictures you left for me to look at, well, one of the names sounded familiar, so I typed it in the clinic database. It seems those two kids of yours, Mike and Leslie, were patients at our sister clinic downtown. Not just that, the Walker couple had other kids that were patients there too, but they have not returned for annual check-ups at any of our clinics. If they were sent back to Mexico, we have no way of finding them. I still don't know where in Mexico they could be if they were for sure taken there. As soon as I get there, I'll ask around. I am taking the envelope you gave me when I go. Oh yeah, one more thing that I thought was weird…"

"Message complete," the machine answered.

"You have no more messages."

I stood by my answering machine, speechless. What? I had to find out what Katy thought was weird. I dialed her number, and the phone rang and rang and rang. I had no answer from her and no answering machine to leave a message. I called her cell and received a recording that her mailbox was full. I decided I would shower and pack. Something would come to me if I needed to know something. My answers almost always came to me in my sleep, so the sooner I got some rest, the better.

I decided to take a long hot shower instead of my usual bath. I lathered up my hair and began to rinse it when I clearly heard a child's voice say my name. It sounded like Mike's voice. I thought someone was in my bathroom. I opened my eyes in a panic and immediately felt the shampoo seep in. Ouch! It burned. I rinsed my eyes and looked down at a pool of blood at my feet. I screamed and hysterically swung the curtain open and climbed out quickly. I grabbed my towel from the counter and looked back at the tub only to find clear water running out of the showerhead and clear water on the bottom of the tub.

After the few minutes it took to regain my composure, I quickly climbed back in the shower just long enough to rinse the soap out of my hair. Was it Mike letting me know something was happening?

35

I called Jack as soon as I could dry myself enough to exit the bathroom. His answering message came on.

"Hey, it's Jack. Talk to me."

"Honey," I said in the calmest voice I could muster. "I have had something come up. You go on ahead. I will meet you at the cabin as soon as I'm done here, promise."

I felt awful leaving the message, but I had to see what was going on. It was only 8:30 pm.

I decided to call Katy again to get the other part of the message.

"Hello," I heard another voice answer. It was not Katy. It was Mrs. Phillips.

"Oh, good evening Mrs. Phillips. I'm sorry; I must have dialed the wrong number." I said apologetically.

"What's up, Ms. Knoes?" Mrs. Phillips asked.

Then she remained completely silent. She had this unique way of asking questions that would grab you and make you surrender the truth before you had the time to conjure up a lie.

"Uh, I think Mike and Leslie are in trouble," I said. "I think something is going on at the house."

"What makes you think that?" she asked in a concerned and probing tone.

"Oh, I just have this gut feeling," I said, feeling like a complete idiot.

"Well, the district won't be happy if we get sued over a gut feeling, Ms. Knoes. Be aware of your boundaries as a teacher. Enjoy your vacation; you deserve it," she insisted.

She spoke calmly; it was her trait. If she received a call at work telling her that her house was on fire, her car had been stolen, and the stock market crashed, I have no doubt that she would react in her same calm and rational voice.

"Yes, ma'am, you're right. Thank you," I said and hung up the phone before I said anything else that was senseless.

I looked at my contact list, crossed my fingers, and prayed Katy would answer the phone. On the second ring, she answered.

"Hey Katy, it's me Jen. Thanks for the information on the kids. What was that last part about something being weird?" I asked.

"Oh yeah," Mike and Leslie both have AB negative blood type," she said. "It's a very rare blood type. Only one in 500 hundred people have this blood type. The interesting thing is that all of the Cardenas kids are AB negative. I hope these kids stay healthy so they can be donors when they are adults. Their blood is so needed."

"Why is that?" I asked.

Katy continued.

"There is a disease called Thalassemia that requires units of blood, sometimes bone marrow, to be transfused into the patient to prevent them from developing blood poising and dying from anemic complications. I know because we have a couple of patients with this condition, and I have to send them for blood transfusions. These transfusions are required every three months or more often. Even though these patients could receive bone marrow and blood from an O Positive donor, there is a risk factor. If the RHD antigen is not present in that blood, it could result in an ineffective transfusion, and the patient will still die. It's safer for the ill patient to receive bone marrow and blood from a person of the same blood type."

I could feel my stomach-turning.

"Thanks for the information, Katy. I appreciate your help."

I hung up the phone. I stood by the phone, took a deep breath, grabbed my purse, and decided to go with my instincts. I sped out of my driveway straight toward the Walker's' house.

I drove fast, but not fast enough to get pulled over with a speeding ticket. The traffic had lightened up. I still witnessed some drivers at stoplights talking on their cell phones or texting. I don't understand why some people can be so inconsiderate and reckless—one more traffic light before I arrived at the residential area. In front of me was a young male texting and not paying attention to the signal lights. Obviously, he was texting someone worth dying for. At green, he did not budge. I honked my horn lightly. Startled, he looked up and sped on.

I was just minutes from the Walker's house. I kept thinking of my reasoning for visiting this late in the night. I also clearly remembered Mrs. Phillip's words: "Know your boundaries as a teacher."

36

I needed a good reason to ring their doorbell, and I remembered I had one. Mike had submitted an invention called Pocket Socks, and it won 1st Place in the 1st-grade level. All 1st place winners received a blue 1st Place ribbon and a notification that their invention would be entered in the District competition. Since Mike and Leslie were withdrawn from school on Thursday, neither had any idea of who won in the Invention Convention. This meant I had a legitimate excuse for visiting their home. I felt better about visiting the home, but not calmer. My stomach was still in knots.

I did not know much about Thalassemia, but I did know that it mostly affected people from the Mediterranean. I recall hearing Mrs. Walker mentioning that she was from the Mediterranean while she chatted with Nicole in the hallway. She did not notice me, and I did not slow down my walk when I passed them. In this instant, my heart was racing. I kept rehearsing in my mind how I was going to introduce the good news so they would allow me in the home, if only for a while.

My phone rang. "Shit!" I said out loud as I pounded on my steering wheel and pulled over on the side of the road to answer it.

"Hey, it's me," Rachel said.

"Hey, what's up?" I asked nonchalantly.

"I was worried about you. Why didn't you tell me your school counselor shot himself. That's got to be devastating," she said, sounding concerned.

I responded, trying not to sound anxious. I wanted to get to the Walker's house to see what was going on. Rachel was up to her ears in murders, and I did not want her involved in this mess.

Innocent Echoes

I told Rachel I was on my way to Walgreens, my favorite 24-hour drug store, for some headache medicine.

"It was an emotional blow to have our counselor commit suicide. I went to the Rosary with Claire, and I'm feeling better."

I tried to sound as convincing as I could. I did not want to burden Rachel with more stress. At this time, she was working on a murder case and had her own share of stress.

"Right now, I am on my way home to pack for my winter vacation with Jack," I said cheerfully.

"Are you sure you'll be okay?" she asked.

"Yes, I will be fine," I answered as calmly as I could. "I have you on speed dial on my phone and voice dial if I can't move my fingers."

Rachel laughed. "Use them if you need me."

"Okay, I'm just anxious to start my vacation, but first, I'm driving by the Walker's house to deliver news about the Invention Convention. My student was withdrawn from school early, so he didn't get the news that he won."

"Alright," Rachel replied, and I clicked off the phone.

37

Mike knew it would be no use to cry out. Mr. and Mrs. Walker had taken care of him by keeping him healthy and giving him a good home. Before the adoption, he was peddling for money on the border from any passerby tourist who would pity him. He lived with his mother and father close to the Mexican border in a hut put together with boards, large pieces of carpet, plastic, and cinderblocks. Since the day he can remember, he had suffered cold nights and days of unbearable heat. He could recall countless days with nothing but a piece of bread or fruit as the entire day's meal. Other days, all he had to eat was what fruit he could find on the fruit trees growing by the streets. Often, the fruit was rotten or had worms. He had two choices, eat what he found or starve.

The Walker's had adopted him and given him a good home. He ate three meals a day without fail. He was taken to the doctor when he was sick and kept safe. It was his duty to repay them; however, he could. Since they brought him to the house, the nurse would also bring him his vitamins and water before bedtime without fail. Taking his blood every once in a while was not a huge sacrifice, he thought to himself as he tried to rationalize what was happening.

He was put through this process every few months and now was no different. The nurse always made him feel well again after every blood donation by giving him his favorite meal of pizza and chocolate milk. He knew the blood was for Mrs. Walker. Silently, he tried to convince himself that it was a good thing for him to give his blood to her. She was sick, and she needed his help, he thought to himself. At his young age, he rationalized that giving his blood to help the one who nourished him and provided a place for him to live and sleep was a good thing.

Still, he dreaded the pain of the needle. His little arm would often remain bruised for a week or so. Mrs. Walker would make sure he wore sleeves that covered the marks until they healed. His body and limbs were strapped to a small reclined bed. He was not able to move his arms or legs. Perhaps this was for his safety to prevent him from moving and hurting himself. Maybe it was to keep him from fleeing. He had a needle in his small arm and could feel the blood being drained from his thin body as he listened to some nature sounds soothing music. It did not soothe him one bit.

Instead, he stared at the round clock that hung on the wall he was facing. It was peculiar to him, for it had no numbers. Just lines, some standing vertically, and others were slanting. He did see the letters V and X but could not understand why a clock that should contain numbers contained only lines and the letters V and X. He let his mind ponder that for a while as he stared at the clock. He was supposed to let the nurse know if he began to feel dizzy. She always stopped the process immediately, and he was sure today would be no different. In the past, all he had to do was say okay to let her know it was time to stop. But now, the room was empty, and all he could hear was the music. His caregiver was not in sight. She had left the room and had not returned.

Mike felt himself drifting off as the blood continued to flow out of his body and into a long red pouch. The music became faint and low as the blood continued to flow. His eyelids were feeling heavy, and his skin cold. The lights were looking dimmer and dimmer as he drifted off into a dark sleep.

38

I was only blocks from the Walker's residence now, and I was still nervous. I could feel the knots in my stomach getting tighter as a person might feel just before an important speech, music recital, or a 1500 foot skydiving jump.

I arrived at their subdivision as the sunset and stars began to show. I could see rows of houses framed with multi-colored Christmas lights and lawns hosting giant snowmen or mechanical reindeer that appeared to be moving in slow motion. The Cardenas kids lived in a house that had Santa in his sleigh being pulled by his eight reindeer on the roof. The home resembled a neat and organized Christmas wonderland with trees in the front yard decorated with red and green lights and the sidewalk lined with three-foot red and white striped candy canes. However, the garden behind the swings had been tilled and appeared to be ready for whatever crop or fruit Mrs. Walker was planting next and possibly donating to the Teacher's lounge.

As I drove along the side of the house, I noticed most of the lights were off, and the driveway was clear of cars. No one appeared to be home, yet something was unsettling. Well, no sense in being a chicken now, I thought out loud. Although withdrawn from school, Leslie and Mike were my students, and it was my job to be concerned about them. Of course, Mrs. Phillips might see it differently.

I was going to the Walker's house to congratulate Mike and let him know his Invention of Sock Pockets would be entered in the District competition. Mike will be thrilled to find out he had received 1st Place in his grade level. It was an excellent idea for joggers who have to keep a key or an ID because the pockets were big enough to hold that, plus change and a few dollar bills if necessary. I was very proud of Mike. The Invention Convention was an exciting event for the entire district, and the awards banquet is a big deal. It's held at the Botanical Gardens Ball Room and always covered by the media resulting in some students even receiving talk show television exposure for winning in the competition. I was entering three of the 1st Place winners from our school this year to compete with hundreds of others in the district.

I walked up the sidewalk and took a deep breath before ringing the doorbell. It took a good three minutes, which felt like an eternity before a tall thin female in a blonde ponytail answered the door. She was wearing blue surgical scrubs. I had never seen her before, but she seemed to know who I was and appeared immediately shaken by my presence. I had a clear view of a study with three walls of built-in bookshelves filled with books. I could also see Leslie in a large brown chair, reading a book that covered most of her lap.

"Hi, I'm Ms. Knoes, Mike and Leslie's Teacher. I was driving by and decided to deliver the news that Mike's invention won school-wide in our Invention Convention. It will be entered in the district-wide competition. Mike was creative with his invention." I said as I looked around to see if he was somewhere in sight, but he wasn't.

I was hoping Leslie would look up from her book, but she seemed mesmerized by whatever she was reading. I looked at the young lady, trying not to notice her agitation.

"You know, I didn't get to see them off, and I heard they are going back to Mexico. Can I just say goodbye to them?" I asked.

"That will not be possible," she said, and she started to close the door.

Quickly moving forward, I held the door open with my hand and pleaded, "Oh, come on! I can see Leslie sitting right over there. Please, may I come in and see them? It will only take a few minutes."

Her expression went from sweet to sour in two seconds flat.

"No, I'm sorry that's not possible," she said and continued closing the door.

It was then that I stuck my foot in and forced myself inside, throwing her back slightly and pushing her aside.

"Look, lady, Leslie is right there. It won't hurt to let me see her."

I begin walking to where Leslie was sitting. She looked away from her book and up at me as I started walking towards her. At first, she had a smile, and then her expression changed to horror at the sight of something behind me. Suddenly, I felt a tight grip around my neck; apparently, a cord of some kind was wrapped around my neck! I grabbed the line with my hands and tried to pull it away without much success. My air was slowly being cut off. I dropped my body back on my attacker, hoping to break the grip, but my attacker would not let go. I could feel myself losing consciousness when suddenly, I heard a gunshot, and everything went black.

39

I must have been out just briefly. I was lying on my back with my arms at my sides. I awoke and began to bring my hands to my throat to pull the cord away. It hurt from the pressure that had been placed on it. I slowly began to open my eyes when I felt a tug and heard a very familiar voice.

"Come on, Ms. Knoes, get your gut feeling ass up and let's look for Mike."

I looked up to see Mrs. Phillips frowning. She extended her hand and helped me up.

"Come on!" she said in a commanding tone as she raced up the stairs in her red heels.

We both entered the first room at the top of the stairs that had the door slightly open. There strapped to the reclined bed was Mike's pale body. Lying on another bed that was against the window was Mrs. Walker. She looked to be asleep. Against a pink flannel gown, her skin appeared pale and gray. She was breathing but obviously very sick.

"Oh no, I heard Mrs. Phillips say as she struggled to unfasten the bed straps.

Before she could begin to undo the first strap, I had cut through it with my switchblade, which I carry in my boot. She opened her eyes wide and looked at me.

"I had a gut feeling I would need this," I said.

I cut through the straps in seconds. I tilted Mike's head and began CPR while Mrs. Phillips called 911. She calmly spoke the information into her cell.

"I have an emergency at 1600 Sawyer Ave. The victims are a young female who has been shot in the chest, a seven-year-old child that appears to have lost a lot of blood, and a middle-aged woman that looks pale and appears to be sick." She listened then said, "Okay, thank you." Suddenly, we heard Claire's voice. Looking over, we found her standing at the doorway with Mr. Walker holding his arms behind him in an unnatural position.

"I found Mr. Walker trying to get in his car. I must have caught him by surprise because he went crazy and ran his head into the garage door," She winked, and then she threw him on the floor half unconscious.

He sat up minutes later and was rubbing his arms when we heard the emergency vehicles approaching. I looked at Claire with wide eyes.

"Who are you?" I asked.

"A karate student who can really kick some ass.".

She raised her eyebrows and turned away. The fire rescue arrived before the ambulance. They began to survey the situation and continued to administer CPR on Mike. Another firefighter was with Mrs. Walker, checking her vitals and speaking to her.

Two ambulances showed up within minutes. To my complete surprise, Rachel arrived in her squad car right behind them.

Mrs. Phillips followed the ambulance that took Mike and Mrs. Walker to University Medical Center. The nurse who had been shot by Mrs. Phillips occupied the other. Soon, after the two ambulances had raced off with sirens blaring and lights flashing, the third ambulance arrived to take Mr. Walker. They placed him on a stretcher, hoisted him into the rear compartment, and shut the doors. Since Mr. Walker suffered from nothing short of a bump on the head, the ambulance did not turn on sirens nor speed through traffic as it departed. Rachel came over to me.

"Are you alright?" She asked.

I felt fine. But my neck was still red, and my skin burned where the cord's friction had rubbed my neck. When the ambulance arrived, I covered my neck with my scarf. I don't want to ride in an ambulance.

"I'm driving to the ER and taking Leslie with me. Can you escort us to the hospital?" I asked.

"Yes, certainly," Rachel replied.

Rachel led the way with her emergency lights and siren. Traffic parted like the red sea as the red lights and siren approached.

We arrived at the emergency entrance. I parked my car and noticed some Lake Worth police officers were waiting at the hospital when we arrived. Rachel exited her car and walked over to her group. I walked into the ER with Leslie by the hand and walked over to the waiting area where Claire and Mrs. Phillips sat. I sat in a lounge chair big enough for two with Leslie, who was still frightened by what she had seen.

After a few minutes, the nurse came out of the room where Mike was and walked over to us.

She smiled and said, "He's going to be okay. He will be kept for observation until the morning, but all looks promising." With that said, she returned to Mike's room.

Rachel entered the ER and stopped at the nurse's station. Minutes later, she walked over to us and reported with an update.

"Mr. Walker just had a nasty bump on his head and has a lot of questions to answer. The police officers are not cutting him any slack."

With an icepack held to his head, they escorted him into a police car that was standing by the ER exit. She continued.

"Mrs. Walker is being given the blood transfusion she needed. She would need a day or two to be back on her feet. Several uniformed police officers will be watching her, and as soon as she is well enough, she will also be taken to the police station. I have no doubt they are anxious to see her in a cell."

I walked over to the room where they had taken Mike. My eyes filled with tears of relief and joy as I watched the nurse handling him gently as she prepped him to receive blood. I sighed and returned to the waiting area after a few minutes.

"Hey, I'm very glad you guys are okay. I hope this is all figured out soon. I have to get back to work." Rachel said.

"Thanks for getting to the house fast. You must have passed quite a few red lights," I said. Rachel laughed.

"I guess old habits are hard to break," she said.

"What do you mean?" I asked.

"When I called you this evening, you said you were going to Walgreens to get medicine for a headache. We both know you do not get headaches. And the last Place you mentioned was the Walker residence. I made sure I stayed in the area just in case. When dispatch received the 911 call, I was just a few blocks away."

I felt my eyes water and the dam of tears broke. How lucky was I to have such a wonderful friend? I laughed and gave her a huge hug. "Okay, Okay, easy on the uniform," she said sarcastically and handed me a tissue she had taken from the end table.

After making me promise to keep her posted, she turned and walked out into the night.

I sat next to Claire and gave her a curious expression.

"How did you know I would be at the Walker's house?"

"After you left the funeral home all shaken up, I decided to go over to your apartment to see if you were okay and bid you a safe vacation. But when I turned the corner of your street, I saw you racing out of our driveway like a maniac. I decided to follow you to see where you were going. When I saw you get off and go into the Walker house, I became concerned. Then, I saw Mrs. Phillips here," as she pointed to her, also drive up in her shiny red shoes, and I figured I better see what was happening since I know that Mrs. Phillips only wears those shoes when she means business. She did not look happy, and she had that 'Oh shit! Time to stop some trouble look, you know?"

Claire looked at Mrs. Phillips.

"That look you get when there's a fight on school grounds, always accompanied with that 'I'm going to kick some ass' walk.

Mrs. Phillips looked at Claire, smiled, and moved her head from side to side. She turned her head to look at me and pressed her hands in a prayer position then in a pleading tone, said, Ms. Knoes, please tell me you don't carry a weapon to school," She glanced at my boots where I routinely kept my switchblade, which I understand is an illegal knife in the United States.

"No, not at all," I replied and smiled a guilty smile.

Then it hit me.

"Wait a minute! You're the one with a loaded gun!"

I stated and looked at her, waiting for some kind of explanation. No explanation was given. She just stood up calmly, looked at me, and said, "That loaded gun saved your ass tonight."

She walked Leslie by the hand to a soft chair about 10 feet away, where a nurse was waiting to check her for shock. The nurse shined a light in Leslie's eyes and checked her pulse.

Mrs. Phillips glanced at Claire and me. She sat across from us and rubbed the back of her neck. She then placed her hands on her lap and took a deep breath.

She began speaking, "I looked up Mr. Brooks' file and discovered some interesting things. As it turns out, he was the lawyer who arranged the adoptions for the Walker couple. It seems what started as an innocent assignment became an entanglement of money and greed. Mr. Brooks was under the impression that the kids were being given better homes and a better chance at life. Perhaps he found out something was very wrong and, when the children started to vanish, he may have wanted out. He tried to stop the adoptions, but somehow Mrs. Walker convinced him that he would be as guilty as they were. I know this because she repeatedly sent messages to his district e-mail. He did not want his family to suffer because of him. The ones who may have driven him to suicide were Mr. and Mrs. Walker, and not his wife. The police confiscated all of his e-mail and phone records after the apparent suicide. They were the ones who shared this information with me. Sadly enough, it turns out Mr. Brooks and his wife had a very happy marriage.

Well, ladies, I believe we have done all we can do here. Let's go home and get some rest. CPS has allowed me to take Leslie and Mike for now until we find them a loving home. You two enjoy your winter break."

She grabbed on to her purse and walked over to Leslie. The nurse who had been examining her looked over at Mrs. Phillips and said, "You may take her home."

Mrs. Phillips took Leslie by the hand, turned to me, and said, "We will be back for Mike first thing in the morning." Then she paused, looked at me, and continued with, "Ms. Knoes, my understanding is you were at the Walker house on legitimate Invention Convention business, after first notifying me by phone and getting my approval."

After her statement, she smiled, gave a quick wink, and exited the hospital.

I decided to wait for Mike to wake up. I will buy him a teddy bear from the gift shop and spend some time with him in the morning. After I visit with Mike, I will go home and finish packing for my trip. I may be a little late, but I was sure Jack would understand.

I jumped in my seat when I heard a loud commotion. Seconds later, a group of emergency paramedics was racing in through the emergency room door. A doctor and three nurses were standing ready to receive the patient.

"Get the patient into OR stat!"

The doctor ordered one nurse as he and the other two nurses raced to the stretcher and began running down the hall towards me. I stood to get out of the way and was curious about what was going on. I heard the doctor ask the patient's name.

"Jack Monroe," the nurse replied.

"Hang in there, Jack," the doctor pleaded. "Hang in there, buddy."

They rolled him into the OR and began cutting clothing and inserting needles in his arms for IVs. I watched in horror as the nurses and doctors fought to keep Jack alive. After an hour, they wheeled him out and placed him in the Intensive Care Unit.

"What happened?" I asked the nurse at the main desk.

She looked up at me and asked, "Are you related to the patient?"

"I'm his fiancé."

"Avalanche accident," the nurse replied.

Those are common, especially early in the season, since the snow hasn't had time to stick. The doctor came out of the ICU room and turned to speak to the nurse.

"He has severe internal bleeding. He's in a coma. Only God and time will tell if he will wake up. Prayers wouldn't hurt." He then turned to me. "You'll have to wait outside, ma'am. We will keep you informed."

"Can I sit in his room?" I asked.

The doctor looked at me, then at the head nurse.

"She's his fiancée," she said.

"Okay, you may sit with him, but he needs to rest. The attending nurse will let you know when you can go in."

He rubbed his forehead, indicating he was probably experiencing a nasty headache. He picked up a clipboard from the counter and passed through some double doors.

Later, the nurse came out of Jack's room and motioned with a nod.

"You can see him now. There's not much we can do." He is heavily sedated to help the pain. He is in a coma."

I walked in slowly with both hands covering my mouth in disbelief. Jack lay still in the bed. I stared at his beautiful face. He had an IV in one arm, and I could see he was connected to a monitor that would send a signal to the front desk if he came out of his coma. I was there for him, and I was not going to leave. I was trying to have faith and believe that Jack would wake up. He had to wake up. It was our destiny to be married and live in a white house out in the country.

I sat in a chair that I pulled as close to Jack's bed as I could. I held his hand and talked to him. The avalanche was meant to happen. Whether Jack was going to pull through was still not known. At 11:55 pm. I was holding his hand when he squeezed. My eyes opened wide, and I looked at him. I could see his beautiful green eyes looking at me.

"You'll be okay, baby. I'll get the nurse."

I was going to get up, but Jack would not let go of my hand. His hand felt cold. He looked at me and pulled me to the bed. I knew what he was asking. He wanted me there, next to him, holding him and running my fingers through his hair as it had always been. Even though he was awake, I heard no bells or whistles alarming the nurses he was awake. I carefully slipped into the bed next to him. He put his hand that was free around my waist and held me close. I looked up at him and kissed him gently. I was afraid I would hurt him, but he leaned into me and kissed me as passionately as he had kissed me the first week we met. I knew this was his way of saying goodbye. I loved Jack's kisses more than anything in the world. Jack gently kissed me and held me. He caressed my body and slipped his hands to his favorite spot, right on my ass. It was a personal inside joke for us. A month after we met, he was often traveling, and he wanted a picture. Jack asked for a picture of my booty.

"I'm an ass man, and you, Ms. Jennifer, happen to have a very nice one," he had said.

I laughed at his request, but I was so stupid in love with him that I took a picture of my behind in a tiny bikini and gave it to him. To date, he still carried it in his wallet.

When he moved his hand to hold me tight to him, I knew that would be the last time I would feel the warmth of his body next to mine. He kissed my forehead gently and drifted off into an eternal sleep. I clung to him and sobbed. My chest was hurting. My heart was shattered, and all of my dreams for a happy ending had disappeared. I clung to Jack, and I pleaded, "I don't want to know. I want to be normal. Please, God, if you can hear me, hear me now. I don't want to know. I don't want to see. I just want to be normal. Please, please, please just let me be wrong! Let him wake up."

All I felt was pain. Even my heart hurt. My pleading was painful. I wanted to die. All I felt was hopelessness.

"Please," I pleaded again. My throat hurt. My head hurt. "If you can hear me, stop my heart from beating. I have no place here now." I clung to Jack and sobbed.

"Jennifer, wake up."

I felt a hand gently tapping my shoulder. Startled, I looked up at Mrs. Phillips. I had fallen asleep on the chaise in the waiting room.

"Hey sleepyhead, we are here to get Mike. Why don't you go home now? If I recall correctly, you are supposed to be on a skiing vacation," she reminded me cheerfully.

I stood up and raced to the nurse's station, where two nurses stood reviewing a patient chart. Another nurse sat behind the counter in front of a computer.

"May I help you?" the nurse behind the counter asked. "

Can you tell me what room Jack Monroe is in?"

The nurse looked at me and asked me when he was admitted. I answered that it was just last night.

"I'm sorry. We don't have a Jack Monroe in ICU." She looked at me, bewildered.

"He was in an avalanche accident." I insisted.

"No, ma'am, we have no avalanche victims," she said as she stared into her computer screen.

"He came in last night, dammit!" I said, now with both my fists on the counter and getting upset.

"Please keep your voice down. We have not had anyone check in with the name of Jack Monroe. I can't help you," she answered in a calm, soothing voice. Are you sure he was admitted to this hospital? She asked.

I turned to Mrs. Phillips, who was now working with one of the other nurses completing Mike's hospital dismissal forms.

I searched in my coat pockets, took out my cell, and frantically dialed Jack's number. His phone was out of range.

"Oh God, no," I quietly pleaded.

I tried again, no connection. I must have dialed his number 20 times. Mrs. Phillips approached me with Mike in tow and said I should go home and get away for a while. I agreed and gave Mike a hug. I found my car in the parking lot, and drove to Jack's home, trying not to go into hysterics, pleading with God all the way there.

"Please take care of Jack. Please! Please! Please!"

I drove up to Jack's apartment to find Jack walking out to his car with his bags. The trunk of his car was open. He looked up at me when he saw me drive up and gave me the biggest smile. I parked my car and ran to him and held him as tight as I could.

"Hey, you made it. We will make it to the ski resort after all," he said enthusiastically.

"Jack, let's not go. Let's stay here and enjoy a whole week indoors, away from the world, just us and take-out food," I said in a soft, pleading voice.

He pulled me close and kissed me gently.

"Now you're speaking my language. Your wish is my command," he said. He closed the car trunk, put his arm on my shoulder, and escorted me back to his apartment with his bag still on his shoulder. If I kept him away from the snow, he was safe from harm. I prepared a hot breakfast of scrambled eggs, hash browns, buttered toast, and fresh coffee for both of us. I took everything to the coffee table in the living room. We ate and watched a very sad movie about a notebook that a man was reading to his wife in a nursing home to help her remember their life together. Parts of the story were funny, and other parts were so very sad.

"Okay, enough of this," Jack said and began to change the channel.

He was looking for the show that had two property brothers that fixed houses for couples. I stood while he channel-surfed. I took two logs from beside the fireplace and tossed them in. The warm fire felt good on my hands.

I collected the dishes from the coffee table and returned to the living room. Jack found his favorite show and lay back on his wide couch. We snuggled together and kissed a little. He told me that since we were not going on vacation, he was returning to work and finishing up some paperwork.

I decided to call Mrs. Flor and let her know that I would be able to take the inventions to Dean Ike Elementary after all. I thanked her for her kindness and continued my evening with Jack.

43

It was Saturday morning, and since I did not go on vacation with Jack, I went by my classroom to pick up the three inventions and deliver them to Dean Ike Elementary. The first one was the Styling Safety Vest, the second one was the Purse Boots, and the third one was Mike's Sock Pockets.

I approached the front door of Dean Ike Elementary. As soon as I entered the building, the Invention Convention Coordinator approached me. Walking beside her were two teens, apparently her helpers for the day.

"How many inventions will you be setting up for display?" she asked.

I answered that I had three. She gestured to the young boys to help me, and they followed me out to my car. I opened the trunk, and without saying a word, each boy carefully took an invention. I grabbed the trifold with the Sock Pockets. Re-entering the building, the coordinator held the doors open and instructed the boys to leave them on top of a long table she was pointing at. "The inventions are displayed according to grade level.

"We will set them up this afternoon for judging tomorrow morning. Tomorrow afternoon, you may return and see if any of your students won District. The doors will open at noon," Please be prepared to take them back to your school tomorrow. She reminded me that the inventions that won in District would need to be displayed at the Botanical Gardens Ballroom. A reception will be held to recognize the winners on Monday, the first day back after the winter break.

"We will see you again tomorrow afternoon. District winners will be identified with a ribbon. The winners of the Most Scientific or Most Creative will have an envelope containing a $500.00 voucher attached to their invention. See you tomorrow, and good luck."

With that, she turned and walked over to assist other teachers who were bringing in their school inventions.

I looked around at a sea of trifold boards and displays. "So many creative minds," I thought to myself. I looked over at my inventions which had already been taken to another table and displayed with the model in front of each entry. I said a silent prayer and hoped one of my students would come away with a District Ribbon or prize.

At 12:15 pm. Sunday afternoon, I was in my car driving to the Elementary school where the district judging took place. Because the roads were icy and slick, the traffic moved slowly and carefully down the long roads and highways. I arrived at the school and made sure to park as close to the main entrance as possible. There were only a few cars there, so I managed to park close. I slipped my coat hood up and pulled my coat closed. I entered the school and followed the sound of people speaking. I went down a long hall and arrived at the gymnasium entrance.

Looking in, I saw long rows of trifold boards on tables. All were holding a maroon District Participation ribbon. The district winners were holding two ribbons, the Participation Ribbon and the blue District Winner ribbon. There were a dozen parents with their children walking around admiring all of the inventions. I walked along the long rows of Invention displays that had been set up by grade level. Upon arriving at the 4th-grade tables, I saw a royal blue District Winner Ribbon hanging on the corner of the Safety Styling Vest. On the next row over where the 2nd-grade winners were displayed, I smiled to find another royal blue District Winner ribbon on the Boots with Secret Pockets. Mike's invention of Pocket Socks did not win District, but it did receive the maroon Participation ribbon. After looking at all of the inventions, I was amazed at the talent of so many young minds.

I begin to fold the Pocket Socks invention when the Invention Convention director walked over to me.

"Ms. Knoes, congratulations! It seems you are taking home a couple of District Winner ribbons. Please remember that our banquet to honor those winners is Monday evening at the Botanical Gardens Ballroom."

She offered to help me with getting the inventions to my car. She turned and looked around, and then she motioned to two young men that had just entered the gymnasium to come over to where we stood.

"Show them your displays, and they will carry them out for you. All you have to do is open your vehicle so that they can place them inside."

She walked over to a table by the entrance and took out a bright red t-shirt with an Invention Convention applique of a light bulb. She held it out to me, saying, "Thank you for participating in this year's Invention Convention. We could not do this year after year without the dedication of our teachers that give up their own time to make it a success."

She shook my hand and allowed me to finish with the gathering of my trifold boards. The two men swiftly loaded the inventions in the backseat of my car and hurried back into the building.

I felt proud that our school had produced two district winners and was excited for the students. That was a record for our school. On Monday, I will have Sam announce the winners over the PA system. Now that it's over, it's one less thing on my shoulders. What a relief. Although the Invention Convention is only for two months, it's many extra hours outside of my regular teaching schedule. I still needed to contact the two students that won District and give them the information to be at the recognition ceremony. Monday evening, I will make sure to have the inventions displayed at the banquet hall with their winning ribbons.

I received a phone call from Jack that afternoon.

"Since we did not go skiing, I decided I would catch up on some work," he said, apologetically. Jack did have a business to run and deadlines to meet. After all, it was one of the busiest times of the year, and business was booming.

After spending Saturday and part of Sunday with Jack at his apartment, I noticed some things that made me uneasy. For example, his apartment looked not lived-in. That made some sense because he spent much of his time at my place. But this was different. Everything was in its place the way a model apartment for an apartment complex would appear. He also had a minimal number of items. In the kitchen, he had four plates, two cups, and three drinking glasses. In the cabinet next to the stove, he had a saucepan and a frying pan. It was the same when I asked to borrow a T-shirt to wear as a nightshirt. In his closet were four sets of clothes and 3 T-shirts. It didn't make sense that nothing in that apartment was a complete set. Still, I had a wonderful time with Jack. I was sure there was a logical explanation. Arriving at my apartment, I found my mailbox filled with what looked like mail from every charity I had ever donated $5.00 to. I heard my phone ringing in my purse and scrambled to answer it before the message mode kicked in. It was from Katy.

"Jen, they took David to Mexico today. They came by the clinic for a copy of his medical records early this morning. I've been talking to my family and friends in Mexico. Cardenas is not just the kid's last name; it's a code name. Cardenas kids are AB negative kids available through the black market. The Walker kids are being sold to the highest bidder! The catch is that legal adoptive papers were

Innocent Echoes

drawn up to clear the parent, in this case, Mr. and Mrs. Walker. Rumor has it that once the child was adopted, they were game for anything. When they started the adoptions, it was only for people interested in their unique blood and bone marrow. They must have gotten greedy and began to sell them to anyone with the money to pay. They began trafficking the children without knowing or caring about their fate after they were sold."

Then she broke down in hysterical sobs. "Los voy a matar! I'll kill them! I'll kill the sons of bitches," She said, now in anger.

Jen, the codes B, and BP stand for blood and body parts!"

I could barely understand what she was saying. I remember David had a BP under his foot.

"What can we do, Jen? Poor baby," she sobbed.

"There is nothing we can do, Katy."

I didn't have a clue where the home was by the ocean, nor did I know how to find the people since the faces were never very clear.

"I appreciate your friendship and your hard work," I said calmly. "I will talk to you later."

I hung up the phone and felt numb. My eyes welled up with tears. Remembering the horse picture he drew for me and the dream I had of the young boy whose face I never saw in that big beautiful mansion with the young nurse. I now knew it was David. I also knew David was gone.

By now, his body had been sold in parts on the internet for millions of dollars. I put the phone in my jacket pocket and placed the mail on the entryway table. I walked to my small dining table and sat with my hands on my forehead. I could not contain my tears. My chest felt as if someone had struck me. I found it hard to breathe as I sat quietly and wept. A beautiful child had been dissected and taken apart, piece by piece. What hurt me the most was the knowledge that he was not the only one.

To be in the presence of an innocent child is equal to being in the presence of God. For their trust is uninhibited, love unrestrained, and forgiveness unconditional. (The book of words unspoken)

The week of Christmas, Jack was not around as often. Christmas was the busiest time of the year, and he said he would be spending most of his holiday working. I was fine with that. I spent my Christmas Eve with my family, sharing childhood stories and exchanging presents. My family is very close. Although we are not in each other's space constantly, we love each other dearly. The only downside to having a huge family is that if I want to get a Christmas gift for everyone, I better start saving money and shopping six months in advance. A few years ago, we decided to put everyone's name in a basket and have each of us pull one name. That worked out well.

This Christmas Eve, I had a very special errand to run. I drove to Ridgecrest Mall and purchased clothes, shoes, some snacks, and three very special items. I neatly placed everything in a large red bag and covered the top with green tissue paper. On the bag, which stood at about three feet tall, was a large red tag that read:

To: Bill

From: Santa

At 7:30 am on Christmas Day, I parked my car away from the front of the rental house where Bill lived. I rang the doorbell twice and quickly hid behind some shrubs that separated the two front yards and prayed for the best. Minutes later, the door opened. Wearing unmatched red and blue flannel pajamas, little Bill stood at the door. His face looked confused for a minute. He looked at the bag, then around to see if anyone else was outside. He moved close to the bag and read the tag. He screamed and started jumping up and down in hysterics.

He began clapping his hands to his face saying, "Oh, boy! Oh boy! Oh, boy!"

He reached into the bag and took out a blue dump truck with moving parts and all. He set the dump truck down, reached into the bag again, and took out a second, larger truck. This one was a bright red fire truck with huge tires and headlights.

Looking back into the bag, he gasped, "Another one!" as he reached in and pulled out the third one, a huge, yellow, construction bulldozer.

He kneeled by his bag, and, using his sleeve, he wiped his face that was now red and streaming with happy tears. Little Bill was filled with joy to a capacity he had never experienced in his life. He carefully placed the trucks back in the bag. He propped open the door and pulled his bag in using both of his small arms. One tug, two tugs, and it was in. The door closed.

Seconds later, he came running out. He was staring at the sky, apparently looking for Santa and saying, "Thank you. Thank you, Santa. I'm sorry I called you stupid."

And with that, he returned inside. When I was sure I would not be seen, I hurried back to my car. Seeing Bill genuinely happy was a great start of my day. Like Little Bill, I, too, was crying happy tears. I wiped my eyes with a tissue that I kept in my bra. I had been expecting the tears. I put my car in drive and headed home.

I had planned a Christmas Day breakfast with Jack. Lately, his visits were few and far between, so I took what I could get. He showed up at my place around 9:00 am. I was home from delivering the gifts to Bill early enough to get a head start on preparing breakfast. But first, I had to call Mrs. Flor.

"Si, digame," she answered the phone.

"Hey Mrs. Flor, I'm still sick. I can't shake this fever. Can you come over and do the egg thing that you mentioned?"

I waited for her response.

"Of course, I just bought some eggs at Marty Mart. Can you believe they are open on Christmas Day? That store is crazy, but good for me because I needed some things. Text your address to my phone and I will have my GPS bring me to your door."

Twenty minutes later, both Mrs. Flor and Jack showed up at the door. Flor had arrived first and was in the foyer when Jack knocked on the door.

"Make yourself at home. Just give us a few minutes, okay?" I said to Jack.

"Sure, not a problem," he answered.

"Oh, by the way, I'm Jack Monroe."

He shook Mrs. Flor's hand and made his way to the area where the TV was and made himself comfortable on the couch. Mrs. Flor and I stayed in the kitchen.

Mrs. Flor had removed an egg from the carton and placed it in her purse before coming over.

"It works better when the egg is close to room temperature," she said as she took the egg from a neatly folded handkerchief. Then she took a white bowl from the cupboard and filled it with tap water about halfway.

"Okay, you need to lay down so I can rub the egg on your body, your head, and the bottoms of your feet."

"What?" I protested. "You're going to rub me with egg? Are you crazy?"

Mrs. Flor laughed. "No, I'm going to rub the egg on you while it is still in the shell. Then when it absorbs all the nasty negative karma, I will break it into a bowl of water. Then keep the bowl with the egg in it close to you for 4 hours. Just keep it in the same room where you are," she said.

We decided to do this ritual while I sat in a chair at the table.

I removed my shoes and placed some slippers next to my feet. Mrs. Flor rubbed the egg on my body, starting with my head and to the soles of my feet while saying the Our Father prayer. She then broke the egg and dropped the contents into the bowl of water. It almost instantly shaped itself into an eye. It looked like a human eye. The yolk was hazed over, and the clear part of the egg was almond-shaped with red spider-like veins on each side. We stood and stared into the bowl for several minutes.

Mrs. Flor looked at me and said, "It's a woman, no doubt. That was some nasty mess. Well, it's out now, but here's the final part. If you want this mess to never come back, you must return it to whoever made you sick. If you don't know who made you sick, it's okay. Just flush the egg down the sink so it will go away from your home. If you know who it was, place the egg close to her, like in her purse or car."

The red veins looked darker and thicker now.

"You must sleep now for a while to rest your body."

She didn't have to say that twice. I was suddenly tired and sleepy.

"Okay, my work is done here. I must go."

I escorted her to the door.

She turned to me.

"Is he your boyfriend?"

Before I could answer, she said, "I don't like him. Merry Christmas."

She walked out into the cold in her long black leather coat and climbed into her car. I slept for a couple of hours next to Jack while he watched a Christmas special.

When I awoke, I felt good as new. No, better than new. I was refreshed 100%. I whipped up some blueberry pancakes served with a pile of fresh blueberries and whip cream. We both had rich espresso coffee. After brunch, we snuggled in front of the fireplace and listened to the crackling of the burning logs.

Jack nuzzled my neck and asked, "Is there any of that whipped cream left?"

I smiled.

"You are a bad boy," I told him in between kisses.

It was a wonderful Christmas day, but like all great days, they have to come to an end.

Jack returned to the store that evening. He said he had quite a bit of paperwork, and this was his opportunity to catch up. He was very busy, and I understood. Even after the Christmas rush, the store was still bringing in quite a bit of business.

"I really need to inventory the departments that had a high sales volume and keep the shelves stocked," Jack said.

"I won't be around much, but I promise to text a goodnight every evening that I don't see you."

"Okay, that's fine," I answered.

As far as I knew, Jack had completed all of the projects he had started at my apartment. Still, if I get really lonely and desperate to see him, I can always throw a large rock through my window. That would undoubtedly prompt him to come and rescue his damsel in distress from the cold.

47

It was Monday morning, our first day back. I strolled into the building with my book bag on one shoulder and coffee thermos in hand. I walked into the office to check my mailbox to find that it was empty. I arrived at my door to find it locked. Maybe Delmon was running late today. I took my key from my purse and unlocked my door. I went inside to put my bag on the reading table, sat down to review my lesson book, and prepared to begin the day. Minutes later, the kids started coming in one by one. In a black tray sat their Math Facts morning work. I glanced over at Mike and Leslie's empty desks. The first bell rang as I turned on my computer to take the role.

I signed on to my computer and heard little feet walk in behind me.

"Okay, who came in late," I asked cheerfully, turning around in my chair.

There next to me were Mike and Leslie with big smiles and their small backpacks in hand. Mrs. Phillips stood behind them.

"Ms. Knoes, Leslie, and Mike will remain in your class until further notice. At the end of the day, please send them to the library. Ms. Bernadette will keep them busy until I am ready to leave," she said in her professional tone.

"Okay, not a problem."

I smiled and gave both of them a great welcome back hug. They both smiled ear to ear and took their seats. Bill came to school today and brought his yellow bulldozer.

"Teacher, can I show the class what Santa brought me?"

"Absolutely, we will do that before we have to go to the computer lab," I said and smiled.

Innocent Echoes

He proudly stood in front of the class and showed them every moving part of that bulldozer. When he was finished, the students clapped. Bill smiled the sweetest smile I had seen yet. Monday mornings the students have computer lab at 8:15. As soon as Bill finished his presentation, I lined them up and escorted them to the computer lab. As the students practiced their reading skills on childrentopia.com, I planned their next reading lesson.

My phone vibrated. "Hello Katy, how was your lunch with Mr. Right?" I asked.

"It was great! He wants to be a couple." she said enthusiastically.

"That's wonderful. Tell me more about it later. I'm at work, so I better go," I said.

"Okay," she said, hanging up the phone.

I waited... the phone vibrated.

"He'll purpose in three months. In the meantime, look your best," I said.

"Thanks," Katy replied cheerfully and hung up the phone.

After placing my phone back in my pocket, it rang again.

"Hello, this is Jennifer," I said and waited for a response.

As soon as the voice spoke, I knew who was speaking. I heard Rachel's voice.

"Jen, the Williams couple has been released on bail pending trial. I don't know how harsh the law will be on them. All of the adoptions were legally done. We don't have any way of proving anything that will keep them behind bars for life. Aside from child negligence, we don't have much on them," she said with despair.

I stood and listened in shock

"What about the children that have somehow vanished? Can you investigate that?" I pleaded.

"Jen, just because you can't find them does not mean they are in danger," she said in a consoling voice.

"Dammit, Rachel, when have I been wrong? When have I screwed up?" I demanded.

Rachel sighed, "Well, dating that Jim guy from San Antonio was a screw-up."

"No Jim was hot!" I said.

She laughed. I laughed also.

"Okay, once, seriously, Rachel, please."

"Okay, I will see what I can do to find the kids. I have friends in those departments that owe me one or two favors. I will keep you posted."

I hung up the phone feeling numb.

The rest of the day went as scheduled. Since it was their first day back, I took it easy on their work and gave them time to get back into the groove of school. At the end of the day, I lined them up and escorted them out.

Tonight was the banquet at the Botanical Gardens for District Winners of the Invention Convention. I had the two inventions that had won, and it was my responsibility to get them to the hall. Putting them in my car and displaying them at the banquet for all to see was a simple task. I notified the student s who won with the Purse Boots and the winner of the Styling Safety Vest via telephone after I had finished setting up their inventions at the banquet hall. I received a text message from both parents notifying me that they would attend if the weather permitted.

The weather was cold, and we were expecting sleet, so I was prepared for two no shows. I would rather they be safe at home than out on icy roads.

48

To my great surprise, I arrived home from the banquet to find Jack under my sink, installing a new garbage disposal. I could see the scattering of his tools all over the floor and him in deep concentration.

"I did not call a plumber!" I said.

He peeked out from under the sink and said, "Well, you got one baby." He winked and smiled.

Since I moved into this garage apartment, I had pledged to get a garbage disposal. It was not until I met Jack that the apartment started feeling more like home. He even went to the trouble of asking my landlord if he could place a small shed in the small back yard to house all of his tools and gadgets. I am sure they are worth thousands of dollars since Jack only uses state of the art equipment and tools.

I was still curious about the brunette he was meeting with at the hotel, if it really was him. Something about the whole situation was not right. I decided to bring it up over dinner to clear it up once and for all.

We were both sitting at the table having my special spaghetti and meatballs, salad, French bread, and red wine.

"Jack, how is work coming along?" I asked.

He looked up at me, wiping his lip with his napkin, and said, "Great. We have a huge company interested in having our store sell many of their tools and hardware. As a matter of fact, I had a business lunch with her at the Halston Hotel, where she was staying a few weeks ago. She is a die-hard business negotiator, that's for sure!" Then he turned to continue enjoying his meal. See, just what I thought, a business deal—no need to worry.

Jack was my happily ever after and, at this very moment, I was very happy. We had not talked about marriage, but I was sure I would be Mrs. Monroe someday. I had seen it when I slept. I had never seen his face, but I felt certain. I anticipated the big white house on a hill with a blanket of bluebonnets behind the house and the golden retriever sleeping in a rocking chair that sat on the front porch. I just dreamt it. Sometimes my dreams are a look at what's to come. I would someday be Mrs. Monroe. Jack ate wholeheartedly.

"Isn't the loss of appetite a tell-tale sign of a person dealing with guilt?" I thought to myself.

I didn't sense any guilt.

We finished our dinner, and I quickly cleaned up so that we could continue with our evening ritual of watching a movie and snuggling on the large sectional sofa. If it was a comedy, we usually slept in each other's arms. If Jack chose an action movie, we would end the evening having sex before the night was over. Action movies had a tendency of making him want to conquer something or someone, that someone being me. I just love action movies, especially those with Arnold Schwarzenegger or Bruce Willis. Bullets could be flying everywhere, but those two were always unscathed and unbreakable, no terminations there! My third action hero, Will Smith, starred in *Men in Black*.

We decided on *iRobot*, a futuristic film about robots taking over people's lives. It was filled with action. Oh yeah, I was already anticipating our memorable action-packed night when Jack said, "Baby, I won't be staying the night. I have meetings early tomorrow, and I have to be prepared for whatever the new company throws at me."

"Aww," I said in a disappointing tone while giving him a playful frown.

"I can still watch a movie and snuggle for a while if that's okay."

"Okay," I said, making my way to the couch where he had arranged pillows and was waiting with a smile and open arms. We snuggled and watched a movie.

When I awoke the following morning, Jack was gone. I must have dozed off last night. He had carried me to my bed and tucked me in. He also made sure he set my morning alarm so that I would not be running late for work.

"What a wonderful guy I had," I thought to myself.

I leaped out of bed and turned on the warm water for my shower. I was dressed and had my bags on my shoulder in ample time to beat the morning traffic and to drive through my favorite coffee shop for a large coffee before arriving at school.

49

Tuesday morning, I walked into the building holding two small trophies that stood no taller than 8 inches. Elegantly placed on a cherry wood base was a large silver lightbulb, identifying the receiver as an Invention Convention 1st Place winner. Both of my winners had not shown, so I brought their prize trophies to school. The banquet had consisted of a table tastefully set with finger foods. I saw two rows of tiny sandwiches, a variety of cheeses and crackers, and two trays containing chocolate chip cookies the size of a small saucer. Next to the snacks were rows of clear plastic cups filled with punch. In the auditorium, they announced the winners one after another. Neither of my winners received a monetary reward. Maybe next time we will win big. It was a celebration that took less than an hour. I was sure it was shortened due to the bad weather, which was certainly understandable.

Walking down the hall, I could still sense the somber air filled with void and sadness. As I made my way to my room, I passed Mr. Brooks' office. It appeared they were removing his items from the office to make room for a new counselor when the time came to appoint one. I could see the open door and the janitor moving furniture around.

"Hey Del, what's up?" I asked, pretending not to know what was happening.

"Oh, we are clearing up some of Mr. Brooks' things," he said as he kept collecting items from a bookshelf. "Mrs. Phillips is taking them to his home later today, so she asked me to help with the packing."

He had placed a box on the floor where he was now putting all of Mr. Brooks' framed pictures, diplomas, and some artwork he had collected throughout the years.

On top of the box was a beautiful 14X18 painting of a Pegasus horse with wings carrying a horseman who had his arrow pulled back, ready to strike a distant target. Delmon noticed I was staring at the striking painting.

"You like it? Maybe Mrs. Brooks would let you have it. It's pretty, but not by anyone famous. The artist was too damn lazy to sign the painting. All he signed it with were those three letters," he said, pointing to three letters on the bottom right side of the painting. It read ABN.

"How does an artist hope to be famous when the art is signed with dumb-ass initials? That, I will never understand. No siree."

He moved his head from side to side as if saying no to himself.

"Anyway, if you don't take it, Ms. Gomez might. I was watching the bitch try to pretend it was under some papers and stuff she was carrying yesterday. She thought I wasn't looking then I said, 'Hold on lady, there is a painting under the stuff you picked up." She pretended it was an accident, but I know it wasn't. Yeah, that's right, I have a strong gut feeling, and I'm never wrong. I know some people don't think I'm smart, but I'm very smart," he said looking away from me. I watched Delmon as he continued with his work, mumbling something or other that I didn't understand. I took my phone out of my pant pocket and took a picture of the painting.

"Delmon, can you show me where that picture was hanging?" I asked without showing any kind of emotion.

Delmon spun around suddenly, obviously forgetting I was still there.

"Oh, yeah, sure."

He began pointing around the room, then stopped at the wall right above his desk.

"There. It was sitting on the floor yesterday," he said.

"Can this one stay here for a while?" I asked.

Delmon looked at me, suspiciously.

"That's fine with me, but at 3:30 when Mrs. Phillips comes in here, it better be in that box," he said and pointed to the box filled with the picture frames and diplomas.

He looked toward the door to see Ms. Bernadette passing by. An ear to ear smile covered his face.

"Good morning Chula," he hollered out.

"Good morning Delmon," I heard Ms. Bernadette respond as she kept walking to the library.

I returned my attention to Delmon.

"Sure, I will make sure it is there, promise."

"Okay, but don't get me in trouble. Mrs. Phillips hates me already," he said.

Of course, I knew that was not true, but I did not think it was time to assure him he was wrong.

The bell was about to ring, and I had kids waiting outside my door, ready to have their breakfast. It was cold out, so I was sure I would have a few students coming in late. I raced to my classroom and opened the door. Leo picked up a breakfast bag, and another student drug the milk bag over by the table where Leo had placed the breakfast bag. I stood at the entryway of my classroom and greeted my students as they trickled in.

Claire was already in her room. I could see the door to her classroom was open, and her students were walking in. After all the children were sitting having breakfast quietly, I signed onto my computer and plugged in my phone cord. I signed onto my Walgreens Pharmacy account and decided to place an order through their photo computer. It took 72 hours to have it ready for pick up.

50

In the winter, students are unable to go out for recess, so Claire and I team up and arrange some kind of activity for the students to enjoy in the auditorium. My students were fond of playing the game Duck, Duck Goose, and Claire's kids seemed just as enthusiastic when playing the game.

The students finished their breakfast and started in on their morning work when I heard Delmon at the door. He informed me that he had left the counselor's room unlocked for when I finished with that painting. The office was empty now, so there was no risk of any school property getting stolen.

"Oh, thanks, I appreciate that," I said with a smile.

"Delmon, did you forget to unlock my door on Monday?"

"No, ma'am, that's the first door I unlock every morning, just like I promised."

He disappeared as quickly as he had appeared. Delmon seemed to always be on some kind of mission. No time to linger.

That day, Claire and I decided to run out for a club salad at Hardy's, a sandwich shop down the street from the school. As we sat in the warm pub discussing grades due and testing weeks coming up, we noticed a young brunette eating alone.

"Hey, that's the lady that I saw with Jack at the hotel," Claire whispered.

"Oh, she's the CEO of some huge home improvement store," I said.

"Really, she looks pretty young," Claire whispered suspiciously.

"Well, she is, and her company is working with Jack to benefit both of their companies," I said assuredly.

We quickly ate our salads and raced back to school in the nick of time.

"We have 90 seconds to spare," Claire said as we quickly walked to pick up our students from lunch.

"Claire, when we pick up our kids, can we team up for the science video and activity? I want to stop in Mr. Brooks' office and see something."

"Sure, but don't take too long. Forty-four kids in one room can drive one teacher insane."

I chuckled and said, "Okay, I won't belong."

We both picked up our kids and headed in the direction of our classrooms. Once they were all settled in Claire's room, I headed to the counselor's office. I stood and stared at the painting and the initials written on it. As I looked, it was the arrow that stood out. If the horseman released the arrow, what would it strike? I walked over to the wall it aimed at and searched for some kind of door, panel, or something, but found nothing. Maybe I was being too dramatic. Perhaps I have been watching too many treasure hunt movies, I thought to myself. It worked in *Men in Black* where a picture of Agent K was pointing to a clue. Not totally discouraged, I returned to Claire's room to find all of the students deeply engaged in evaluating a variety of rocks with their magnifying lenses and enthusiastically writing their rock's properties in their Science journals.

"What did you find," Claire asked.

"Nothing, I can't figure out what I am supposed to be looking at. Perhaps I need time to think," I said. "I will go back later and see if something comes to mind. I know the answers are in that painting, but where?"

The students finished their science work and documentation with just a few minutes to spare before the bell.

"Okay, kids, line up! I need a boy line and a girl line."

The kids lined up to put away their journals and magnifying lenses. I allowed them a trip to the water fountain and a bathroom break before I started the dismissal routine of calling each table to gather their backpacks, jackets, and line up. Every student put on his or her jacket and hat. I started to the door as the bell rang. It was only a few minutes until all the students had been picked up by either the bus or their parents.

Locking my classroom was a routine when the students left, so I was not in a hurry to return to my class. I decided to stop by Mr. Brooks' office again before I had to place that painting in the box for Mrs. Phillips to take. As I stood there by the door, I heard Nicole coming down the hall with a cart loaded with strawberries and grapes.

Innocent Echoes

"Wow, Nicole, that's a lot of fruit," I said.

"Yeah, but probably the last fruit we will get. Mr. and Mrs. Walker have that house up for sale. I gather they have returned to their hometown somewhere in the Mediterranean."

As she was speaking, I was staring at the painting.

Then she said, "You know Ms. Gomez likes that painting too? I can just stare at it for hours and admire the majestic horse and that hot God on it. But not as much as Ms. Gomez! We came in here yesterday before they started cleaning and admired it. I guess she admired it so much the damn thing fell off the wall. The nail fell out of the wall, so I quickly picked up the darn thing, thankful it had not broken, and I placed it against the wall behind the desk. Oh, gotta go. I have to pick up my child from school." She raced off.

Suddenly a thought came to mind. Ms. Gomez was the one that put Ojo on me. I had a surprise for that crazy lady in my lunch bag.

So, that was not the original home of that painting. I approached the wall and examined it inch by inch, and moved around the room. Behold, there on the wall beside the door was a small hole where it appeared a nail had been. I took the painting and held it up there. The arrow would be released into the wall covered with classy textured wallpaper. It was a new trend, so that wallpaper should be available at most home improvement stores. I quickly walked back to my classroom to retrieve a hammer from my small toolbox. I was walking back to the counselor's office when I saw Charles coming down the hall toward me.

"Hey Charles, how's it going?"

"Great," he replied.

Charles was delightful to have as a friend. Not only could he teach, but he was also a wiz at computers and quite a handyman. Sure he did not have state-of-the-art tools, but he made due. He once broke his screwdriver while helping me connect my computers and put up shelves.

"Oh no, I will get a new one for you," I promised.

He smiled and said, "My tools are mostly flea market specials or tools I was given as gifts. Don't worry about it."

Still, Charles worked wonders with what he had, and he always did it with a giving spirit.

He looked at me, frowned, and then he asked, "Where are you going, and what are you doing with a hammer?"

"Oh, Charles, come with me. Do you have a minute? "I asked in a whisper.

"I already have all my grades posted and confirmed, so sure; I have a minute." He followed me into the counselor's office. I stood where I was, getting ready to knock a hole in the wall.

"Charles, if I make a hole here, do you think you can fix it before Mrs. Phillips finds out?"

"Sure, but she will find out if you do it now because she announced that she was taking these things to his home and asked if we wanted anything delivered to him? Unless you wait until she leaves, that's the only way she might not notice. I would need an hour or so to fix the wall, depending on the damage you do. Maybe you can ask Delmon to keep it locked after you make the hole and only open it for me to work on."

"Okay, Mrs. Phillips won't be here tomorrow, so let's do it then. I will bring some tools from home." He gave me an assuring look as he reached to open the door.

Then he looked at me puzzled and said," Should I ask why you are making a hole in the wall?"

I smiled. "It would be better if you don't."

He smiled back. "Okay."

I placed the painting in the large box to be delivered and exited the office.

51

I returned to my classroom to put my hammer back in my toolbox. I cleaned and organized for the next day. I went by Claire's room, but she had left for the day. I decided to do the same. Tomorrow was another day, hopefully, one filled with answers.

Upon arriving at my apartment, I found no sign of Jack. Usually, he could be found lounging on my couch or fixing something around the apartment. That's okay. I have Kayla and Chloe here to keep me company. Speaking of the ladies of the house, they managed to make the effort of at least meowing when I walked in. Kayla was lying on the large sectional and was Chloe nestled in an empty shoebox Jack had evidently left on the living room floor. He is the only man I know that buys as many shoes as I do. I picked up the box, and Chloe scampered out of it with much disapproval. This evening was going to be like many others recently, TV dinner, some television while I sifted through papers and looked at my school to-do list, grading papers, the ten o'clock news, and a hot shower.

I kicked my shoes off by my bedroom closet door and grabbed some lounging clothes. I entered the kitchen area to find my phone almost vibrating off the table. It was from Jack.

"Hey, honey. I am calling you to let you know that I really feel terrible. This cold weather is not being nice to me at all. I hope I don't have the nasty flu. Unfortunately, I have all the symptoms. I think it's better that I stay away from you until I get better. I would hate to make you sick, and you make your little ones sick."

I laughed. "Yes, sweetie, that's exactly how it works. Thanks for caring about my little ones and me," I said sweetly.

"If I am not feeling better by tomorrow, I am going to the clinic for antibiotics or something. I can't work feeling like this. I will keep you posted," he said in between coughs.

"Sorry, baby. I hope you feel better and get some rest. I love you, and call me if you need anything," I said in a caring voice.

"Okay, I will," he replied in a weak tone.

"Bye, honey," I answered and hung up the phone.

I was still trying to figure out the ABN on the painting. I took a long, warm shower and climbed into bed. The temperature was in the low 30s tonight, and I love cold weather. Sometimes, I sleep so well that I don't often dream, but tonight would not be one of those nights.

I was standing on the other side of the Mexican border. It was twilight. I could hear vendors speaking in Spanish, trying to entice tourists to buy their products. The stench of urine, beer, and sweat coated my nostrils. I heard others talking behind me; I turned around and found myself watching some women sitting against a concrete wall with their children eating what looked like a biscuit. Then I heard a familiar voice.

I could only see his backside and an arm with a large tattoo of a Boa Constrictor. He was offering money to the women for the kids. He was telling the women that their children deserved a better life. His demeanor was friendly, and I could see that these women trusted him. He told them how he would bring them back when they were doctors, lawyers, and community leaders. They smiled, took the money, and the children piled into a white van. I counted ten little bodies climbing into the van, looking hopeful. Unknowing to them, they were headed to a slaughterhouse. I wanted to scream, "No! No! Don't let him take your children," but my words were mute.

The laughter of the children echoed as the van drove away. On the driver's side, I could see the smoke of a cigarette. The driver was smoking.

52

I arrived early at school to find Charles waiting by my classroom door.

"Hey Jennifer, I'm ready for whatever wall you are going to make a hole in," he laughed.

He had the sexiest Latin accent. I could see that he had his tools in his tool bag.

"Okay, we have 30 minutes before anyone starts to arrive. Want to do it now?" I asked.

Charles had become my favorite male teacher after our first chat. He always helps me when I need computer help or when I can't hook up my media equipment in the classroom. Now, he will help me vandalize our school by patching up my mess before anyone notices. Now that's what I call a true friend, I thought to myself.

With his hammer, he knocked a hole the size of a 12 inch by 12-inch box. We found nothing.

"Oh man," I said, disappointed.

I looked at Charles, and he shrugged his shoulders.

"Do you want me to patch it up?" he asked.

"Shit Charles! It's here. I know it's here, but where?"

What was it that Mr. Brooks wanted me to know? We had 5 minutes before other teachers would start to trickle in.

"Charles, I am going to my room to get a poster. I will just stick it over the hole for now. We don't have time to patch it. This afternoon when everyone is gone, you can do a quick patch job with tape and that wallpaper."

"Okay, Jennifer," he said with a smile and picked up his tools.

A tool that looked like a screwdriver with a round tip fell out of his bag through a hole on the side of the bag.

"Oh, heck," he said in a low voice and returned to pick up the tool and took it in his hand. He looked up at me and blushed. "I am going to my room, Jennifer. You should go to yours. I don't want anyone to see us come out of this office together. Rumors would fly like crazy."

He walked out, and I stayed to try to think. All I came up with was frustration. After a few minutes, I headed to my classroom and grabbed a numbers poster to stick over the hole. I quickly took care of that and went back to my room as if nothing had happened. I brought in the breakfast bags and did a quick scan of the room to ensure all was in place. I was standing outside the door greeting my students and parents like I did every morning when I saw Claire coming down the hall with her book bag in tow.

"Claire, I found ABN signed on a painting Mr. Brooks had hanging in his office," I said in a low voice.

"Really?" she leaned forward.

"He was the one who left me the note. Dammit, Claire. What am I missing?" I whispered.

"I don't know, Jen. Give it some time, and maybe an idea will come to you," she said, hugging me. "I have to get to class, talk later."

She headed to her classroom, and children began pouring into mine. I was standing at my door with my hand on the doorknob, ready to close it as soon as all the kids were inside. I spotted little Leo coming down the hall with a backpack that was half his size.

"Well, hello, little one," I said as he approached my door.

Rene was walking down the hall right behind him. He looked over at me and crossed the hall to my side. He approached my room and smiled with a sly grin on his face.

When he reached me, he leaned in and whispered, "I saw you and Charles coming out of Mr. Brooks' office. Is there something juicy going on that I should know?"

He put his hand over his mouth in a dramatic, teasing way. He then walked away backward, doing the shame, shame signal, sliding one index finger over another. He winked, turned around, and continued on his way.

Rene was a real character. Nothing worth gossiping about escaped him. He was loaded with secrets.

53

During lunch, I checked my mailbox to find a phone message from Rachel that the secretary had taken for me. I decided to skip lunch and call Rachel.

"Hey Rachel, what's up?"

"Jennifer, I want to share the information we have so far. Most of the information gathered comes from the files Mr. Brooks left behind. The murders of the Whitman couple are connected with Mr. and Mrs. Walker. The Whitman couple had adopted as many as 20 kids they had scattered in different school districts and schools. The kid's last name was Racesand. They registered kids in different schools, so no one would get suspicious. The good part is all of their kids except for four can be accounted for. They were also being used as blood or marrow donors. Those kids have been taken away and placed in a safe house until we find someone to adopt them. It's all in the last name. The last names of these black market kids have the same letters. The name Cardenas and Racesand contain the same letters. The same was true of the Cardenas kids. Mrs. Walker and her husband adopted over 30 children from Mexico and had them scattered throughout the district in different schools. Those kids we can't find. We only know the whereabouts of two, Leslie and Mike. Until we find the kids or their bodies, Mr. and Mrs. Walker will more than likely walk away with minimal charges and not do jail time." Rachel said.

She also told me that the information in Mr. Brooks' computer suggest that there were fifty couples in the United States who adopted children. They still had to find the other 48 couples. So far, they had individuals figuring out last names that contain the same letters and investigating. Perhaps they could locate some of the couples that way. I knew we were running short on time.

"I will keep looking, Jen, but this case is so twisted," Rachel said in frustration. "I will keep you posted."

"Okay," I replied.

I only had ten minutes left of my lunch period, so I decided to make copies of next week's calendar and homework contract. I walked in to find Nicole setting up a beautiful table with strawberries and peaches.

"Hey Nicole," I said when I walked in.

She turned to look at me.

" Hey Jen, we have been given permission from the realtor to clean out the fruit garden in the greenhouse since the house is vacant and up for sale. This is the last fruit batch we will get, and these strawberries are very, very sweet," she said as she took one and took a big bite. "Mmmmm, these are so good. You want one?"

I had placed my master on the copier, and the copies were smoothly coming out through the side end.

"Sure, I will take one," I said, and I took one that Nicole handed me. I bit into it and tasted a bitter stale taste. I turned and kept the piece in my mouth until I grabbed my copies and walked out of the lounge.

I immediately spit it out in a trash can that is kept by the water trough the students use to wash their hands before lunch. I took a drink of water from the water fountain and proceeded to pick up my kids from lunch. Yuck, what the heck was wrong with Nicole's taste buds? Was she sick? Maybe she had a cold and couldn't taste anything, I thought to myself. I held my stack of papers and headed to the cafeteria. The cafeteria monitor had already lined up my students to be picked up.

I looked at her and, as if she was reading my mind, she said, "Oh Ms. Knoes, you're not late or anything. The kids were just finished eating, so I thought I would line them up to keep them from playing with their food tray."

"Okay, that's fine. Not a problem," I said with a smile and made a hand gesture for the kids to follow me out of the cafeteria.

54

I met Charles again, and we decided we were looking in the wrong place. It was not the original wall the painting had been hanging on. Perhaps the other wall contained all the answers we needed to see where the kids had gone to or been taken to. Charles made a second hole on the wall where the painting hung initially. This wall was also wallpapered but had no pattern. It would be easier to fix. Charles made an 8 x 8 inch square in the wall and found nothing. Charles could sense my disappointment.

"Okay, Charles, I give up. I keep finding nothing." The pointing picture worked on *Men in Black*, and *The National Treasure* had a trail of findable clues. I was getting tired of going in circles, but at the same time, I could not get that painting out of my head. I decided to finish off the day optimistically. Tomorrow will be a better day.

At the end of the day, all of the kids had been lined up and escorted out of the school building at exactly 3:00 pm. By 3:10 pm. they were all gone. This afternoon I was determined to go home, take a long bath, and rest my brain.

As soon as I had entered my apartment and placed my bag and keys in their place, my phone rang. I answered and was happy to hear Jack's sweet voice.

"Hi, honey. I broke down and came to the clinic. I thought my head was going to explode. I think I am going to be in bed for a while. The doctor informed me that I am very dehydrated, and my fever is at 103 and going down slowly. He advised that I take it easy," he sighed.

"Honey, the important thing is that you will be taken care of," I said.

Innocent Echoes

"I am not planning on staying in bed any longer than tomorrow," he said. "I have work to do." I thanked him for keeping me posted and hung up the phone feeling sorry for Jack, but I was glad he would soon be feeling better.

Chloe sat in the corner of the sectional couch. Kayla had sprawled out on the other side. When I walked into my living room, they both meowed simultaneously. I knew they were waiting for me to get home. I can always tell when they are hungry, tired, afraid, or when they just need love because their meows are different for each one. I went to their food dishes, washed them, and refilled them with fresh food and water. They both followed me to their food dishes and started to eat as soon as the dishes were placed on the floor.

Before I changed out of my school clothes, I decided to go to Ted's Tools to get some more of the wallpaper that covered Mr. Brooks' office in case we needed more. It was still very cold but dry. I could feel the wind stinging my face the instant I walked out into the open. In times like these, I am glad the store is only 8 minutes away. I walked inside and headed straight to the wall covering aisle, where I picked up a roll of the same wallpaper used in Mr. Brooks' office.

I approached the counter to find the same brunette I had seen in the sandwich shop at the cash register. Jack had not told me that the CEO of the other company was managing the store while he was out ill. But then again, why would he? He kept his business to himself, and I didn't ask boring questions.

She smiled a pearly white smile and asked, "Did you find everything you needed?"

"Yes, thanks," I replied.

She rang up my wallpaper, and I handed her my debit card.

"You can swipe your card there," she said, pointing to the small gray box sitting on a small ledge in front of me.

I swiped my card and proceeded to punch the appropriate numbers. She bagged my wallpaper and handed me my receipt.

"You're new here?" I asked.

She smiled a big smile and replied, "Well, you could say that. I was away for a few months. I am a photographer, and when I am here in the city, I usually stay home. I would not be here today, but the cashier called in sick." She made a slight frown. " My husband is usually the one in charge. I decided to come in and help since he is laid up with flu symptoms. I don't want him getting our customers sick. If he knew I was here, he would kill me. He says this store is his space, just like the camera, and our home is mine. How old fashioned is that? But he loves me. Us, I mean." She touched her belly that showed early signs of pregnancy.

Suddenly my head started to spin. I could feel a salt taste building in my mouth. I quickly walked out the door with seconds before the puke spilled onto the sidewalk. My head was aching, and my heart was pounding against my chest. I could feel the tears streaming down my face and freezing halfway down.

"Oh, God, how can this be? No! This is not possible."

I kept repeating to myself as if caught in a bad dream. I could feel my head spinning and my pulse racing. I hung on to my bag. I opened the door to the car and sank in the seat. I tossed the bag on the passenger's seat, closed the door, and cried uncontrollably. The tears would not stop. I felt my heart shatter into a million tiny pieces.

Sitting in my car, still in shock, my phone rang. It was Rachel.

"Hey, do I have some news for you," she said enthusiastically. I tried not to speak. Rachel would pick up on my emotions. No way to pull it off. Even when I said nothing, Rachel picked up the vibes.

"What's the matter, Jen?"

"Nothing, I was listening," I answered.

"Bullshit! Are you hurt? Do you want me to call a unit for you? Where the hell are you?"

In an almost inaudible tone, I answered, "I'm okay, Rachel, I'm okay. Seriously," I said, trying to sound convincing.

"You sound like shit Jen, I know you. Now, where are you?" she demanded.

"I am in the parking lot of Ted's Tools. I am well enough to get home." I said.

"Do you want me to come over?" Rachel asked. There was a long silence. I was crying without making a sound.

Finally, I said, "Yes, come over to my place. I will be home in 5 minutes."

"I am on my way." She clicked her phone off.

I arrived at my apartment and grabbed my bag with the wallpaper in it. I got out slowly, still in shock of what I had heard. Rachel was already there waiting for me in the driveway. She walked over and hugged me without saying a word. I sobbed and sobbed and clung to her. She didn't ask any questions; she just held me.

After I calmed down a little, she asked, "What can I do, Jen?"

I replied, "There is really nothing you can do unless you have a cure for stupidity."

I laughed and cried at the same time.

"Come inside. It's cold as hell out here," I said in a low tone.

It was now drizzling and starting to snow.

55

We sat on pillows by the fireplace. I kept a couple of striped afghans on the couch. Rachel tossed one on my shoulders. Next to the fireplace was a small wine rack holding four bottles of red wine. Next to that was a tall TV tray containing two wine glasses.

"I am having some red wine; want some?" I offered.

"No thanks. I am still working." Rachel replied.

I looked at Rachel and spoke the words that barely came out of my mouth.

"Rachel, Jack is married," I said in a low, almost inaudible tone. "All of this time, his wife was on some photography assignment, and he pretended she did not exist. He lied. Lie after lie, after lie. How can a person be so cruel? I am such an idiot! That's why he said he did not want kids right away. That's why his apartment is empty. It's his fucking fuck pad!" I began to cry again.

I put my head on my knees and cradled myself.

"All you did was love him, Jen. You trusted him and believed him. That's what people like you do. You're not an idiot," Rachel said gently.

"Thanks for coming over. Here." I handed her my phone and asked her to erase and block all messages from Jack. I never want to hear from him again. "I still can't believe he was so cruel," I said, trying to hold back my tears. My heartfelt like it had been trampled on by a stampede of horses.

"I'm glad you're here, Rachel. Your calls are timed perfectly. Were you in the area?" I asked.

Innocent Echoes

I poured a glass of wine and took a sip. I looked over at the TV that I have programmed with a timer for on automatic on and off. I had ignored it until now. The talk show, *Ellen*, was on.

"I'll bet she's never anyone's sap," I said.

"Who, Ellen?" Rachel asked.

"No, she's an awesome talk show host. What do we do now?" I asked Rachel.

"The only thing you can do, you move on. You hold your head up and move forward."

Then, we heard the talk show host say, "My Show, My Rules."

"Let's ask her what she would do in our situation," I said in a low tone.

Rachel laughed, "Seriously?"

Before she could talk me out of it, I was on the laptop that I keep on my coffee table.

"Found it!" I said enthusiastically.

"Okay, go to the contact Ellen window and tell her what we have," Rachel said.

I was starting to feel better, although nothing had changed in the last 15 minutes. I was hopeful for a bright future, or maybe it was just Rachel being there with me. I typed:

Dear Ellen,

If you were investigating a mystery and the only clue was a painting with three written letters on it, what would you do?

Signed,

Clueless

Rachel reached over after reading the message and pushed send.

"She's not going to answer," Rachel said. "So don't get your hopes up. For all you know, she is in Vegas or Tahiti getting material for a new show."

"You're probably right," I agreed.

"Besides, rich people don't even read their own mail. She might even have someone that wipes her ass," Rachel said.

I laughed.

"I'm desperate. Desperate times call for desperate measures." I said.

I took another sip of my wine.

"Oh, what was the news you had for me?" I asked.

Rachel looked at me puzzled and then said, "Oh, I almost forgot. Mr. and Mrs. Walker were on the road early this morning. I don't know why. The television news broadcasters kept asking people to stay home if they did not have to be out due to icy and slick roads. At four o'clock this morning, they were involved in a fatal car accident. It seems they were driving down Interstate 820 when the car lost control. The vehicle rolled over several times before it slammed into the median. They were both pronounced dead at the scene. Talk about severe head injuries. I am surprised they still had their heads on their shoulders with how torn up they were."

"Could there have been foul play?" I asked.

"I don't think so, maybe. With scum like that, it's more like good riddance. I doubt anyone would follow up on it. People like them are bad news and don't deserve to live. Maybe someone provided a public service of their own. I, for one, am glad they won't be using taxpayer's money for their incarceration," she said.

Rachel was on duty, so she left after a while. I was feeling better and couldn't wait to take my bath and sleep. I still had to be up early for work the next day.

It was 3:00 am. when I woke up with an upset stomach. I raced for the toilet and vomited out every ounce of what was initially in my stomach. It was not the wine that made me sick. Red wine had never made me sick since I usually only drink two glasses. But I had this horrible sick feeling. I was rinsing my mouth of the foul taste of old strawberries. Then the answers came.

Oh, my God!! I ran to the bedroom with a towel to my mouth and dialed Rachel. She answered on the third ring.

"This better be good if you are waking my ass up this early in the morning."

"Rachel, wake up!! It's me, Jennifer. I know where the kids are!"

I could hear Rachel spring out of bed and rustling with her clothes as she quickly dressed.

"Keep talking, Jen."

"Rachel, the kids are buried under the strawberry field at the Walker's house. They died in the house. When the Walkers tried to take their blood and marrow, they hired shady medical staff to keep their secret. Many of the kids died of malpractice and infection. It was not until Leslie and Mike that they hired a real nurse. That's probably why they were still alive."

I could not breathe. My head was spinning, and tears were flowing uncontrollably.

"How do you know this Jen?" Rachel asked.

"I don't know how I know! Rachel, please listen to me. Get the police to dig it up. You'll find them there. You'll find all of them there! The children were buried naked with no caskets. I don't know why. I can only tell you they were not wearing clothing. I only see parts."

By now, I was pleading and weeping at the same time. I was amazed that Rachel seemed to understand what I was saying.

"Okay, Jen, I will call my boss. But if you are wrong, I am going to be in a pile of shit. You are hearing me, right?" she said sternly.

"Yes, Rachel, I hear you. I am not wrong," I said, barely audible.

"Okay, I will call you when we find something," Rachel said.

"Thanks," I answered.

I hung up the phone, numb and tired. I sat on my sectional with my feet up and my arms wrapped around my knees. I leaned into a corner and slept. At 6:00 am, my eyes automatically opened. I looked at the clock on the wall. I yawned, took a deep breath, and headed for the shower. I was ready to go to school in under 20 minutes. I only had a few hours of sleep; somehow, that is never a problem. My body is conditioned now. I don't even feel sick or tired. The days I don't sleep at all aren't any different than the ones I have after a good night's sleep.

56

I arrived at work and prepared the breakfast tables for the kids. I decided to get a cup of coffee from the teacher's lounge. The secretary makes a pot of coffee every morning for the teachers. Teachers are allowed to help themselves for a small donation. I took 75 cents from my purse and headed to the lounge, hoping there was some made. Nope, no coffee, I sighed.

"Okay, I will make the darn coffee myself," I said in a low tone.

No one had arrived, so I made a full pot of coffee. I looked around for cups but did not find any in the lounge. I went to my classroom to get the coffee mug that I kept in my cabinet for times like today.

I returned to the lounge with my cup, and I encountered Nicole.

"Hey Jen, would you like some more of those juicy strawberries? There is just a small bowl left. Boy, they went fast! You should have seen Amanda loading up her lunch pail to have something to snack on later. She kept talking about how they gave her psychic energy. That girl is not playing with a full deck, that's for sure."

"Oh no, thanks, I appreciate it," I answered and quickly stepped out of the lounge with my coffee cup in both hands.

Ms. Bernadette was just unlocking the library.

"Hey Jen," she said as she opened her door.

"Good Morning Bernadette" I answered. From behind me, I heard Delmon addressing the librarian.

"Chula, Chula, Chula. When are you going to go out with me?"

Bernadette laughed.

"Never," she replied.

I chuckled and kept walking to my room.

Claire was in my room on my computer.

"Hey, Jen, my computer is messed up. Can I check my mail on yours?" she asked as she put her book bag on the floor.

"Sure, go ahead," I answered.

I glanced over at Claire.

"What does he call her? Every time he sees her, he calls her Chula. That means pretty or beautiful right?" I asked.

Claire exited the computer and stood to grab her bag from the floor.

"Chula, that's her name."

She chuckled.

"We call her Ms. B, but her name is Bernadette Chula."

Claire raised her eyebrows at me.

"I will talk to you later."

She walked past me as I waited by the door, turned, and headed in the direction of her classroom.

It was almost time for the kids to start arriving. I had five minutes to check my mailbox, so I hurried down the hall. In my mailbox, I found a sample box of chocolates from Sam, who every Valentine's holiday, gives all of the teachers a small, four-piece box of chocolates. I took my box of chocolates and hurried back to my classroom. I quickly placed it on my reading table in a black paper tray and prepared to start the day. I made it in the nick of time, feeling glad I had already set up the breakfast table. I stood by the door awaiting my little angels and ready for a great day, when I heard the low roar of kids coming down the hall.

"Good morning, little ones," I said cheerfully as they trickled in and took their breakfast to their table.

I stood by the door and greeted my students and those parents who escorted their children to the classroom. Bill was dropped off in front of the school, so he walked to the classroom alone. I was hoping to see all of my kids. They are so precious, and I adore every last one of them. When they had all arrived, I closed the door and instructed them to please hang their jackets in their cubby and not drop them on the floor.

After breakfast, I begin the day with our morning circle literacy lesson. Our focus for this week was nature's giants. I started the morning by asking them who had ever seen a mountain, an ocean, the moon, or a very, very tall tree. The kids raised their hands and began telling stories about their encounters with these giants. I introduced their vocabulary for the week and asked them to listen for those words as we read our morning big book titled Nature's Giants.

The day went relatively smoothly. The children had their routine down to a science. I called them by name and directed them to their morning center. In center 1, the students were constructing new sentences using their weekly vocabulary words. In center 2, the students were putting together a large 3-D puzzle of dinosaurs. In center 3, students were building a city using building blocks. In center 4, the students were listening to grammar and spelling songs. In center 5, students were drawing something big and writing about it. In center 6, students were working with math flashcards. In center 7, students were working on the computer playing grammar and spelling games. They loved center time and were eager to go to them every single day.

Before I knew it, lunchtime was upon us. I rang my bell and instructed each group to clean up. The children sang a clean-up song as they placed all of the pieces belonging in their centers into the appropriate tubs.

57

I escorted the children to the cafeteria. They walked single file with their finger vertical to their mouths, staying quiet. Ms. B. walked by the group and gave the kids thumbs up on hallway behavior. The kids love being complimented. They entered the cafeteria and went through the line quietly. They all have set seating spaces, so they sat and ate their lunch using their quiet voices to chat with their classmates. Since I made the call to Rachel, I had been waiting for news from her to see if she found the tiny bodies. I was wondering what was taking so long. I did my best not to think about it and continued with my day.

At 12:30 pm. the phone vibrated in my pocket. I had added Rachel to my contact list, so her name automatically flashed on the screen when she called.

"Hey Rachel, what did you find?" I asked anxiously.

"Jen, there are nobodies! The whole back yard was taped off, and they have been digging since this morning."

My heart sank, and I was speechless. Rachel kept talking.

"What we did find is indescribable. I have never in my life seen such madness. There are piles of mulch and compost, all containing human remains. The insane bitch treated the mulch with salt, dry leaves, coffee grounds, and baking soda. It threw the police dogs off at first, but then they figured it out. No telling how many kids they tossed in the wood chipper. That's beyond fucked up. There are three gardens with human remains. The dogs are also checking around the large, green turtle sandbox. The sandbox was filled with salt. It's unbelievable that two people could do such a thing and then plant gardens using the remains of their victims. These individuals went beyond monsters. That is like something out of a fucking Steven King horror movie. There is no way of knowing how many, and since they were more than likely adopted from Mexico, we have no way of identifying them. That department does not have the workforce or the equipment to use DNA to figure out who is who. Besides, the kids are from Mexico. That country is so poor that many kids are born at home. Only God knows how many of them didn't even have birth certificates."

I could hear the disappointment in her voice. I had a way to help.

"Thanks for believing me, Rachel. I appreciate it. You know, since we were kids, you have been the only solid friend I could convince to do some stupid shit without proof," I laughed. Then she said, "That's because you have never been wrong. You're out of whack, sometimes, but never wrong. I would say it's your track record. That or I'm just a sucker for adventure."

I smiled.

"Rachel, if you're interested in collaborating with the Fort Worth Forensics Department and speeding things up, I have a connection for you. Call the Forensics Department and tell them you want to speak to Raul Arroyo, the Department Chief. There's no need to mention my name; just say, 'I have a 10 and 5.' Let him know what's going on and tell him what you need. He will make sure your findings take priority. I will text you his office number in a few minutes. I've got to go."

I hung up the phone and continued with my day. I was glad I was able to talk to Rachel and offer some help. Now it was time to focus on my kids and monitor them as they created their own patterns of two and three parts in their math journals. I passed out their journals and a basket of one-inch squares in a variety of colors. I watched as they chose their squares and passed the glue. I listened as they shared ideas and helped each other glue their patterns on the pages of their journal. Watching children who have been taught to work together working together is amazing. When squares of paper dropped on the floor, they took turns picking them up. Little Leo refilled the center glue plate so that everyone working at the table could have what they needed. They laughed and complimented one another. I sighed and smiled.

After arriving home tired, disappointed about Jack, and sad about the children, I received a very interesting phone call from Rachel. She called to tell me that after the stunt Jack pulled, she decided to see if he had any outstanding tickets or something she could give him a hard time for that would not entail breaking the law.

"Guess what I found Jennifer? You won't believe this shit! Your old boyfriend was using a fake name! His name is not Jack Monroe, it's Roy Miller, and he has a rap sheet for public intoxication, assault and battery, and resisting arrest. He also has a warrant out for his arrest for outstanding traffic violations. To top everything off, he's a high school drop-out. I guess he figured he would inherit his dad's business, so why bother with school. What gets me is that I will bet his wife does not have a clue. It's something like a *Who the Bleep Did I Marry* episode. If he is home, he is going to be arrested tonight. I wanted to let you know. Some of the other officers will break the news to his wife about his background. If she's smart, she'll take half of all he owns in the divorce and ride into the sunset. I will touch base with you later and keep you posted," she said.

"No, don't bother. I just want to put Jack, or whatever his name is, behind me. Thanks." I said appreciatively.

I hung up the phone, determined to leave Jack behind and move forward with my life. I felt sad for his wife and her baby, but I was certain she would be fine.

58

It was late at night, and I was standing in a warehouse building that appeared to be vacant. The sounds around me were of the wind, some crickets, and other insects. The building stunk of urine and dust. There was trash tossed around in different areas along with broken glass bottles and cans. Toward the center of the building, I saw sheets of different colors that had been vertically hung on wires that extended horizontally throughout the place. I saw two young ladies, covered with only a dirty beige towel, being led to where I was. They looked to be barely 18 or 19 years of age. Both were slim and appeared to be slightly over 5ft tall with long brown hair. One girl had a small red rose tattoo on the side of her neck. The other young lady had four or five ear piercings. Both ears were riddled with tiny silver hoops. They looked to be in a daze. They did not speak. Behind them was a tall, slim man that was leading them on to a mattress covered with a black sheet.

"Lay down," he demanded as he pulled the towel off one of the girls, revealing her innocent body. He pushed her to the center of the mattress and told the other young lady to sit at the edge of the same mattress.

I could smell stale cigarette smoke on the thin man's clothes. Both girls were scared and confused, looking at the man and repeating, "Please home," in the few English words they presumably knew. These young ladies did not look to be from Mexico. I would guess France or Russia. They appeared to be drunk or drugged. Then, from behind a curtain, came another man. He was tanned and had a large boa constrictor tattoo wrapped around his entire left arm.

"Oh, shit, you brought two? This is going to be a night I will never forget. You outdid yourself," he said to the skinny-faced man.

He took out a roll of money and placed it in the thin man's hand.

"Paid in full," he said.

He walked around the two young girls as a lion would around its prey.

"You did great, man. I should be in the market for a few more this coming week. I've got friends that will definitely be interested in your merchandise," the tanned man said enthusiastically.

He approached one of the young ladies and reached for her breasts. She moved his hands away and crossed her arms across her chest, frightened. He smiled.

"Okay, you wanna play hard to get?"

He followed the question with a right punch to her face. She screamed and crashed down to the dirty floor. She was silent.

"You think you can make choices bitch! I own you!" he yelled out as he repeatedly kicked her. First came a hard kick to her abdomen, and then a kick to her face. Blood was spurting from her mouth and nose.

I was frozen. The inside of my head was screaming, "Stop! Stop! Stop!" I could feel the hot tears streaming down my face and nausea beginning to build in my throat. I could see my hands shaking. My chest was heavy, and I could barely breathe. I tried to memorize what I saw. I tried to see the faces of the men, but I couldn't make them out in the shadows.

I took long looks at their bodies and tried to memorize some patterns that I might recognize if I saw them in person. I looked over at the skinny man as he reached into his front shirt pocket and took out a cigarette. When he lit the flame, it did not reveal his features. He took a deep drag and exhaled only through his nose, making him look more like a dragon than a man. He just stood there, as if watching the premier of some fascinating movie. I sensed not an inkling of remorse in those men.

59

At 10:00 am, I awoke in a cold sweat. I could feel the wetness of the tears I had cried in my sleep. I wanted to vomit; my head was spinning. Oh my God, Oh my God. I took hold of my pillow and sobbed. I don't always know if what I see in my dreams is real. I also don't know if what I see is past, present, or future. After I calmed myself down, I took a long shower and managed to pull myself together.

I decided to call Mrs. Brooks and ask about the painting. I waited until after 2:00 pm to call her. I remember Mr. Brooks always saying that his wife liked going to the 9:00 am church service and then going to lunch at 11:00 am with some of her friends. At 2:15, when I called her, she answered the phone.

"Hello, Brooks' residence."

"Good afternoon Mrs. Brooks. This is Jennifer Knows from Coronado Elementary."

"Oh, yes, Ms. Knoes. How can I help you?"

"Well, I'm very interested in the painting of a flying horse your husband had hanging in his office."

"Oh, that silly thing, what about it?" she asked.

"Well, I would like to purchase it from you or, if you are disposing of it, I would very much like to have it."

"Oh, I am very sorry dear, just last night I drove by the Goodwill on 3rd street and donated many of Mr. Brooks' things to charity. Of course, I kept some of the more important mementos, but that painting was just something we both bought together at some flea market when we were young. It was not worth anything. The store was closed when I arrived with the boxes, so I left everything at the door of the store. There were plenty of other boxes and bags that had been left before me, so I figured it would be okay if I left my donations as well. Maybe you can find it and purchase it. Since I just left it last night, I would imagine that they are still trying to sort through things and get the items out on the floor for sale," she said, sounding hopeful.

Well, at least I knew where to look, I thought to myself. I thanked her and decided not to waste any time. If I was lucky, maybe I could find the painting and purchase it before anyone else did

Goodwill stores usually close at six on Sundays, so I had a few hours to get there and look around. If I got lucky, maybe the painting would still be outside or in the back somewhere. I drove up to find two young boys sorting the bags of donations that had been left outside of the store. I saw furniture that had been moved alongside the building and four rolling carts. The two young boys were sorting the donations. They were sorting books, music, and movies in one cart, toys in the other, clothes in the third cart, and household items in the fourth. I walked up to the young man closest to me as the other continued to sort items.

"Excuse me. Can you tell me if you have found any paintings donated today?"

He looked at me and stopped working.

"We still have to sort through all this." He pointed to what looked like fifty or so bags and boxes of donations. "If there is art here, we have not seen it. Perhaps it has already been put on the floor. We try to put stuff like that out as soon as we get it because it sells quickly. I can tell you I have not seen paintings or art out here yet."

He picked up his sweaty T-shirt, wiped his face, and continued working.

I thanked him and decided to go inside. I walked up and down the rows of frames and paintings and saw nothing that even came close to the painting I was looking for. Perhaps, the painting was somewhere under the pile of items that still needed to be sorted. I looked down at my purse; that was not my purse, but my lunch bag. No big deal, I won't need any money anyway, I thought to myself. To my complete surprise, I heard a familiar voice behind me.

"Hey, Ms. Knoes. Looking for antiques?"

I turned to see Ms. Gomez with a cart containing a couple of jeans and a rolling piece of luggage.

I examined what she was carrying in her cart and asked, "Going somewhere?"

"I'm planning a cruise, and I always like to bring an empty piece of luggage to hold the new clothes and souvenirs I purchase."

"I see. Well, that's a very nice piece of luggage," I said.

I noticed it had a bottom compartment that was assessable to me as it sat in her cart. Perfect! I had my lunch bag, and she was distracted looking at blouses. I had to move fast. When I heard her accidentally drop a blouse and hanger on the floor and bend to pick it up, I unzipped part of the bottom and slipped in the bag with the egg Flor had used to cure me from Ojo. I quickly zipped it back up. She never saw or heard anything suspicious. I walked on down the aisle past her.

"See you later, Ms. Gomez. Have a good day," I said without even looking back at her and headed for the door.

"Okay."

I decided that I would return later. Maybe by this afternoon or tomorrow, the things will have all been sorted and put out on the floor. If they see a painting of a flying horse, surely someone would remember it. I walked outside and over to the donation side of the building. The two young boys were still working, sorting items into baskets. The one I had been talking to before looked up at me and shook his head from side to side.

"Nothing yet, but we still have quite a few bags and boxes left. If we can't sort them before closing today, we will finish tomorrow."

"Listen," I moved in closer to him. "There is a painting of a flying horse that was accidentally donated. It's a very special painting, and if you find it and hold it for me, I will be glad to give you a nice tip."

The young man looked at me, suspiciously.

"We don't accept tips, but if I see it, I can have someone call you. Leave your name and number and what you're looking for again with the front desk. We'll see what we can do."

He smiled and continued working. I did as he asked and crossed my fingers. I would still be coming back to see for myself tomorrow.

60

I arrived at school early Monday and checked my mailbox. It was empty, which to me was good news. Mr. Brooks used to say, "No news is good news." I was walking out of the office when Mrs. Phillips came out of her office and greeted me.

"Good Morning Ms. Knows. I have some information for you. I received a message from the foster care home, notifying me that Leslie and Mike have been adopted into a perfect home."

Mrs. Phillips smiled, winked, and returned to her office. I wonder about Mrs. Phillips. I just know someday I will read a headline about how she was an undercover Navy Seal or something.

"Thank you," I replied and walked on to my classroom.

At 12:30 that afternoon, I had my lunch in my classroom, still boggled by the ABN on the painting. Rachel called me that morning to let me know that although they can't be sure who the children are, they were making an effort to find out how many different DNA samples were in the pile found at the Williams house. She said they had discovered a total of 32 so far.

I looked up at my door to see Claire knocking. She came into my room with a panicked look on her face.

"What's wrong?" I asked.

"I just came from the teacher's lounge. I don't know what happened, but poor Charles is in there crying. I mean, he is really crying! Do you know why he is crying?"

I put my bottle of water down, and I smiled a big glorious smile.

"I calmly walked into the lounge a while ago while he was sitting alone at the small square table by the window. I wanted to thank him for his patience and help with trying to find a clue in Mr. Brooks' office. I told him I was very grateful and that I used to have a friend like him that liked to do handy work around the house. With a big smile, I handed him the key to Jack's tool shed and the inventory Jack kept of everything in it. I told Charles it was all his."

Claire shook her head in approval and smiled.

"That's a good one, Jen. Good for him!"

"From your description, I can conclude that Charles is very, very, happy," I said.

She smiled, turned, and waved as she left my room.

Rene came in a little later and asked, "Okay, what did you do to the poor cutie crying in the lounge?'

"What? Me?" I looked up at Rene.

"Okay, I'm going to come clean and tell you the truth."

I looked at Rene with the most serious expression I could muster and said, "I told him he couldn't have me, and the young man just fell apart."

Rene laughed. "You're so full of do-do."

A thought came to mind as I looked at Rene.

"Rene, would you like to go to Goodwill with me? I have to find that painting that Mr. Brooks had in his office. His wife told me that she donated it to them two nights ago."

He looked at me as if I had just asked him to do something terribly dreadful.

"Are you kidding me? No way!" he said.

"Come on, Rene, it's not that bad. I really need your help. Please come with me," I pleaded. Rene looked at me, defeated.

"Okay, girl, but if I go in there, I am wearing a disguise. That's for poor people. I have never set foot in a thrift store. Do I have to wear gloves? Aren't those stores disgusting? I mean, it's all used stuff," he said.

"Rene, get a grip. Just come with me. I need help looking. Bring a bottle of sanitizer and wipes if you want. Here, I have them right here," I told him and pointed to the Clorox wipes on my desk and the medium size bottle of clear sanitizer.

"Okay, I will come, but bring the wipes. Are we going right after school?" he asked.

"Yes, as soon as the clock strikes 3:20 pm. I will meet you there at 3:45, okay? Don't be late!"

"You better not just be telling me this to embarrass me," he said.

"I would not do that to a friend, especially you." I looked at him reassuringly.

"Okay then," Rene said. Then he repeated, "You told him he couldn't have you," he chuckled.

That was a good one Jen."

He walked out into the hall, still chuckling.

61

I met Rene at the Goodwill on 3rd at 3:45. He had parked far from the front parking lot and was wearing a hat and sunglasses. He waited for me in front of the store, trying to look inconspicuous. He actually looked very handsome, standing there incognito.

"Hey Rene," I shouted happily.

"Shhhhh," he said. "Don't say my name."

I laughed. "Come on."

I opened the door and walked in. I remembered the frames and paintings were flanked on the left wall of the building. Rene stood next to me and removed his sunglasses. He appeared to be in awe staring at all of the signs.

"Wow, this place is very organized and unexpectedly clean. It's nothing like I imagined," he said.

"Come on; let's go check out the paintings." I tugged him along by his shirt.

We both walked to the art section on the left. I was very surprised to see what could have easily been over 100 frames mixed with paintings ranging from very large 72X48 wall size to 11X8 notebook sizes. Next to the paintings were rows and rows of women's shoes.

I quickly begin sifting through the rows of paintings, making sure I did not overlook any piece. My focus on the paintings was broken when I heard Rene say, "Girl, I found some Neiman Marcus shoes!" In his hand, he held what looked like a pair of red ruby slippers, like the ones worn by Dorothy from *The Wizard of Oz*.

"Come on, Seriously? You're supposed to be helping me find a painting. Put those fucking shoes down before I shove them up your ass," I said in a low growl.

"Ouch, that's nasty," he said.

He put the shoes in a carrying basket he held on his arm that I was unaware he had picked up.

"Okay, where do I start?" he asked.

"Go to the other side, and we will meet in the middle," I instructed.

"Okay. I do love those shoes," he said as he walked to the end of the row of paintings and frames.

After what seemed like an hour, we found two pieces of art I recall seeing in Mr. Brooks' office. The first was a good copy of a Vincent Van Gogh, and the other was an eleven-inch box containing a well preserved, once living African Walking Stick. Other than that, we found nothing. My hands were filthy from the rummaging. Thank goodness for the wipes and mini bottle of sanitizer I kept in my purse.

Before we left the store, I decided to ask the attendant if they had any paintings in the back. Maybe some that did not get put on the floor.

"No, ma'am. We put all the paintings and frames on the floor pretty much as soon as they come in. People are always buying art and frames," the young man said.

I was so disappointed. If only I would have done what Delmon said and just asked for it when it was still at school. Damn, I could have just taken the thing, and she would not have even missed it. I guess it's too late now. I did not even have the slightest clue of where to look next. I decided I would call Mrs. Brooks and ask if, by chance, it had stayed behind somewhere in her garage. Perhaps if I showed her the picture I took of it, she would remember if she definitely donated it to Goodwill or if she gave it to a friend or family member. I walked out of the store empty-handed and frustrated. Rene, on the other hand, walked out with ruby slippers, a Louis Vuitton purse, a suit by Calvin Klein, and a pair of black slacks by Ralph Lauren. After spending all of $23.75, he cheered.

"Oh my God, I love this place! How come nobody told me I could have been saving hundreds of dollars all this time?" He took his bag, and we walked out the double glass doors.

His car was parked further than mine but along the same row. I unlocked my car door automatically as we approached. I said thanks to Rene for taking the time to come with me.

"Jen, why didn't you tell me these stores are so awesome? Did you see the six racks of dresses? Oh, honey, I'm coming back very soon with some of my gay sisters."

I playfully pushed him.

"Thanks again."

I turned to climb into my car. Rene was still beside himself over his great finds, hugging his bags as he continued to his car. He was elated. I, on the other hand, just wanted to strangle him.

62

Claire and I had arranged to meet for dinner at Tony's at 8:00 pm. At 7:55 pm, she drove up right behind me as I entered the parking lot. Claire had the best timing of anyone I have ever met. We walked in and sat in our usual booth.

"Should we start with some music?" I asked as I reached into my jacket pocket for change. Claire gestured to the waitress who was coming in our direction.

"We will have two of our usual drinks and two club sandwiches with chips."

The waitress smiled and winked.

"Two Pina Coladas and two subs with chips coming up!"

By then, I had loaded some quarters in the jukebox and pressed in the numbers for two songs: That's Alright Momma by Elvis Presley and Here I Go Again by White Snake. The first was an upbeat song, and the second to remind me not to be a sap when it comes to men.

"Men suck!" I said.

Claire looked over at me and said, "Who, Elvis?"

I smiled. "No, not Elvis. I love Elvis."

"Well, so far, Brian is really good to me," Claire said. "I hope it works out. We have passed one of the critical steps in a relationship."

"That step being?" I asked.

"We both know what we look like in the morning. You know, sleepy eyes, hair going in all directions, and bad breath. We still can't get enough of each other! Isn't that crazy?"

I laughed. "Okay, it's time to focus. What are we going to do about the ABN on the note and the ABN on the painting?"

What was it with the painting? I know Mr. Brooks knew I liked the Pegasus horse because I would stare at it whenever I was in his office discussing upcoming events or asking him for school supplies for my little ones. I don't remember ever seeing the letters ABN written on it, though. Poor Charles patched up two holes on the walls and found nothing.

"You know what Claire? Mr. Brooks wanted me to have that painting. He gave me the paper with ABN on it so I could make the connection and claim the painting."

"You think so?" Claire asked.

"The Cardenas couple adopted an unknown number of kids. The records Mr. Brooks kept of the adoptions do not mean they did not adopt others using another lawyer once Mr. Brooks wanted out. Leslie, Mike, and David were the only three we became aware of. There are more children out there, and we have to find them."

Just then, my phone rang. It was Mrs. Brooks.

"Hello, this is Jennifer. How can I help you?"

"Well," Mrs. Brooks said, "I just remembered something about that painting you were asking about. I remembered that I had also given boxes of paintings and household items to an organization called ARC. It's an organization that helps mentally challenged individuals succeed in the workforce and society. I remembered today because I received an invitation to their upcoming dinner and silent auction. The date is scheduled for Saturday. You might find the painting there. It's the only other place I donated items to," she said.

She told me the tickets sold for $10.00 in advance through the internet or $15.00 at the door. The auction was going to be at the Red Gallery Ballroom. She said she would mail me the invitation in case I needed it at the door. I sent a text message to her phone number and in minutes, she replied with the information about the auction and said she would drop the invitation in the mail for me tomorrow morning. I was in disbelief. Just when I thought all was lost, I get the phone call that might just save the kids.

"Thank you, Mrs. Brooks. I appreciate your help."

I hung up the phone with a big smile.

"I know where the painting is," I told Claire.

We finished our drinks and bundled up before going out into the bitter cold.

It was sleeting, and visibility was low, but I was going straight home. I was prepared to take it slow. I could sense danger, and I wanted to drive as safely as possible. I hugged Claire and reminded her to drive safely.

"You too," she said.

I quickly climbed into the car. I turned on the heater, fastened my seat belt, and waited until I could see through all of my windows. I patiently waited to exit the parking lot.

63

I was waiting for approaching lights to pass before pulling out. When the vehicle moved closer to me, the driver suddenly lost control. I heard the loud screech of breaks and saw the bright lights shining on me. I didn't even have time to react. The next thing I heard was a loud crash echoing in my head. I could feel the car moving and spinning. I think it flipped and over several times and slid. I could hear screaming, my screaming. The seatbelt was so tight I could barely breathe. Something was compressing my chest. Time passed; I couldn't tell how much time; I only recall the chill of the cold rain.

I could hear the commotion, and then I heard a very familiar voice.

"Jen! Jen!"

Someone was gently slapping my face. Ouch, I thought. But my lips did not move.

"Jennifer, open your eyes, dammit. Hang on!"

It was Rachel. I could see only gray and black shadows. I felt people moving about me and heard what sounded like hundreds of people talking in the background. I knew they were speaking, but I could not understand a word. I could hear police officers telling people to get back and stay away so the paramedics could do their job. Rachel was next to me, unfastening my seatbelt.

"Jennifer, open your eyes," Rachel insisted as she leaned close to push my seat back.

The paramedic lifted me out of the car and laid me on a bed that felt hard and cold. Rachel was now holding my hand, standing next to the stretcher.

"Jen, open your eyes!" she demanded.

To my amazement, I answered, barely moving my lips.

"No, I am tired. I want to sleep."

And I let myself rest.

"No! Jennifer," Rachel practically yelled. "Dammit, you're not getting off that easy. You have no fucking clue how many times I thought about our adventures to lift myself up during hard times. You don't know how many times I wished I would someday run into my old friend. Then, out of nowhere, you found me! Now you are going to sleep? Oh, fuck that shit! No you don't, missy!" "You've never been a quitter Jen, don't quit on me now." I had never seen or heard Rachel cry, until that night.

She held my hand and kept telling me I was going to be just fine.

One thing about Rachel is that when she becomes very angry or hurt, she curses. A lot!

Claire took my hand, and I heard Rachel say, "I will meet you there." After what seemed like an eternity, I finally heard the sirens stop. We had reached the hospital. I was brought down from the ambulance and the medical staff raced me into the emergency room. I saw the lights on the ceiling and the half faces of doctors and nurses. Then, all of a sudden, the noise stopped, and everything went pitch black.

I woke up to someone taking my pulse and asking me softly, "Ms. Knoes, are you with us? Can you hear me? Smile for me, sweetie, if you can hear me."

I smiled.

"Very nice, you have been out for a while. How do you feel?" The nurse asked.

"Like shit, weak, hungry," I mumbled.

"I will get the doctor to come in and talk to you. You got a little banged up there."

The nurse raised my bed slowly and gently placed a pillow behind my back.

"You must be a very special person," the nurse said in a low calming tone. "You have some very good friends that care for you very much. Your friend Claire just went to the cafeteria to grab a bite. She and your other friend, the police officer, have divided the time so that you were never alone since you were admitted on Monday."

"What day is it?" I asked.

The nurse answered, "It's Wednesday. The police officer slept on that very uncomfortable chaise last night."

She pointed to a chaise still with the wrinkled hospital blanket sprawled on it. She had just finished her sentence when both Claire and Rachel walked in.

"Hey! Aren't you a sight for sore eyes?" Rachel said.

They both came to my bed and hugged me. They were both crying.

"Stop being weenies," I said, also crying.

"Watch the IVs," the nurse said as calmly as she could. "Her veins aren't very cooperative."

"You were pretty lucky," Claire said. "The airbag caught you from busting your head, and the belt kept you from ejecting the vehicle. Unfortunately, you did fracture a rib and bruised your legs. You were purple and blue from head to toe when you came in. No broken bones, just a lot of bruising."

I heard a male voice at my door. Then in walked a tall, dark-haired, blue-eyed doctor with the prettiest smile and the pearliest white teeth I had ever seen.

"Good afternoon Ms. Knoes. You gave your friends here quite a scare."

He was about to introduce himself when the intercom interrupted with: "Dr. Grant, you're needed in OR stat!"

He looked at me and said, "I will return before my shift is over; I promise."

He sounded like an old friend, and somehow, I knew he would always keep his promises. With that, he turned and exited my room. I slept soundly after that. I woke up later that evening to find Rachel playing solitaire on the table next to my bed.

"Dinner time, sleeping beauty," Rachel announced as she moved the cards and set my tray on the table.

The nurse had brought a tray containing a baked chicken breast, green beans, mashed potatoes, red gelatin, and unsweetened tea.

"Yum," Rachel said sarcastically.

"Want to share?" I asked.

"I'll pass," she answered.

I sat up to eat when I heard the doctor.

He walked in and paused, "Okay, where were we?"

He gave me a genuine smile. He looked at my dinner and said, "Just in time. I better examine you before you eat that." He laughed.

Rachel stood and said, "I'm going to the cafeteria to get some real food. I will be back in about an hour."

She tapped the door on her way out and waved. Dr. Grant checked my lungs, heart, eyes, and body for bruising.

"Well, you are recovering nicely. This brings good news and bad news. The good news is that you will be moved into another room, not in the ICU for one more day. I want to make sure you will be able to move about normally before you go home."

"What's the bad news?" I asked.

"The bad news is that you are stuck with me for one more day. I will be checking on you first thing in the morning and right before I dismiss you."

"Oh, I think I can handle that," I said with a smile.

64

He came in twice the next day to visit with me and conduct a quick overall check.

"How are you handling the food here?" he asked.

"Well, to be honest, I can't wait to dig into a bowl of spaghetti and meatballs with a glass of red wine on the side."

Dr. Grant laughed. "Now that is a meal. How would you feel about an Italian dinner with me? My treat for being the easiest patient I have had all year."

I was a little surprised and nervous at beginning another relationship so soon after my heartbreak. I decided I would listen to my intuition and go with it.

"Okay, I would love that," I said.

"How about I pick you up at 7:00 pm tomorrow, Friday? It won't be formal or fancy. I don't think your body is in the mood for any tight-fitting clothing. How about casual and comfortable?" he asked.

"That's a date," I responded with a smile.

He touched my hand and with a wink, said, "I will see you tomorrow."

The nurse came in minutes later and had me sign some dismissal papers. She was holding a paper bag that contained some items they had removed from me when I arrived. Claire had gathered my things and checked the bathroom for the last time to make sure I did not leave anything behind. An attendant appeared with a wheelchair. Claire stood next to me and made sure I did not lose my balance. I slowly settled into the wheelchair and placed my feet on the foot plates. The nurse handed my bag to Rachel as she walked into the discharge area. The discharge nurse patted my back and said, "You know you're special when you have a uniformed officer escort you to your car and carry your bags." The nurse smiled and returned to the nurse's work station.

Rachel looked over at Claire.

"You want to take shifts looking after our pal here?"

"Oh, stop it, I will be fine. I did not break any bones. I can get around fine. You both enjoy your time away from work. You have been the best friends I could ever ask for."

Claire looked back at Rachel and said, "I will be over at Jen's in a few hours."

"That's settled; I am taking you home," Rachel said. "I will help you get settled in, and then I will have to go to work and arrest some bad guys."

Rachel drove me home in her vehicle, brought up my bags, and helped me into my apartment. I sat on the couch and took a deep breath. Oh, so good to be home. Where are the kids? I called their names, and they came running. Rachel took the things out of my bag, putting my dirty clothes in the laundry and my toiletries in the restroom.

"Rachel, can I ask you something?"

"Sure," she said.

"Dr. Grant asked me over for dinner. Do you think I'm moving too fast? I mean, he's funny, kind, gentle, honest and I like being around him. Something about him makes me feel good inside."

"Wow! I like him more than you already," she laughed. "Jen, just follow your heart." She handed me my car keys and my cell phone.

I took the charger that I kept plugged into the wall by the couch and plugged in my phone.

"Well, any progress on your case?" I asked.

"We are still trying to find something Mr. Brooks may have had in his computer that identifies the other families. So far, we have found nothing."

Then I heard my phone ding telling me that I had new e-mails. I picked up the phone and unlocked it. There, on the very top, was a reply from Ellen. I laughed.

"Hey Ellen responded. I told you she would," I said.

"What did she say?"

Rachel came and sat close to me on the couch. I opened the e-mail:

"Dear Clueless,

If all I had was a painting as a clue, I would take that sucker apart inch by inch and examine it with ultraviolet lights, a magnifying glass, lemon juice, and multicolor lenses to look for symbols and other clues that could be in the painting.

Good luck!

Ellen

P.S. If you discover a national treasure, e-mail me I would love to have you on my show."

"Well, that's all good, but we can't take it apart if we don't have the damn painting!" Rachel said as she stood and paced the floor with her hands on her head. "Well, it was worth a try. I've got to go to work. You get some sleep and recover so you can go back to work soon and not go batty in this small apartment."

She kissed my forehead and locked the door on her way out. I didn't tell Rachel I knew where the painting was. Something told me to hold off until later.

65

Claire arrived about five minutes after Rachel left. On my phone was all the information that Mrs. Brooks sent regarding the dinner and silent auction. In the pile of mail Claire collected from my mailbox, was the actual invitation to the auction.

"Will you be up for a fancy dinner and silent auction on Saturday evening?" I asked Claire.

"What? Are you kidding? It's the middle of the month. I can't go and spend hundreds of dollars purchasing a painting that may or may not be helpful in finding the other couples," she said.

"That's okay; I know who can come and buy the painting," I said confidently.

"Who?" she asked.

"Rene," I answered.

Claire laughed. "Rene is a volunteer. He doesn't even get paid!"

I looked at Claire. "Rene is a volunteer at our school, but at the Burlesque downtown, Rene is Rene-Rene, one of the best female performers around. He makes in one week what we make in a month," I informed.

"Oh well hell, let's call him," Claire insisted.

I knew it was late, and I figured I would leave a message. He was probably out or working. I picked up my phone and heard it ring.

"Hey girl, how are you?" It was Rene.

"I'm fine. I should be back at work by Monday," I answered.

"I heard you were banged up pretty good. I prayed for you, girl, but you know I can't stand the sight of hurt friends or blood. My skin crawls and I cry like the girl that I am. Trust me, honey, you don't want to see that," he laughed. "Anyway," he continued, "I wanted to let you know that I have been feeding your fish while you're out. Yesterday I went to feed them, and Ms. Gomez was coming out of your room. I figured maybe she was offering to help the substitute with something. When I entered the room, the sub was not in there. So what the hell is Ms. Gomez doing in your room? I don't like the bitch. She's weird."

I laughed.

"As soon as Sam heard you were in an accident, she set up a sub for Tuesday, Wednesday, Thursday, and Friday. She was lucky to find one that could do the four days in a row. I went into your room and pulled your lesson plan book. You are the only teacher in history that plans two weeks ahead. Mrs. Phillips came in and took your subfolder off of the shelf where you keep your Teacher Editions. That lady almost went into shock. She said it was the most complete subfolder she had ever seen. She freaked when she saw you had even pre-made name tags for the students! I thought it was wonderful," Rene said. "Anyway, I got you covered. You relax, and I will see you Monday."

"Wait for a second Rene. How would you like to attend a silent auction on Saturday?"

I explained the situation with the painting and why we needed to find it.

"The auction starts at 6:00 pm, and we might need your wallet. You, Claire, and I are going if you're up for some adventure."

"Okay, honey, I could use some adventure. Let me call work and have someone fill in for me that evening. I've been waiting to wear my ruby slippers since I bought them," he said excitedly.

"Oh no, hold the phone! Rene, you are coming as the handsome man that you are," I said.

Rene made a dramatic "aww" sound.

"You really know how to hurt a girl," he said.

"Claire and I will have to find something semi-formal, which brings us to the other problem. Can we peek into your closet?" I asked.

"Sure. I will allow you to play dress-up with my clothes. Arrive at my place at 5:00 pm, okay? I will see both of you Saturday," Rene said and hung up the phone.

Claire stayed with me that night and helped me with my bath and getting dressed. I was taking pain medication, so I slept most of the time. I was glad a substitute had been arranged for the days I was out. I was also glad that a week ago, something inside told me to get my subfolder up to par and to prepare lessons for two weeks. As I said, I don't always know why I do what I do. I simply pay attention and follow instructions. The doctor assured me that I could return to work on Monday if I followed the instructions he had provided. They were the usual, no lifting, no strenuous exercise, no contact sports or physical activity that would interfere with the recovering period.

66

Friday evening, I was nervous about my date with Dr. Grant. I had thought it through and decided I was going to take it one date at a time. He was flirting with me almost the instant he met me. He was so gentle when caring for me. He would joke about the hospital food and how the frozen dinners he prepared himself were no better, hinting that he did not have a wife or significant other caring for him at home. He was dedicated to his profession and worked long hours. I genuinely enjoyed his company, and something about him felt so right. I was still afraid of being let down again, but how will I ever find the right one if I hide away because of a bad experience? I reminded myself that what's worse than doing something wrong is doing nothing.

At 6:59 pm. Dr. Grant knocked on my door. I decided to wear a calf-length floral silk wrap dress with gold strappy sandals. I pulled my hair in a classy up-bun. Although the swelling and bruising on my legs and arms had gone away, I did not feel like wearing anything tight on my body. I stood by the door, took a deep breath, and slowly exhaled before I opened the door to see the handsome Dr. Grant standing there on my front porch. He was wearing a gray silk shirt and some black slacks. He smiled and stood quietly as if he had no idea what to say. He glanced at his watch.

"Right on time," he said. "Wow! You look gorgeous."

He scanned my body from head to toe.

"Thank you," I responded.

I grabbed my beige purse from the table in the entryway and blew a kiss to my two little ladies sprawled out on the corridor.

"Shall we?" Dr. Grant said as he stepped aside and made a gesture to say after you.

He walked next to me. I could feel his hand on my back as he led me to the car. He was playing some classical music I was not familiar with. The piano and violin together sounded so calming.

We drove onto the outskirts of Lake Worth to a country setting. It was beautiful. The sky was filled with more stars then I had ever seen in my life. He swiped a plastic gate card on the silver box that stood before a large metal gate. In seconds, the two large gates parted in the middle and invited us in. We followed a driveway that led to a ranch style house with a large porch and a carefully groomed lawn.

"This will be my home for the next six weeks or so. I'm renting it from a friend while I find a permanent residence," he said as he led me up a long sidewalk that extended alongside the house. He unlocked the door and led me inside. From the entryway, I could see a table set for two with white dishes and silverware wrapped in a royal blue napkin. A goblet sat next to each place setting. In the center of the table was a vase of fresh, colorful flowers that made the dining table look very elegant.

"Come into the kitchen. I have dinner ready. I turned everything off when I went to get you, but I am certain it is still hot," he said.

He smiled and headed to the kitchen. He took the goblets from the table on the way and served some chilled wine he had sitting in an ice bucket on the counter.

"Here you go," he said as he handed me a glass of red wine.

The kitchen smelled delicious with the aroma of fresh vegetables, meat sauce, and French bread.

"Wow, you really went all out. I hope this patient didn't cause you too much trouble," I said and smiled.

He lifted his glass.

"What should we toast to?" he asked.

I smiled and hesitated.

"To health," I said shyly.

He smiled again and looked at me with his mysterious blue eyes.

"To us, and good health."

He toasted as he touched my wine glass with his and took a sip. I just held my glass and stared at him, wanting so bad for this to not be a dream.

He slowly leaned in and kissed me. I gripped my glass of wine, not wanting to spill it, and returned his kiss. I felt a tingle beginning at my lips and traveling down my spine. He held me close, but gently, aware that I might still be hurting from the bruising. I wanted him to take me in his arms and make love to me. I know he saw the yearning in my eyes.

He smiled. "You still need to recover. You are amazing. Thank you for saying yes to the invitation. I'm going to serve you dinner and keep your wine glass fresh. You, Jennifer, are going to enjoy the attention."

He placed both hands on my arms and kissed my neck.

It was the most wonderful meal I ever had. Dr. Grant was actually an excellent cook. As he said, he served me, and I don't recall how many times he refreshed my wine glass. We talked for hours. I never wanted to leave. My heart was falling, and I didn't care because it felt so good.

67

Saturday evening, we arrived at Rene's apartment at 5 o'clock in casual clothes. I had taken the time to put on some make-up and curl my long locks of auburn hair. Claire had also applied a little bit of lipstick and had curled her hair up in a French roll. Rene opened the door, looking dashing in his pajama pants and muscle shirt.

"Oh my God!" he said as he looked at both of us with a pitiful look. "I don't know if we have enough time to make you two beautiful." He laughed. "What's with the big bag?" he asked as he moved back to let us enter.

"Shut up and let us in. We have clothes to try on," I said, as we both walked into the living room where Rene had already displayed what looked like ten outfits with matching shoes and purses. I brought a big shopping bag with some extra clothes and things I figured I might need.

"Oh wow," I said in complete surprise. "What in the world? You are a diva, aren't you?" Claire walked around the display of garments and started to feel and choose those she liked. I pulled a dress with a low bust line and handed it to Claire.

"Here, you'll need to wear something like this."

She looked at me with disapproval.

"Oh no, I don't wear low necklines. The only thing I wear with a low neckline is my bathing suit in the summer," Claire said, moving away from the dress.

I laughed. Claire reluctantly took the dress and matching shoes.

"Okay, here goes nothing," she said and started to remove her clothes.

"Whoa, ladies have some modesty, will you?" Rene said as he pulled a tri-fold dressing divider into the room. Claire did not care one way or another.

We only had 30 minutes to get ready and arrive at our destination. I grabbed a dress I liked as well and began to get dressed. Surprisingly enough, Rene's wardrobe fit us relatively well.

"Hey Rene, if you ever take a collection of garments to donate to Goodwill, let me go through them first," I hollered at him from the other side of the tri-fold. "You have the cutest clothes.

Claire walked out from behind the tri-fold, looking stunning.

"Where are the shoes?" She asked as she looked for them in the row of shoes Rene had lined up by the back of the couch. I walked out from behind the divider, also ready to try on some shoes. Claire had already found a matching clutch, and Rene was showing her some jewelry to match her outfit. I walked over to the couch and found a flattering pair of shoes and a matching clutch. Claire was admiring herself in a full-length mirror Rene had rolled out from his bedroom. She was touching up makeup and lipstick. Rene looked over at me and clapped his hands in a hurry-up gesture.

"Okay. My turn," he said and hurried to his bedroom.

Minutes later, we heard Rene's voice.

"Come on, ladies, it's time to go."

He stood there in a perfectly tailored suit. He looked gorgeous.

"Wow, Rene, you look great," I said.

He laughed, "tell me something I don't know honey." He walked over to a silver bowl on his kitchen counter and took his keys.

"Come on, we have a painting to buy," he said.

He patted his coat to make sure he had his wallet. I placed the invitation and my wallet in my clutch purse. I had my lipstick in my hand and was touching up my lipstick when Rene said,

"Come on. We have to go!"

We walked out looking and feeling great. Rene unlocked his BMW. I sat in the front passenger's seat. I was excited and nervous at the same time. It was now 20 minutes before seven. We would be there right on-time. I was so glad to have my two friends supporting me.

"Hey, did you tell Rachel we knew where the painting was?" Claire asked.

"No, I didn't see any reason for it. I'm still not 100 percent sure the painting will be there, so technically, we don't know where the painting is until we actually see it," I said, justifying my action.

"Well, it better be there. I did not make myself this hot for nothing, honey," Rene said as he moved his head from side to side. "I have never been to this place, so I hope we find it."

"It's called GPS, Rene," Claire said and laughed.

"Oh shut up, slut in my clothes," Rene retorted as he laughed and put the car in reverse.

68

The three of us walked into the Red Gallery Ballroom and quickly melded into the low roaring crowd. I decided to wear a little black dress with black high-heeled, strappy shoes and a gold clutch. I talked Claire into wearing a low neck, peach chiffon dress with silver strappy sandals, a beige clutch, and a long strand of pearls that Rene loaned her. Rene looked handsome as ever in a black silk suit that was tailored to perfection with a white shirt and skinny tie. Rene was handsome enough to make women gawk at him and pretty enough to turn men's heads. As we walked around scoping out the place, we did not see anyone we knew.

There were small groups of people chatting and holding plastic champagne glasses. We walked to the table and took our own glass. Rene's attention was focused on a young man who was chatting with a brunette.

"Look at that handsome devil. I would like to be locked in a closet with him," Rene said, taking a sip of his champagne.

Claire looked at Rene and said, "You know that is so wrong on so many levels."

I chuckled at their exchange.

Two years ago, Rene decided to share with us that as a child, his mother would lock him in her walk-in closet with a coffee can to pee in, a box of pop tarts, and a bottle of water while she went out to party with men. He told us sometimes she would not return for days. When he was eight years old, his mother died of a heroin overdose. He was adopted by an aunt and began a better life where hope, love, and encouragement were given freely. After several years of therapy, he can now jokingly talk about it.

We decided to walk around and find the auction room. The first set of double doors was open to disclose a dimly lit dining room decorated with floating candle centerpieces. The second set of doors opened into a large round auction room.

"Bingo," I whispered.

The large room was lined with tables along the walls of the round room. Three feet separated each table. The tables displayed items like brass pieces, jewelry, antique dishes, and many other small valuable knickknacks for auction.

Claire looked in astonishment and said, "How in the hell are we going to find the painting in this mess?"

I looked at her.

"All I can tell you is that it's in a box," I answered.

We walked around looking interested and pretended to look at the bidding cards.

"Hey, I'm bidding on this one," Rene said as he picked up a Louis Vuitton wallet. "I have the matching purse."

"Hey knucklehead, you're dressed like a man," I reminded him.

"Then I will buy it for my blow-up wife," he said and busted out laughing.

We continued walking until we came to the last 30 feet of the circles of tables.

There against the wall, were a slew of paintings standing on the last four tables. The painting wasn't there.

"Oh, dammit," Rene said.

"It's in a box," I said.

"How do you know that it's in a box?" Rene asked.

"I just know. Stop being stupid and look in a box."

I picked up the skirt around the table to find two large boxes filled with paintings.

"Well," Rene said, "if it hasn't been put out, we can't bid on it. But if it hasn't been put out, it won't be missed," he said slyly.

"What if they don't put it out? I mean, look at all those beautiful paintings already out," I said, disappointed.

"Rene, we have to take the painting," Claire added. "There is no other way around it if we want it today."

I looked around and noticed the emergency exit about 10 feet away from the table with the paintings underneath.

"Rene, go outside and move your car close to this exit door, pop open the trunk so I can lift it quickly, and wait for me."

I looked over at Claire.

"Claire, in two minutes, you're going to flirt with the two security guards coming our way to tell us to get out. Get them away from this area. I'm going to be under the table rummaging through the boxes. I'm determined to find that damn painting. Text me when you have them away so I can exit this door once I find it."

With that, I crawled under the table in my short dress, revealing my black garter and stockings. I didn't care because no one was looking.

Claire looked toward the entrance and saw the two security guards wearing blue polo shirts with the ARC logo and khaki slacks walking her way. She lowered her neckline, boosted her breasts up, and met the men halfway. One of the men looked at Claire and then began looking around as if expecting someone to be with her.

"Excuse me, miss," the other guard said. "The auction will not start for another 30 minutes. Would you mind waiting in the main hall?"

"Oh, I'm so sorry. I wanted to get a sneak peek so I would be ready to bid on the items I like," Claire said. She continued. "This is a beautiful ballroom. The way it's set up for the auction is totally genius. Did you gentlemen do that?"

While Claire was rattling on, she walked toward the large double doors that exited the auction room and back into the large opened area.

She sighed. "Alright then, I will wait out here and have me a glass of champagne."

The guards quietly closed the large wooden doors. Claire strolled over to the champagne table and picked up a glass. She took a sip and placed the glass on an empty tray of a host walking by. She reached into her clutch purse, retrieved her phone, and sent a text message to Jennifer.

All clear!

69

I was frantically looking for the painting in the two boxes under the table. After not finding it in those two boxes, I realized that there were four more boxes that had paintings in them at the other end of the table. I crawled my way over to the other boxes and began searching. Rummaging through the last box, I found it. I grabbed the painting out of the box. Suddenly I heard the security guards unlocking the doors and asking people to wait back until the doors were completely open. It must be time for the auction to begin. I checked my messages and saw the all-clear from Claire. I quickly crawled out from under the table and darted out the emergency exit door.

Right as the doors swung closed, the other opened, and a crowd of noisy people poured into the building auction room. I found Rene right outside the door, standing by his trunk. I slipped the painting in and walked around to the passenger's side. I sent Claire a text.

Got it! Come out the front door.

Claire read her message and began to head toward the front of the building. She had just reached the front door when she heard a voice behind her. It was the security guard.

"Excuse me, Miss, the auction is just beginning. Weren't you going in?

"I left my pocketbook in my car. I can't bid without it," she said.

Then she noticed she was carrying her clutch in her hand.

Nervously she said, "I better hurry now," and she turned to walk down the front stairs.

Just then, coming up the stairs, was their security police officer for the evening.

"Hey, Claire," Rachel called out. "Is Jennifer with you? I went by her place earlier, and she wasn't home."

Rachel noticed the nervous look on Claire's face.

"Are you leaving?"

Before Claire could even answer, Rene came speeding to the front of the building and stopped two feet from Claire. She climbed in the back seat. Rachel noticed that I was sitting in the passenger's seat. She walked over, appearing to want an explanation for the bizarre behavior. I smiled and said, "We really need to go."

"Should I even ask?" Rachel said as she looked at me, suspiciously. "Did you do something illegal?" she probed, not really wanting to hear the answer.

"I will tell you later, promise."

By this time, Rene had exited the car and was standing next to Rachel.

"Will you do me a huge favor? Can you bid on that Louis Vuitton wallet?" He handed her five one hundred dollar bills. "My sister would really like to have it."

He flashed Rachel his handsome smile.

"I don't know if I can even bid." Rachel said.

"Just try; that's all we ask." Rene said.

He patted her hand as he handed over the money and returned to the driver's seat. Rachel sighed and put the money in her front pocket.

"Okay, but be prepared for me to hand this back to you later."

"Thanks, Rachel," I said. "We can't talk right now, but call me or come by later. I will fill you in on everything. Hopefully, we will have some good news for you."

Rachel took a deep breath and tapped the top of the car before walking away and into the building.

70

We arrived at Rene's townhouse and raced up his front porch stairs. I was holding the painting with both hands, anxious to start examining it. Rene opened the door and invited us in. Claire and I walked in, taking excited breaths. I was holding the painting, anxious to get a closer look at it. I sat it down on the couch while I change my clothes. Claire stood by the sofa and whirled her dress over her head. Then she sat on the love seat and removed the silver shoes. She hung the chiffon dress on a fabric-lined coat hanger Rene handed her. Then she handed him the shoes.

"Thank you," Claire said.

"You're very welcome, my dear," Rene said as he walked into his bedroom holding the items.

"Oh, and don't think I forgot that you're still wearing my pearls!"

Claire laughed.

Rene was walking back into the living room, saying, "A real hottie gave me those pearls after a night I'll never forget."

"Well, spare us the details, or tonight will be a night we'll never forget," Claire said.

I laughed.

"Jealous bitches, that's what you are," René said as he plopped himself on the couch and pointed at a rose-colored bowl in the center of the coffee table.

Claire removed the pearls and gently placed them in the bowl. While that was going on, I removed and hung my little black dress on a hanger identical to the one Rene had handed Claire. I removed the black shoes and headed to Rene's bedroom.

"Just place them on the bed, dear," Rene hollered from the couch.

We had left our clothes on the back of the couch. Claire put on her jeans and pullover pink top. Then she grabbed her beige flats from under the coffee table. I slipped back into my khaki slacks and black shirt. Claire threw my black flats my way. While we dressed, Rene made himself busy in the kitchen,
Rene returned with three wine glasses.
"Here you go," he said. He left the room and returned with a hammer, a wedge, a magnifying glass, some scissors, and a box cutter. I sat on the couch, took the painting, and cut the paper along the side with the box cutter. I completely exposed the back and removed the brown paper backing. There wasn't any writing on the back. Claire and Rene released a disappointing moan.
"Well, go ahead and take it out of the frame. Maybe something is on the sides."
Rene was now sitting on the couch wearing Marylyn Monroe pajama pants in black and white paired with a black muscle shirt. He took the painting and, with his hand, he gently slid it out of the frame. I saw nothing at all inside the frame. I examined it inch by inch while René and Claire were examining the painting with a magnifying glass. Rene put down the magnifying glass, took a sip of his wine, and crossed his legs.
He leaned back on the couch and said, "I am glad the painting was free."
We had a couple more glasses of wine and kept looking for another 30 minutes.
After finding nothing to guide us in the right direction, Claire and I decided to call it a night. We handed our wine glasses to Rene, and he walked over to the kitchen and carefully placed them on his counter. While he was busy in the kitchen, and Claire was in the ladies' room, I placed the original painting in my big bag and took out the duplicate that I had made at Walgreens.
"Rene, I'm going to leave the painting with you and take the frame to fix it," I hollered from the living room.
I put the frame in the large bag along with the original painting and covered it with the extra clothes I had brought. Rene agreed to keep the painting safe; unaware that it was a duplicate.
I called Rachel to let her know we had the painting and had found nothing in it to help us find the missing children. She said there was a huge turnout at the auction, and she had to work late so she could not make it to Rene's.

I took the large bag, and we said our goodbyes to Rene. I knew we were either being watched or heard. I could not say anything or appear suspicious. Rene is such a stickler for locking doors and setting alarms that I was not too concerned about him. Still, I made him promise to lock his doors, close the blinds and set his security alarm before going to bed.

"I always do that," he said. "Call me if anything comes to mind. I'm up for more torture."

He laughed, waved, and closed the door. Claire drove me home. My car insurance was providing me with a rental tomorrow so I could return to work Monday.

71

Sunday, I was sitting at my desk in my bathrobe, my wet hair pulled up on my head with my towel and a cup of freshly brewed coffee, reviewing my plans for the last week before Spring Break. My phone rang, and I answered on the third ring. It was the very handsome Dr. Grant. I decided I wasn't going to predict, anticipate, or rush anything.

I decided to let life move along. Jack had disappointed me so much, but really, it was my fault. If I had paid attention to the signs, I would have known he wasn't the one. I was so wrapped up in him being the one that I saw nothing else.

"Are you up for a visitor? I have been thinking about you since you left," Dr. Grant said.

I smiled.

"Sure. Come on over."

"I will be there in 30 minutes," he said softly.

I hurried to finish my work and make a note of what I had to do first thing in the morning.

I had just written in my last activity for my next week's lesson plans when I heard the doorbell ring. My heart was pounding with nervousness and excitement.

"Take out from Ching Wok, my neighborhood Chinese restaurant. I hope you haven't had lunch," he said. "I wanted to surprise you. I'm sure you've been under a pile of papers."

I laughed.

"Come in," I said with a smile as I moved aside.

He walked into my apartment and placed the bag containing 4 square boxes, utensils, and two fortune cookies on the dining table. He turned and held me. It felt so good to be in his arms again.

He leaned down for a kiss that quickly ignited into a wildfire. After a soft kiss, our tongues danced together in perfect rhythm. I took him by the hand and led him to my bedroom. Our bodies pressed together. I felt his lips traveling to my neck. I felt a sharp pain as he sucked on my neck. He untied my robe belt and opened my robe. His hands move softly on my breasts.

"Here," I said, "let me do this."

I started to unbutton his shirt. I pulled the shirt off his back and began to caress his flawless body. His hands helped me out of my robe. The towel I had on my head had long hit the floor. I could feel my body aching and the moistness collecting between my legs. My nipples were hard with desire. I unbuckled his slacks and reached in to cress a hardness that confessed he wanted me as much as I wanted him. He removed my robe and slipped his hand between my legs. My breathing was heavy now; my entire body was aching.

I moaned.

We moved to the bedroom. He removed his slacks and moved toward me. He kissed my breasts and sucked on my stiff nipples. The sharp pain was delicious. I moaned again as he slipped his fingers into my moistness. My blood was racing; every part of my body was tingling. He was breathing feverishly as he moved his hands to separate my legs. Working his way between them, he guided his long, thick hardness into me. I moaned in ecstasy and pain as he completely filled me. He moaned as he entered me. We moved in perfect rhythm. With every thrust, he filled me again and again. I felt myself peaking to orgasm.

"Keep doing that," I moaned. "Don't stop!"

Then came the climax and release of multiple orgasms. As my muscles squeezed his hardness, I felt a hot release inside me and Dr. Grant's body slowly relaxed.

"Oh heaven," he said.

He held my body and turned on his back. I was now lying on top of him, kissing him gently.

"I can still feel you inside me," I whispered. "Does that family jewel relax after your orgasm?"

He kissed me and whispered, "It has."

"Seriously, but I can still feel you inside me," I said.

"Humm," he responded.

"I am one lucky lady," I giggled.

Grant sighed, "And I am one starving, lucky man."

"Oh no, our take-out is on the table!" I said, laughing.

I grabbed my robe from the floor and raced to the dining table. I loaded a T.V. tray with our Chinese take-out, took two wine glasses and a bottle of wine from the small bar by the fireplace, and headed back to the bedroom. We laughed, talked, and fed each other with our chopsticks. It was the best take-out meal I had ever had.

72

Monday morning, I arrived at work with my usual 20 minutes to get prepared and make some copies. If I know I have to make copies for the week; I always arrive before the other teachers so I can get them done without interruption. I was almost finished running my copies when Ms. Gomez and Nicole entered the lounge. They were chatting about the spring vacation they had arranged to take together.

"Oh, you'll love it. It's so sunny and beautiful there. The beaches are as blue as can be. Let's plan to sit at the beach at least an hour a day," Ms. Gomez said.

"Oh definitely," Nicole agreed. "When we come back, we will be the tannest hotties at Coronado Elementary!"

They laughed and then stopped when they noticed I was there.

"Welcome back," Nicole said with a smile

"Yes, welcome back, Ms. Knoes," Ms. Gomez added.

"Did you get the flowers we sent to your home?"

"Yes, I did. Thank you," I answered.

"Oh, it's from the Hospitality Committee. We were all wishing you a quick recovery," Nicole said.

"Well, thank you, ladies. I guess your recovery wishes worked. I really do appreciate it," I said with a warm smile. I grabbed my papers off the copier tray and headed out of the lounge before Ms. Gomez attempted to reread my palm lines.

I was standing at the door greeting the children. I pushed the panic button by my door and informed the office that I needed the assistance of Mrs. Phillips and the Vice Principal in my classroom STAT! Then, I heard the dreaded voice I knew was coming.

"You fucking bitch! Did you report me to CPS?"

There, 10 feet from me, was Bill's mother. She was heading straight for me with fists clenched and a face of rage.

"Why did you report me?" she yelled.

I remained calm but prepared for her to strike. Other parents had heard her and were stopping to see the commotion.

"Do you really want me to answer that in front of all of these witnesses? I asked. "I don't think you want that. If you have been a good parent, then you have nothing to worry about," I assured her, still in a calm tone.

"You think you're so fucking smart, you bitch. You better watch your back. If they take my Bill, I'm coming for you." She glared at me.

By that time, Mrs. Phillips, the V.P., and the school security guard were surrounding Bill's mother. She was escorted out of the building, still calling me all kinds of colorful metaphors. Bill did not attend school that day, and I was a little worried.

Considering the rough start of the day, the rest of the school day went relatively smoothly. Routines and procedures were followed, literacy centers were ready, and the children enjoyed their new center activities. Mondays were always rough, but today the kids were very self-regulating and working quietly with their partners.

When dismissal came, Mrs. Phillips and our security guard decided to escort my students and me to the dismissal area. In case Bill's mother decided to return with a vengeance. I did not like threats. Especially hers because she seemed to be out of her mind most of the time, and I knew she meant business. Thankfully, by 3:15 pm. all of the children had been picked up. We walked back into the building and shut the doors to lock automatically. I knew it was not over. I was expecting her to return for me. Maybe she would not return today, but soon.

73

The next day, I awoke to find Chloe nestled next to my arm and Kayla at the foot of my bed. They normally sprawl their large furry bodies in the corridor or on the couch, so this came as a surprise to me. I have read how sometimes cats can detect death and how they sometimes visit the soon to be departed. I was hoping that was not the case. Perhaps my fear of Bill's mother was detected by my cats. I climbed out of bed and found my phone plugged into the charger on my nightstand.

This morning, I woke up with numbers in my head. I called Rachel.

"This is Officer Brinks," she answered.

"Rachel," my eyes began to tear up, "there are 248 other couples in the state of Texas that have adopted children to sell. Brooks arranged those adoptions, but I don't know who they are."

"Oh God," Rachel sighed. "Do you have any idea where or how we can find the children?"

I could sense her frustration.

"No. All I know is that it has something to do with that painting."

"You told me that you, Claire and Rene, looked at the painting and found nothing," Rachel reminded.

"Just because we didn't find it doesn't mean it's not there," I said. "I will keep you posted," I assured her and hung up the phone.

I knew the final clue was in the painting. I will keep the painting until I figure it out. We still haven't tried multicolored lenses and lemon juice, I thought to myself.

I decided to focus on my classroom, and hopefully something would come to me that I had not thought of. It was up to me to try to figure out what I was supposed to find. I decided to let it rest for now and get ready for school. My two ladies jumped off the bed when I left it and proceeded to the corridor.

I took my shower, still worried about Bill's mother and my safety. I dressed in some khaki capris, a dark blue school polo, and beige flats. I grabbed an orange from my fruit bowl, blew kisses to my two furry young ladies, and headed out.

The school day began as usual. The kids placed their folder in a plastic tub by the entrance and chose their lunch by moving their names to the menu item posted. Today it was pizza or a chicken burger. After selecting their lunch, they took their breakfast and milk from the breakfast bags and sat quietly to eat.

Bill arrived just as I was moving the breakfast bags out to the hall to be collected. He was wearing clothes that appeared to have been slept in, and his hair was not combed.

"Hey little one, have you had breakfast?"

He looked up at me and smiled at my question. He told me he had not eaten since he was here. He went on to explain that he did not get much sleep because his mother and father were drinking. Then they started fighting because his mother called his father a mutter flutter, and he became angry and started chasing her with a bat. He said his mom ran out, and the police came and took both of them. He said he had stayed with the neighbor and she was the one who brought him to school. My heart sank. I hugged him and handed him his breakfast.

"You can eat at the back table. When you finish, take what you want to take home for later and put it in your backpack, okay?"

Bill smiled and nodded.

"Okay," he said and took his breakfast to the back table.

As soon as he reached the table, he began to eat. Never uttering a word, he just ate. When he finished eating, he placed three cereal breakfast packages in his backpack.

I asked the rest of the students to focus on their morning writing work. This morning, they were sequencing a story. They were cutting the six sentences on the sheet and gluing them in order on another sheet. I allowed them to work with a partner, so you could hear a low roar of children talking and debating.

The day was relatively uneventful, and at dismissal, all of the students were picked up on time, including Bill. I approached the lady that was there to collect him and asked to see her identification. There were only two other names on his information sheet that were allowed to pick him up. She was one of them. I thanked her and released him into her custody. He climbed in the back seat and buckled himself into a booster chair. He smiled at me, padded his backpack, and waved goodbye.

74

Wednesday morning, all of the students filed in like the day before. They each placed their folder in the plastic tub by the door and entered the room to choose their lunch posted on the board just inside the door. Once they chose their lunch, they put up their backpacks and took breakfast from the red bags. The children ate quietly at their tables. Bill did not show today. While the children ate their breakfast, I dialed the phone number of the neighbor that collected him the day before. The mailbox for the phone number was full, and I was not able to leave a message. The other numbers on the form were not working numbers. The morning Literacy learning centers went as I had planned. My students were in Specials. Specials are what we call Music, Art and Physical Education. It's also the 45 minutes we have to make copies or do what we need to do to finish our day or prepare for the next.

    Claire came by the teacher's lounge while I was making copies to ask if I had learned anything new regarding the case of the children. I looked at her with disappointment in my eyes.

    "I don't know where to go Claire. It's never been this difficult to figure things out. I'm only sure of one thing. The answers are in the painting."

    Claire responded, "We looked everywhere, and that's not possible."

    "Is Rene here today?" I asked Claire.

    " I have not seen him today. Maybe he took some time off to stay at home," she replied. I sent Rene a text message and asked him where he was keeping the painting. He replied minutes later, letting me know that he had it hanging on the wall in his game room. He noted that it actually looked nice hanging on his wall.

He even sent a picture of the painting's new home. I returned an emoji smiley face.

Just then, Nicole came out of the restroom.

"Hi ladies," she said as she walked out in a fast pace.

I looked at my watch. It was time for me to pick up my students from music.

"I have to go Claire. We will talk later."

I decided to go by my classroom and drop the copies off on my desk. I saw Nicole and Ms. Gomez walking away from my classroom. I hurried in, placed my copies in my tub of homework, and hurried to the music teacher's portable to collect my students.

The children arrived at the classroom and proceeded to take their science journals from the tub on the writing-table. Today's topic was the four stages of a plant, from seed to flower. On the Promethean board was a large model of what each student was expected to draw or, at the very least, resemble on their journal. On the bottom of the flower was a list of words that they were to write on the correct part of the flower. They enjoyed coloring their flowers and labeling them. Science is a brief 20 minutes, but it's important to have something they can do quickly to allow time for discussion.

At ten minutes till 3:00 pm., they had all finished with their science journal entry. I lined the students up for dismissal. Mrs. Phillips met me at the door and joined me to dismiss the children. By 3:15 pm, all of the children had been collected. I walked inside to prepare my classroom for the next day.

75

When Friday arrived, things had pretty much gone back to normal. This morning, Bill was wearing fresh clothes with his backpack in tow. In his hand, he held a piece of paper, which he handed to me as soon as he reached my door. It was an excuse for being absent, explaining that he had some kind of stomach virus. It was a good day, and since it was the last day before Spring Break. The kids had popcorn and a movie after art class. The weather was a perfect 74 degrees. I gave them some extra recess, and they all took full advantage of an empty playground. There is nothing better than having an entire playground to play in. They played tag and a few of the boys asked to play with a soccer ball, which they kicked around the entire playground. A small group of girls huddled together and blew bubbles at each other. There was so much laughter. The kids were having a blast.

At 3:00 pm. I had everyone lined up and was preparing to exit the classroom. I waited a while and saw Rene coming down the hall.

"Hey Rene, will you please watch my kids while I use the restroom?"

"Sure," he responded and stood at the door with my students while I entered my classroom restroom.

The bell rang just as I walked out.

"Thanks," I said.

Rene looked around.

"Where is Mrs. Phillips?"

"Not here. I guess she is comfortable believing things are back to normal, or she had a meeting to attend," I said.

"Well, you're not going out there alone. I'm coming with you," Rene said.

"No, you're not. You stay here or watch from the door. I don't want you outside," I demanded. I proceeded to take my children out the door to the dismissal area. By 3:15 pm, all of the students had been picked up. Even Bill had been picked up promptly by his uncle. Rene came outside when he noticed everyone had been picked up.

"Well, ready to start a much-deserved spring vacation?" Rene asked.

I took a deep breath.

"Is that a trick question?" I asked and laughed.

We turned the corner of the sidewalk and started walking toward the building. Both of us anticipating days filled with fun and rest. Before we reached the door, two shots rang out. I felt the burn of both shots on my back and collapsed on the concrete floor. I was in a lot of pain. I felt like I was being pressed between two walls. I was struggling to breathe. I heard Rene screaming like a girl! He was banging on the window to the library.

"I need help! Call 911! Call 911!"

Ms. B came out after she heard Rene screaming, only to scream herself.

"Oh, My God!"

Rene remembered he had his cell phone in his pocket and called 911.

"Hello, this is Rene Ross. I'm calling from Coronado Elementary. The address is 3020 Louise Lane. My friend has been shot twice in the back. I need an ambulance now!"

Then he lost it.

"Oh shit, she's going to die. You better hurry or she's going to die!"

Rene was sobbing.

"Rene, shut up! You're freaking me out! Get off the phone! We need to help Jennifer," Ms. B. demanded.

"Is she breathing?" Ms. B asked.

Rene answered, "Yes, she is. Thank God! Thank you, Jesus. I hope Mrs. Phillips doesn't mind that I called 911 without letting her know."

"Oh, forget protocol, my best friend was shot twice, and I needed an ambulance. That's all I was thinking," he said.

Then in a whisper, he said to Ms. B, "Just don't tell her I thought that. It would be unfortunate to get fired from a job where I don't even get paid."

Rene held my hand and kept telling me I would be just fine. I found that humorous since Rene knows nothing about anything medical, much less injuries. Still, he was comforting.

76

Rene was kneeling next to me, holding my hand and saying, "Hang in there, girl. It's okay."

It reminded me of how I talk to my cats when they are sick or getting shots. I wanted to laugh, but I was in too much pain. I could hear the sirens getting louder and louder. The ambulance arrived just seconds later. The fire department had responded to the call as well and arrived almost at the same time as the ambulance. Two firemen approached the paramedic that had exited the ambulance.

"We got it covered," the ambulance driver stated loudly, raising his hand.

The firemen nodded and returned to their vehicle.

Ms. Phillips was outside now. She kneeled next to me.

"Ms. Knoes, can you hear me?"

I nodded.

"Rene will be going with you. I will follow you in my car to the emergency room. You hang in there."

People who live across the street from the school had come out to see what was going on. I could hear people talking and asking questions. I had no doubt that at least half a dozen people were holding their camera phones, ready to get the juicy gory scene to post on youtube.

Youtube.com is an internet site where people post videos, pictures, events, and various other topics. A video posted on Youtube.com will be there for the whole world to see.

Two paramedics raced to my side with a gurney. They rolled me over and gently placed me on it. My eyes were calm, but I kept my hands on my chest, which was now feeling like someone had stomped on it. Before they began to examine me, I signaled with my finger to one paramedic to come closer.

"Put me in the ambulance before you assess me, please. I don't want all these people looking at me."

He looked at the assisting paramedic and said, "Let's load her in."

The assisting paramedic methodically placed a neck brace on me and slid me into the ambulance.

One paramedic quickly began checking my vitals. He was looking into my eyes with a light he was moving from side to side. The other paramedic began to assess the damage by unbuttoning my blouse. He stopped and stared down at my chest. Then I heard his laughter. Rene was laughing and crying at the same time.

"Holy smokes, now that's my kind of call," the paramedic said. The two paramedics laughed and gave each other a high five with flapping fingers at the end. Both paramedics carefully removed the Styling Safety Vest that now had two bullets lodged on the backside.

"Be careful with that, I have to return it to the student it belongs to. This bedazzled bitch won District. It better work! I hope she doesn't mind that I put it to the test," I said in a whisper.

My forehead was hurting from the fall on the pavement, and I could feel the burning of small pebbles and dirt caught under the skin of my forearms.

The paramedic spoke clearly and slowly as he looked at me.

"Ms. Knoes, you have suffered quite a bit of bruising from the gunshots. You don't appear to have any broken bones, but we would like to take you to the emergency room to be examined for further injuries. You do appear to have some scrapes and cuts that will need to be tended to." The other paramedic interrupted.

"You also have a nasty bump on your forehead. It looks like you hit your head pretty hard."

Before he finished speaking, Rene said, "Yes, please take her. I'm still coming, Jen, but I'm going to drive my own car. Don't worry honey; I will be right on your tail."

Then he laughed out loud as if he had made a joke. I like Rene, I thought to myself. He was so cute. Then I fell asleep for a while, or maybe I passed out.

77

The E.R. doctor on duty examined me and gave me the good news of no broken bones. I already knew that. He said he was going to have me taken down for an MRI to check that bump on my head and, although he did not see any broken bones, he still wanted to take X-rays of my chest in case I had any newly fractured ribs. I was in a room waiting to be taken for X- rays to be followed by an MRI (Magnetic Resonance Imaging).

I heard a knock at the door and was happy to see that Rachel came to pay a visit.

"Hey, I heard you were shot. What in the hell happened? Do you have any idea who it was?" she asked.

"It was Bill's mother's boyfriend," I answered.

"Did you see him? Can you describe him to a sketch artist? I can get one in here."

"No," I answered, "I didn't see him."

Rachel was looking at me with confusion in her expression. I began to cry.

"If you didn't see him, how can you be sure?" Rachel asked.

"Cause I know, dammit! I know! I swear it, it was him."

"Oh God, help me," I sobbed.

My brain hurt, my heart hurt, my whole body was in pain. Rachel stood next to the examining table where I sat. She paced in a circle then paused for a while. She looked at me with sadness in her eyes.

"You're telling the truth, aren't you? You're serious, you just know?"

"Yes," I answered in a voice barely audible and sighed.

Rachel sat on a doctor's stool and looked at me.

"You know Jen, in all the time I've known you, you've never been wrong. It must be a bitch living a life where you can't speak what you know. That's how you always knew what to study for in school, isn't it? How you knew what teachers would be absent or late? That's how you knew Mr. Morales was calling in sick that day we had that card arrive at his home."

She looked at me.

"Always one step ahead, but pretending you don't know, so people won't think you're weird. That's why you once told me your biggest fear was to be considered a freak. That's gotta suck," she said.

"Jen, I'm going to find out where he is. That asshole is going down," she assured me.

I was quiet now, just listening and thinking.

"We're going to get him, don't worry."

She stood and hugged me.

"I have to get going," Rachel said, stopping at the door to look at me.

"We are going to get him, right?" I smiled. "Yes, you will. Tomorrow he will be at a place called Burger Hut at 1:00 pm," I paused. "Maybe 3:00 pm. I don't know what Burger Hut looks like, and I can't give you an address. I do know that there are train tracks close to it."

She smiled.

"I will call you tomorrow with the news," she said.

"Rachel," I called out.

Rachel turned.

"The bullets that were lodged in the vest were taken to keep as evidence. He will be armed with the gun he shot me with, so be careful."

"I will. I'll call you tomorrow, promise." she said.

She was walking out of my room as the X-ray transport came in.

"Transport for Ms. Knoes," the tall, skinny young man wearing blue scrubs said, pushing a green wheelchair in my direction.

"Oh, I can walk, just lead the way," I said.

"I am sorry, ma'am, but I have to transport you in this wheelchair. It is not safe for you to walk. Those are my instructions. Please sit in the chair."

I reluctantly sat in the chair as he wheeled me down the hall and into the elevator. When we reached the 3rd floor, the doors opened into a very large busy section of the hospital. Two X-ray technicians met us upon arriving and wheeled me in for X-rays. The process was simple. I simply sat in a medical chair, and a machine moved around me. In just a few minutes, the process was complete, and the transporter arrived to take me for an MRI.

I did not mind the nurse asking me to be completely still, and the machine circling me as much as being in an enclosed tube. I could feel a hint of claustrophobia creeping up. I tried to take myself away to a beach somewhere in the Pacific to calm myself. It worked. In minutes, I was out of radiology and being transported back to a waiting room.

78

I was tired and wanted to get home. The doctor came in to let me know that the X-rays looked good and that there are no signs of breaks or new fractures.

"You do have some swelling from the hit and some scratches and bruises from the fall, but physically you're fine." He noted something on the computer that held my files then said, "I am dismissing you. Go home and get some rest. Do you have someone to take you home?"

"Yes," I answered.

"Very well, then. Gather your things; a nurse will check you out and you are free to go."

Rene had followed the ambulance and stayed with me through the check-in process. He was waiting in the waiting area.

I straightened my blouse and slacks and exited the examining room. The front desk clerk completed some paperwork and dismissed me. Rene was not in the waiting area. Dr. Grant stood and smiled when I walked in.

"I told Rene to go home and get some rest. I will be taking you home this evening."

I smiled. He came to my side, gave me a quick kiss, and held me as we walked out. We drove out of the E.R. parking lot, and I felt a sense of relief to be out of the hospital. Dr. Grant started speaking.

'There is something I have wanted to clear up, but I think I should just show you. We drove out to the country in the opposite direction as before. I wanted to ask where we were going, but I decided it was just time to listen. We drove down winding roads until we came to a large metal gate with a card keypad.

"Close your eyes. We are entering my future home, and it's pretty torn up outside because it's under construction."

I kept my eyes closed until I heard a garage door open and close.

"Alright, open your eyes," Dr. Grant said as he walked around the car and opened the door for me. He took me inside by the hand and led me along a hall decorated with paintings from the Renaissance era.

We entered a study where he displayed his diplomas and medical accreditations.

"Here's the first confession. There are two doctors with the name of Monroe on my floor at the hospital. One of us is the head of education and has a Ph.D. I am the E.R. Doctor, and I have an M.D. The nurses chose to call me Dr. Grant to prevent confusion. My name is Dr. Grant Monroe."

My eyes began to tear up. This was him. I still had not said a word. He leaned in for a long passionate kiss, and then he smiled his beautiful smile.

"Okay, one more confession," he said.

He took both my hands and led me into a dining room. The table was set with beautiful china and crystal wine goblets.

"I can only cook Italian for dinner," he laughed. "I can't cook anything else."

After thirty minutes, dinner was ready to be served.

We ate spaghetti and french bread with goblets of red wine. After dinner, we snuggled on the large leather sectional.

"Would you like to go to bed and rest?" he whispered.

"Yes, I would," I answered. "But I won't promise I will rest."

He took my hand and led me into the bedroom. I was still sore and bruised. I lay on the bed with a soft pillow. Grant slipped onto the bed next to me and propped up on his elbow. He kissed me and stroked my hair. I slept.

"Good morning, sleepyhead," he said as he kissed my forehead and presented a tray with pancakes, orange juice and apple slices.

"Ummm, thank you," I said.

I ate breakfast and was anxious to get home to my two cats that had been left alone since the day before. I also needed to call Rachel and Rene to get some updates on the missing kids. Grant and I drove out of the garage onto the drive and away from the house. On the lawn laid a golden retriever that stood as the car drove by.

"Oh, that's Lucy," Grant said.

I smiled, remembering the golden retriever from my dreams. I turned to look back at the house I had just left and saw a white house with a wrap-around porch and a pair of rocking chairs by the front door.

79

I had set my phone to silent while I was at the hospital and had forgotten to change the volume. I was entering my apartment when I remembered. I took my phone out of my purse and quickly checked it. I had a call from Rene and a call from Rachel. I decided to call Rachel first.

"Hey, I just noticed that you called last night. Anything new on the missing kids?" I asked. I was hoping for some good news.

"No, but I do have some serious information on the guy who shot you. You were very right, the bastard decided to have the Burger Deluxe and a basket of onion rings with a cold beer at the Burger Hut on Kettle Street. He was going to be apprehended on his way out. We wanted to avoid causing negative commotion for the restaurant owner. That side of town is poor and the business owners need all the customers they can get. We watched his every move and had at least two officers at every exit. After thoroughly enjoying a nice lunch and waiting for the restaurant to be at its busiest peak, the piece of shit pulled out his gun and splattered his brains on the booths and people around him," she said.

The gun had been sent to forensics to be matched with the bullets taken from the kevlar vest I was wearing when I was shot. The 911 call from Burger Hut was made at 1:00.pm. I had placed my purse on the table and was now sitting on the couch listening to Rachel.

"Bill's mother was picked up for questioning. She swears she had nothing to do with the shooting. We have nothing to hold her on, so we had to let her go," Rachel paused. "Here's another strange turn of events. At 3:00 pm, another call came in about a couple by the name of Scardean that was found dead in their home. It turns out that Mr. Scardean had a nurse that visited him every other day. They were killed the day before. This couple also had children scattered around the Metroplex that had been adopted. Mr. Brooks' signature was found on the adoption documents that were found in an office safe. Jen, someone is cleaning house, and I have a feeling that they are going to wipe the slate clean of everyone involved. You might be one of them," Rachel said.

"I was shot by Bill's mother's boyfriend for reporting her to CPS. That's not connected with the murders of the missing children and the couples adopting them," I reminded her.

"Yes, that's correct, but who's to say that if you discover something big, the people cleaning house won't add you to their list?" Rachel said. "If the painting holds some kind of clue and the wrong person realizes you have it…"

Rachel had not finished speaking when I interrupted.

"Oh no, Rachel, we have to get to Rene. He has the painting that is being sought after. I think Ms. Gomez or Nicole is going to try to steal it from him. I'm not sure Rachel, but I know we have to get to Rene," I urged.

I gave Rachel his address and hung up the phone.

I was aware that Ms. Gomez and Nicole were very interested in getting whatever Mr. Brooks had left for me. What other reason would Ms. Gomez have for snooping in my closet and going through my purse? She was the one who kept locking my door. Since Mr. Brooks' death, I had noticed them around my classroom more often than before. They were looking for some kind of clue to find out what Mr. Brooks had told me. By now, they were aware that I believe, with certainty, that the painting held some kind of clue. Twice I had been discussing it when either Ms. Gomez or Nicole was within hearing distance. I was certain that they were going to take the painting from Rene and I was afraid I was too late. I was not concerned about the painting. I was concerned about Rene's safety.

Rene had started his day by going to the gym at 6:00 am for his two hour workout. He returned home, showered, and went to Central Market to do his weekly shopping. He called Claire that morning and invited her to have lunch with him at Central Market. While they sat enjoying their shrimp gumbo and rolls, they tried to figure out if maybe the clues were in what was painted and not in a literal sense.

"Okay," Rene said while impaling a small shrimp with his fork. "Let's look at the painting again with fresh eyes from the picture perspective. We might get lucky."

Claire agreed to return to Rene's apartment and take another look at the painting.

"What if we don't find anything again?" Rene asked.

"We will. If Jen says it's there, I believe it's there somewhere."

Claire looked up from the booth they were sitting in to see Esperanza Gomez in the next booth. She gestured to Rene to be quiet by putting her finger vertically on her lips. She grabbed her purse, and they both left the restaurant, pretending not to see Ms. Gomez.

Rene drove his car home and Claire followed. Rene disarmed his alarm system, and they entered his apartment.

"That gumbo was delicious. I'm feeling like a nap," Claire said as she plopped herself on the couch.

Rene said, "After my morning workout, I could use a nap too. Let's take a break before jumping into our mystery painting."

He laid on the love seat, took his T.V. remote control from the coffee table, and turned it to *America's New Model.*

"Oh, I love this show. It's my favorite. This one is good, I have seen this one before," he said with excitement.

"Where's the painting?" Claire asked.

"When Jennifer left it, she said to just hang it somewhere so, I hung it in my game room," Rene answered. "Let's not worry about that and take a break for just a few minutes longer. I want to see who wins. I did not get to see the ending the first time it was on."

Rene kept his attention on the television.

After a few minutes, there was a knock on the door. Rene ignored it. Ten seconds later, another knock.

"Are you going to answer that?" Claire asked.

Rene rolled his eyes.

"No, I want to see who wins and it's coming up next. Besides, I didn't invite anyone else over. It's probably one of those Jehovah's Witness people. I can't stand them dropping in whenever they feel like it."

He turned to watch the T.V. and ignored the knock. I could see that there were only two contestants left.

"I hope the ginger girl wins; she's cute. The other girl has a shitty attitude. I don't like her," Rene said.

Another knock.

"Dammit!" Rene stood up to answer the door.

Claire stood at the same time

"Hey, while you get rid of whoever is at the door, I'm going to use your facilities."

Rene reached and opened the door to find Nicole standing there.

"What are you doing here? Don't you believe in vacation Nicole?" Rene asked sarcastically.

"Send me a text or e-mail with whatever you need. I'm in the middle of something important." He began to close the door, but did not move fast enough. Before Rene could notice the gun in her hand, she rushed in and pointed it at his chest. He stood in shock, not believing what was happening. He did not say a word. She motioned Rene into the living room. Claire was coming out of the restroom when she heard Nicole's voice. She began to walk back into the restroom, thinking she could probably climb out the window and get help. Then, she heard Nicole raise her voice.

"Hey Claire, bring your ass out here, or I will blow his fucking head off."

Claire walked out quietly into where Rene stood.

"Where's the painting?" Nicole asked. "And don't tell me you don't have it, because Esperanza heard you talking about it at Central Market this afternoon. Now, where's the fucking painting?" She asked again.

"There is nothing written on it, and there is nothing in it. We already took it out of the frame," Claire said.

"I'm only going to ask you one more time. Where is the fucking painting?"

Nicole was beginning to sound very impatient. Actually, it was more like she was getting ready to explode.

"Okay, take the fucking painting and get the fuck out of my house," Rene said. "It's in the game room, there to the right." He gestured with his hand to point the direction. "You don't need a gun; we are not going to stop you. We can't report it because hell, we stole it," Rene said. "I'm sure as hell not interested in dying on my vacation."

Claire and Rene looked at each other, communicating without saying a word. They waited, and as soon as Nicole turned into the game room, Rene and Claire darted out the door, leaving it wide open, and ran as fast as they could away from Rene's apartment. Claire had her cell phone in her hand. When they were a good distance away, they rested at a bus stop, both panting and breathing heavy. The bus stop was empty.

"Did you call the police?" Rene asked.

"I called Rachel. She's on her way."

"No, the real police dammit! You know the ones with tough attitudes, multiple marriages, big guns and explosives, that police!" Rene said, sounding disappointed.

Claire looked at Rene.

"Rachel's better. Besides, what are we going to tell the police? You said it yourself; we stole the painting!"

81

I quickly left my apartment and drove as fast as I could, trying not to break the speed limits or pass too many red lights. Traffic was lighter than usual and it turned out the traffic lights were on my side. Almost on cue, the lights turned green when they saw me coming. I arrived in a matter of minutes, speeding up the street to Rene's apartment and parked along the street.

I felt dirt and gravel under the wheels of my car as I slid to a stop. I looked over to find the front door wide open. "Oh no, please let Rene be safe." I said out loud to myself. I walked around to Rene's side of the building and found nothing suspicious. I walked inside and found no one there.

The T.V. was alive with the loud noise of a game show. I slowly approached the T.V. and turned it off. I was listening to hear if anyone was still in the apartment. I called out Rene's name and received no answer as I slowly canvased the apartment. I called Rene's phone with my cell only to hear his phone ringing on the coffee table. I clicked off my phone and slowly walked toward the game room.

I was startled when my phone rang in my hand. I looked at the screen, and it was Rachel. I answered.

"Hey, it's me, Rachel. I caught up to Rene and Claire at a bus stop. They ran away from Rene's house without getting hurt. They are both fine, but have a hell of a story to tell. When you arrive at Rene's, stand by for me. I'm on my way." she said.

"Rachel, I am already here. The apartment is empty."

By that time, I had already walked into the game room to find a bare nail hanging on the eggshell painted wall.

"I'm guessing that the painting is gone?" Rachel said. "Who did they say took it, Esperanza or Nicole?" I asked.

"Rene said Nicole showed up with a gun and threatened to blow his head off. She was the one who took it. Claire said that when Nicole turned her back to enter the game room, she and Rene raced out the door, never looking back until they reached the bus stop where I caught up to them."

"Okay, Rachel, bring them to my apartment. I have quite a bit to share. You need to be there. Can you stay for a while?" I asked.

"Sure. I am on duty, so if it's related to our case, I can stay as long as I need to. Today might be the last time I will be riding solo. I was told this morning that I am getting a new partner." Rachel said with some disappointment in her tone.

"If Rene and Claire are fine, don't worry about the painting."

"What?" Rachel asked, perplexed.

"Just come to my place in a few minutes and I will meet you there. Tell Rene I found his keys in the silver bowl and I will lock up his apartment and bring his cell phone in case he needs it.

"Okay, will do," Rachel responded.

"I will see you later," I said.

I hung up the phone and slipped it into my pocket. I walked around Rene's apartment, making sure his windows and doors were locked. His apartment was very elegant and organized. Rene had very rich taste in Ming carpets and expensive Laura Ashley furniture. In the corner of his living room was a beautiful Grand piano. On his kitchen bar, he kept crystal wine glasses that accompanied expensive brandy labels.

I turned off the lights and scanned his stove to make sure that the burners were not on. Rene had an electric stove, so it was difficult to tell if a burner was on unless you could see the burner knobs. I remembered Rene likes scented candles, especially the sandalwood scent that lingered in his apartment now. I made a quick surveillance of the two restrooms and his bedroom. No candles left burning. I felt Rene's keys in my hand and headed out the door, making sure I locked his door lock as well as his heavy bolt lock.

82

The four of us were sitting in my small living room. Rene was on my recliner, Claire and I sat on the large sectional while Rachel straddled a small wooden chair and placed her arms across the top.

"The skinny bitch had a gun! I can't believe it!" Rene was saying.

"Would you happen to know what type of gun it was?" Rachel asked, looking at Claire and Rene.

"No, I don't know anything about guns," Claire answered.

Rene stretched his neck, looking at the ceiling, and then said, "Don't look at me. All I can tell you about guns is that they shoot people and the bitch had one

"Okay, this is what I know," I said, coming from my kitchen with a pitcher of lemonade and a tray of Girl Scout Cookies. I placed the pitcher and tray on the coffee table and began. "When Mr. Brooks killed himself, he left me what I would need to clean up the mess he unknowingly made. He left me the note the Friday he left the school allegedly going to some important meeting. Because the office is around the corner and we did not follow him that far, we did not know he had entered the administrative office and left the note in my mailbox. When you and I," pointing to Claire with a cookie I held in my hand, "walked out the door later that same evening, we did not stop to check our mailboxes. The next morning when I was collecting my mail, I unknowingly dropped it. I didn't get the note until later when Rene found it on the office floor. When Nicole and Esperanza found out that the painting had the letters ABN on it, they were instructed to find out what Mr. Brooks had left behind that might incriminate them. Nicole and Ms. Gomez were instructed to find the painting and send it to the Head Honcho. All this time, they thought maybe some other clue was hidden in my classroom, which is why my door was sometimes locked when Delmon had unlocked it. Someone entered my room and then locked it without thinking that it should have been left unlocked. There were several times that I entered my closet to find things that had been tipped over or moved. I woke up this morning knowing where the clue is, which is why I hurried to get home."

I walked back to my bedroom and came out carrying the painting.

"When I first saw the painting in Mr. Brook's office, before Delmon could take it away, I took a picture of it. Later that same day, I took my phone cord and sat at my computer. I uploaded the picture to my Walgreens pictures and ordered a picture on canvas the same size as the painting. I picked it up a few days later and kept the copy in my closet. When I went to your apartment to get dressed for the auction, I placed the painting in the large bag I was carrying. When we took the real painting out of the frame to examine it, I took the opportunity to switch it out while you were in the kitchen and Claire was not paying attention. I brought the real one home after the auction and locked it up in my safe. The one I gave you to keep is a copy. Ms. Gomez or Nicole heard us talking, mentioning that we had taken the painting out of the frame. They weren't surprised when the painting was not framed. Nicole stole the copy. I woke up knowing the location of a blue-chip with information that will help Rachel blow this whole case out of the water."

I took the painting and undid the staples on the lower right-hand corner that held the canvas to the wooden frame. The painting was double layered with two canvases. I pulled one back, and a dark blue square thin chip slipped out when I tilted the painting.

"What is that?" Claire asked.

"It's a chip that needs to be inserted into a small adapter that is then inserted into the USB portal of the computer," Rachel answered.

"It's like a thumb drive, but flat and tiny," I said.

83

Rene crossed his arms and looked over at me.

"So I had a fake painting all this time?"

"Yes," I answered.

"I could have been shot by that crazy bitch over a fake painting! Well, that sucks out loud if you ask me," he said.

I looked at him with affection and said, "I couldn't tell you because you're such a poor actor and so dramatic. I had to be one hundred percent sure that whoever took it thought it was the real deal. Nicole was under so much stress that even a hint that it wasn't the right one would have had her pull the trigger for sure. I had a strong feeling you would not get hurt. I don't even think her gun was real, to be honest," I said.

I took a small adapter from my purse and inserted the blue-chip.

"Okay, here goes," I said as I signed on to my computer and opened the chip. I was silently praying that we would have all of the couples that adopted children on that chip. Rachel looked at the screen, waiting for something to appear.

We were staring at the screen hopeful. The first screen flashed static then turned blue.

"Oh no, Seriously?" Rene said, sounding as if he was in agony.

"Wait," I said. "Give it time."

The screen came up asking if we wanted to open my documents or SIM. Rachel clicked SIM. Then another screen popped up asking for a password.

"Password? Are you freaking kidding me?" Claire said.

Rachel looked at me and asked, "Do you know?"

I took a deep breath and typed in children. The computer responded with an incorrect password message and warning that I only had two attempts left before being locked out for security reasons. I placed my hands on my forehead and felt a sense of hopelessness. My eyes began to water, and I could feel the tears streaming down my face. I looked at Rachel, who was now sitting quietly, staring at me. Then it came, as another tear streamed down my face.

"Forgive me, I said, feeling Mr. Brooks' sadness.

Rachel typed it in and took a deep breath as we waited. Suddenly, rows and rows of information flashed on the screen. The couples that had adopted children with the services of Mr. Brooks were all listed in alphabetical order.

"How many couples did you say?" Rachel asked.

The numbers I had in my head the day I called her to tell her were 248. The three of us stared at the screen in disbelief. My eyes were weeping because I knew that most of these children were dead. Rene and Claire stared in shock. I was also aware that more than half of these children would never be found. We were staring at a list of 842 couples, of which 248 were in Texas. The rest were scattered around the world.

"We won't be able to save them all. Jurisdictions will get in the way, but I can sure as hell share the information with the world," Rachel said determined.

In Texas, the first four couples on the list had already been executed or killed in some freak accident. The number of children on the screen was 16,837, roughly 20 children per couple. Rachel was trying to absorb what she was looking at.

"You have to get this to the precinct ASAP. All of these couples have to be located before they are executed, and the children have to be accounted for," I said in a whisper.

Rachel stood.

"Shit! Motherfuckers! Fucking monsters! Pieces of shit! Cock sucking sons of bitches!" Rachel screamed, putting her arms on top of her head as she paced the room. "Where do we begin?" Rachel asked rhetorically.

I stood and gently pulled her arms to her side.

"You begin at the beginning. What matters is that you begin."

I gave her a reassuring hug.

She took her cell phone from her pocket, and in a couple of minutes, she was on the line with her chief making plans and reading off the names and addresses of the couples living in Texas.

"I have to go," she said. "My chief wants me to bring in the chip that contains the information. Before I take the chip, I want you to download all the information into your computer in case something happens."

"Okay, give me a few seconds," I said as I begin saving the files to my computer. "I will pull a flash drive from my desk and save it on that also in case my computer crashes. It's old so, just to be safe," I said.

I decided to visit the Lake Worth Police Department and pay a visit to Bruce Wells. I walked straight up to the window where two officers played sentinels to the police precinct. I was professionally dressed in a gray fitted suit with a white silk shirt and appeared to be on a mission. Today, I was wearing my perfectly applied makeup and my friendly, don't fuck with me expression. I smiled at the officers and said, "I am here on police business and have a lead for Officer Wells. He's expecting me," I lied. "May I step in to see him please?"

The officer checked my I.D., searched my clutch purse, and had me walk through a metal detector. I walked back into a noisy area of cubicles, where at least twenty officers were on the phone talking and taking notes. Some were talking to each other and reviewing videotape.

I stopped to find four rows of desks, all piled with papers and folders. Some had pictures displayed of things I did not care to see. Officer Wells was sitting at his desk filing papers. He looked up at me in surprise. After a minute of silence and me staring at him calmly, his expression turned arrogant as he stopped filing. I sat in the black metal chair he had beside his desk.

"Officer Wells, my name is Jennifer. I am Officer Brinks' friend."

"What can I do you for?" he asked sarcastically.

"I am aware that you gave her a hard time after she provided an escort to the hospital for me without permission. I know you are a veteran officer, so you of all people should understand that sometimes shit happens and you just have to use your judgment. The four-day suspension without pay was uncalled for. She took up a security job to make up for her loss of income. She did not deserve that," I said.

"She told you I had her suspended?" he asked.

"No, she didn't. Someone else told me," I responded, lying through my teeth. "She holds her own. She doesn't even know I am here and I expect you won't tell her."

He looked at me and said, "So you came in here to tell me to lay off your friend. Are you trying to save her from me?"

He laughed and placed his hands behind his head as he leaned back in his chair.

"No. Actually, Officer Wells, I came here to save you."

I held my gaze on him. With that, he sat up in his chair, placing his arms on his desk as if he was going to type on his computer, but he didn't.

"Officer Wells," I continued, "That is your beautiful family there in the picture, I presume?"

I pointed to an 8X11 framed family photo that sat on his desk.

"Yeah, you presume right. So what?" he said with a cocky attitude.

"And you are working until 5 pm this afternoon, correct? I'm guessing your beautiful wife will be in the school building to pick up your two very pretty daughters at 3:00 pm, yes?"

"Yeah," he answered. "Now get to the point or get the fuck out." he said in a low authoritative voice.

I took a deep breath and ignored his comment.

"Well, there is going to be a gas leak at your daughter's school in a couple of hours or so."

I looked at the digital clock on the wall. It was 1:00 in the afternoon.

"I know you have already taken your lunch break. There is going to be an explosion sometime before 4:00 pm. You see, Officer Wells, I can see things in the future sometimes. The question is, do you leave your workplace when you are on the clock to pick up your children early to be on the safe side or do you just wait until school lets out at 3:00 pm and hope you get to see your wife and daughters again? Sometimes, Officer Wells, people have to make their own judgement calls. I understand you were under the peer pressure of your little posse, but what you did to Officer Brinks was wrong. Both you and I know that I didn't have to come here today," I smiled and stood.

I looked over at the clock, then at Officer Wells, and tapped my watch.

"Have a good day," I said in a professional tone and turned to exit the maze of desks.

85

It was late in the evening, and Rachel was still working. She had managed to locate fifty couples and was reviewing notes and sorting files. Rachel was applauded for her success in the child trafficking case. That was it. She did not get any kind of special recognition medal or award. No monetary bonus like they show on those fancy television cop shows. For her, it was just another day at the job and she was satisfied with it being just that.

She was sitting at her desk reading her files when Officer Wells approached her. Rachel looked up and took a deep breath.

Sounding agitated she asked, "Now what? You're going to fucking write me up for working too hard? Maybe this time it will be for liking my fucking job? What is it Wells? What do you have up your ass now?" she said, glaring at him as she crossed her arms across her chest. She waited.

Officer Wells sighed.

"I've been an ass, I get it. I just wanted to say congratulations. You have solved the biggest case we have ever had in Lake Worth and did it in pretty good time too. I know you will have a lot of paperwork. If you need any help, I'll lend you a hand. Welcome to the team. You're an excellent cop."

He held out his hand. Rachel hesitated, then stood and shook it. Officer Wells turned to walk away. Before walking too far, he turned and said, "Oh, that friend of yours you helped out with an escort is okay too, scary as hell, but okay."

Then he walked away.

On a small television that sat on a distant countertop, the news anchor reported, "This afternoon a gas leak was reported at Edgewood Elementary after an explosion in the school cafeteria. Thankfully, all of the children had already been dismissed. There were no injuries to report, and there was no major damage done. The school will resume classes as usual tomorrow, back to you, Angela."

No, no medal for Rachel. What Rachel received for her long hours and dedication was worth more than that. What she received was the respect and recognition from her Chief Officer and her fellow officers. She was respected for doing her job. That was her job, to stay up nights and to drop Everything when a call came in for her assistance. It doesn't matter that she will help save thousands of children and many adults. Saving one or two individuals would be just as important. Rachel was true and blue. She sat back in her chair and watched Officer Wells exit the workroom. Her eyes had teared up, and now she reached for the tissue box she kept on her desk. She had just finished wiping her eyes dry when her phone rang.

"Officer Brinks speaking," she said.

"Hey Rachel, it's me Jennifer. Do you still have that security job at the coliseum?"

"I have one more night and then I'm sticking to my regular job. Why?" she asked.

"Well, I was wondering if you could return that painting to the ARC Foundation. I fixed the frame so it's framed as it was. It was in a box with paintings that had not even been sorted or numbered. Only the pictures that were numbered were on the bidding log. I will bet that they didn't even miss it. They probably don't have a clue that it was once briefly theirs," I laughed. Rachel was quiet. I could tell she was not smiling.

"You stole the painting and you didn't even tell me, Jennifer."

"I didn't tell you because you are an officer of the law and you have always been the straight-arrow kind. I knew you wouldn't be comfortable knowing what we were up to."

After a long pause, she finally spoke.

"I will not put it back for you. What I can do is tell you that I will be working there tonight and I take my break at 9:00 pm in the back lounge. The front door automatically locks at 9:30 pm. Anyone can come in before 9:30 and exit anytime since the doors open from the inside. The alarms are not on because I will be there in the back with the radio cranked up so loud that I will not be able to hear anything that might be going on in the front."

She sat in silence after that.

"Okay, thanks."

I could tell by her silence that she was smiling. I clicked off my phone.

86

Mrs. Brooks and the Director of the ARC Foundation, a 28 year-old brunette, were sitting at a table in the round auction room discussing future plans for using the money that had been collected at the ARC Auction. It turns out that the auction had brought in over $20,000 in just that one evening. They brainstormed a list of items needed for the home, also listing equipment required for the office. Together they started working on scheduling other events to continue raising money for the foundation.

"Well, we still have plenty of new donations as well as some items that did not even have the chance to be shown at the last auction. I think we will consider another auction this summer," said the brunette.

"Oh, that sounds wonderful," Mrs. Brooks said. "I will collect other items from my attic to donate once again."

In the background, in a large box of paintings, was the framed Pegasus painting donated by Mrs. Brooks.

It was evident that Mrs. Brooks had found her purpose. Without Mr. Brooks, it appeared that she took his place in helping needy families and children. She busied herself, making a difference in her community. She worked as a counselor at Sunnyvale, a home for orphaned children. Sometimes she would take a handful of children on field trips or doctor visits.

She even took the time to volunteer twice a week at our school, tutoring those little ones who struggled with reading and math.

Today she had two young ladies sitting with her at a back table with several books while she focused on a little boy who needed math tutoring. "I arrived at the library with my students in a single file line, their little faces eager to see Ms. B., knowing she would be delivering a story that would stimulate their imagination. I sat at a table while Mr. B. read the children a story about a cat named Pete. The children were chanting something about buttons. I could hear their laughter and Ms. B's animated voice. I took my green milk crate of books up to the counter for check-in. David, her assistant, stood and emptied the books onto the counter and said, "Here, let me check those in so we can see if you have any missing books before they check out new ones."

He smiled and began checking in my classroom books.

David was very handsome with a perfect, pearly smile to match his smooth complexion. He was tall and slim, not scrawny or toothpick skinny. Slim with muscle in all the right places. I could tell he was happy with his job. Ms. B. had developed a certain skip in her step since he had arrived. A person would have to be blind to not see the chemistry between those two. I don't know what the regulation is for a male's hair in the school district, but it was clear someone had made an exception. David's hair was past shoulder-length, wavy and full, and he wore it well. He looked very professional in his beige slacks and a black collared shirt.

When Ms. B. finished reading to the children, they were allowed to check out another book. I looked over at David after he scanned the last book to see if I was missing any books from the previous week. He smiled and gave me a thumbs up. "You're all clear. They can each take another book," he said, moving his lips but not making much noise and smiled.

While the students checked out their books, I stood to line up my students. I looked over at the young ladies. One had a rose tattoo on the side of her neck, and the other had five silver rings on each ear. They looked to be 18 or 19 years of age. I heard one ask the other to hand her a book please. Her voice carried an accent I could not recognize.

I walked over to Mrs. Brooks as she was finishing her tutoring session.

"Hello Mrs. Brooks. Where are you off to today?"

Mrs. Brooks looked up at me and smiled.

"Oh, these two young ladies are exchange students. I allow them to stay with me while they attend college. They have been working so hard, so I'm showing them some historical sites today. Tomorrow we are going to the zoo."

I smiled.

"You're a godsend, Mrs. Brooks. Have a great day. It was good to see you."

I thought for a moment before turning around.

"Hey, Mrs. Brooks tomorrow is going to be hot, humid and a terrible day for the zoo. Why not take them to the new World Aquarium? I will bet they would love that. "

Mrs. Books looked at me.

"You know, I had not thought of that. The girls would probably enjoy the aquarium more."

She looked at the young girls.

"Tomorrow, we are going to the World Aquarium."

The girls smiled with approval. I lined up my students and escorted them to the classroom. I was certain that the thin-faced man would be at the zoo, but he would not find what he was looking for.

87

Two blocks over in the hidden crevasses of downtown, the Wild Cactus restaurant was at its peak. They served only those with appetites for the exotic and only those with thousand dollar appetites dined here. The restaurant was so famous to the elite that a person had to make a reservation months or years in advance. Some delicacies on the menu were so exotic that they were served just minutes or hours after birth or upon hatching. The restaurant was clean and dimly lit. The tables were wooden with high backs and intricate carvings on the armrests, each chair was cushioned with a royal blue velvet fabric. Indeed, it looked rich and inviting, but most of all, elegant with an illusion of royalty.

In the center of the dining room sat the tall man with the boa constrictor tattoo on his left arm. He treated himself to a game of Russian roulette from the menu, always ordering the same thing and dining alone. This evening was not any different. The waiter approached the table with a bottle of wine and poured it into the crystal glass. The waiter handed the man what looked like a palm pilot. He took it, marked some items, and returned it to the waiter. He took a sip of his wine and was soon presented with a basket of fried butterfly larva. They were the size of small peanuts and very tasty. Crisp to the touch, but exploded with a creamy substance once in the mouth. He was enjoying his appetizer when he glanced over to a table in front of him. There sat a gentleman who had just been presented with a small silver pot of oil. Next, he was presented with a saucer covered with a silver dome. When he removed the dome, something squirmed on the bed of lettuce cleverly placed on the saucer. He wondered what they were as he spooned another bite of appetizer into his mouth.

The man sitting at the table noticed he was being watched, so to be polite, he lifted his saucer slightly to show the delicacy he was about to enjoy. The saucer contained a dozen or so small snake-like creatures. They were no longer than 3 inches or so. He picked one up with a silver pair of tongs. It wiggled. He dipped it into the hot oil, took it out, and waited for it to cool. Then he ate it. The man's attention was brought back when the waiter offered to fill his wine glass.

In the kitchen, the phone rang. A female voice asked to speak to the head chef.

"Please tell the chef it's a 10 and 5."

Minutes later, Master Chef Ernie Davi came to the phone.

"Okay, got it," he said and returned to his work.

Ernie Davi was one of the finest chefs in the world. People came from all parts of the world to sample his exotic dishes that were prepared so perfectly. He owned two other restaurants, both equally successful.

The man with the boa constrictor tattoo had ordered the Japanese Puffer Fish. He ordered it every time he came in to dine. Puffer Fish is not ordered often, and it has to be served fresh. These fish are shipped from Yamaguchi, Japan, and are not killed and prepared until an hour before the dish will be served. The Puffer Fish contains the poisonous deleterious substance Tetrodotoxin. For Puffer Fish, there is no adequate sampling scheme that can assure a safe lot being transported into the U.S. Any single fish may contain a lethal dose of toxin. To date, there is no known antidote for Tetrodotoxin poisoning.

It was the rush of knowing that he was playing a deadly game of chance that kept him coming back. He watched with anticipation as the waiter approached the table and placed an oval tray covered with a silver dome in front of him. Next to the tray, the waiter placed a small bowl of white rice. The fish was beautifully cooked with a buttery lemon sauce on the side. The waiter smiled and walked away. The man began to eat and savor every morsel that entered his mouth. This would be a meal he would never forget, compliments of the chef.

The sun was rising the next morning, and traffic was beginning to move along the roads of downtown. The car was parked at a meter and the meter had timed out. The driver's arm, wrapped with a boa constrictor tattoo, was on the edge of the door window, resting. When the police officer approached to question the driver, he found the driver dead. Apparently, his luck with the Puffer Fish had run out. He looked at the dead man, remembering his face as one he had come across several times in the precinct. This guy had a rap sheet as long as the snake tattooed on his arm. The police officer smiled.

"Justice is good," he said to himself as he called it in.

88

Nicole and Ms. Gomez began their cruise as planned. Both were excited about this great gift they were receiving. Their secret friend, who was introduced to them only by web via Mrs. Walker had promised to reward them for their efforts in helping with the minor task of obtaining the painting and shipping it to the address provided. Soon after shipping the painting, they received $20,000. The hundred dollar bills were in two leather wallets, $10.000 for each of them.

They made sure to tell their friends that they would not be available to chat on the phone because they were going to take full advantage of their dream vacation, and they did not plan on even thinking about work. They boarded the large ship, giddy as two school girls. They made sure to bring some extra stretchy clothes and an empty piece of luggage for all of the souvenirs they planned on purchasing at every stop the ship was scheduled to make.

All morning they had been boasting about how good their friend was to provide such a luxurious cruise for their efforts.

"Just think, " Nicole said, "if this is our reward for simply finding a simple painting and mailing it off, imagine what rewards we could get for doing something more difficult."

Ms. Gomez agreed.

"I'm just glad you were able to get that painting. Do you think they called the cops?" she asked.

"How could they? They stole the painting, I heard them say so. Besides, the gun I had was a toy gun. It's not my fault they were too dumb to figure it out," Nicole laughed.

Ms. Gomez and Nicole didn't have a clue what they had gotten themselves into when Mrs. Walker befriended them.

Ms. Gomez was pouring some suntan lotion on her palm and rubbing it on her arms while Nicole was making herself comfortable in her chaise, tugging on her floppy hat and straightening her sunglasses. Ms. Gomez had finished putting lotion on her arms and was now looking out at the sea and enjoying the view. A tall, slim male approach them with a stand holding a chilled bottle of wine and two wine glasses that had already been poured. These two glasses had been heavily laced with enough pure caffeine to cause a cardiac arrest in seconds.

"Oh, yum, thank you," Nicole said, as she took the full chilled glass and handed the other to Ms. Gomez.

They took a deep breath of the cool breeze and looked at each other with a smile.

"Cheers," Nicole said as they both lifted their glasses and took a cool long drink of chilled red wine.

The tall waiter took their glasses and placed them on his tray. He left the untainted wine bottle chilling in the bucket by Nicole's lounging chaise and placed two clean glasses on the center table. There was nothing suspicious about that setting. He unlocked the door to their cabin, took the two leather wallets from their purses, placed them in his jacket and exited the room. He disappeared as quickly as he had appeared. At the next port, he would exit the ship.

The sun was shining, the sky was blue, and the breeze was cool. Nicole was oiled up and prepared to sunbathe in her brand new bikini. For now, she wore a long sheer blue bathing suit cover that was elegantly sequenced. Her sunglasses and floppy hat were covering most of her face. Ms. Gomez was wearing loose-fitting silk pants that covered her legs, a white cotton shirt, sunglasses, and her floppy hat to cover most of her face. A small round table sat between them. On it sat both their cell phones, turned off, and two goblets awaiting some red wine from the bucket that sat near. With the breeze blowing downwind, it would be hours or maybe a day or two by the time anyone noticed that they were dead.

89

The church was filled with friends and family. Ms. B., Jennifer, Dr. Grant Monroe, Rachel, Rene and Mrs. Phillips stood with pride and smiles on their faces. Brian Blake turned to behold his beautiful bride. As the pianist began to play the traditional wedding march, Claire walked onto the long, carpeted aisle. She was beautiful beyond words, wearing a lace dress with a train that must have been 15 feet long. Everyone stood in awe of her beauty.

After the exchange of the rings, the Minister spoke the final bonding words.

"You may now kiss the bride."

Music began to play as the bride and groom exited the church. The bridesmaids had assembled themselves along the side of the aisle and tossed handfuls of pink rose petals at the bride and groom as they passed.

The best man, Brian's younger brother, approached the microphone on the podium and announced that the reception would be taking place in the Rose Hall across the corridor. The crowd slowly poured into a beautiful banquet hall. Front and center was the table where the Bride and Groom were taking pictures.

The round tables were decorated with lace table cloths and beautiful centerpieces of clear cylinders holding floating candles and purple flowers. The guests had settled themselves at the tables. We were sitting at a table distant from the front, closer to the dance floor. On the other side of the hall, the D.J. was preparing for a night of dancing.

"Wow, Claire looks gorgeous" I sighed.

"Yes, she sure does," Rachel replied.

Just then, a very handsome Brian, resembling a young Mel Gibson, was escorting his new bride to the dance floor for the first dance of the evening. They kissed and danced the evening away like the ending to a fairy tale and the beginning of a beautiful life together. Claire deserved a happily ever after.

Rachel flirted with her new partner, who was instantly taken by her strength and dedication. He enjoyed helping her with the workload of the ABN case, as put by the local newspapers. A few minutes later, Rachel came and sat at my side as I watched the guests dance. That Forensics Chief has been a godsend. He has been more helpful than any department I have ever worked with in Fort Worth."

I looked at her and smiled.

She looked at me inquisitively and asked, "What does 10 and 5 mean?"

I smiled.

"It's a code word. It means family," I winked.

Out of nowhere, her partner appeared, took her by the hand and on to the dance floor.

Ms. B was standing by the dance floor, holding her champagne glass and mingling with the guests. Realizing that the chances of me being asked to dance would increase if I were standing by the dance floor, I approached Ms. B.

"Hey, where is David?" I asked.

"Oh, he said he had some flying to do. It's still light out, so he wanted to get in a few hours before twilight.

She found out that working as an assistant librarian was just something he chose to do to stay social. He had finished flight school and was now just trying to meet his flying hours before he could become a pilot.

"He will be around soon enough," Ms. B. said confidently.

Grant came up behind me, and we joined the dancers on the floor. Out on the terrace, beautifully decorated with flowers and antique lace chair covers, Grant was holding me as we danced to the love song "Almost Paradise."

Grant leaned down and said, "There's something I want to ask you."

"What would that be?" I looked at him and smiled.

"Do you like airplanes?" He asked.

I was perplexed and disappointed by the question, but I hid it well.

I smiled and said, "Well, planes can be fun as long as they don't crash."

I laughed and thought nothing more of it. The song ended, and we were walking toward our small table when Grant stopped.

He took my hand in both of his and said, "What about that plane?"

I looked up and, to my amazement, saw a white Cessna plane flying a yellow banner with black letters that read "Marry Me Jen." Grant knelt on one knee and took a gold ring out of his inside coat pocket.

"Well? Do I get an answer?"

"Yes!" I answered with tears in my eyes.

He slipped a diamond engagement ring on to my finger. Now there were wedding guests looking at us. Claire and Brian were smiling over at us and clapping. I would finally get my happily ever after. Ms. B came up to me and hugged me.

"I told you he would be around here soon enough." She winked. "Congratulations, Jen."

She walked over to chat with Mrs. Phillips, who had attended the wedding as a party of one.

After several hours of laughing, dancing and exchanging stories about our adventures at Coronado Elementary, Mrs. Phillips said her goodbyes to me, Ms. B, Rachel, Rene and the Bride and Groom and exited the reception. Outside waiting for her was a jade Jaguar with a very handsome George Clooney look-alike standing with the door open, waiting for his wife. He took Mrs. Phillips by the hand, helped her in and closed the door. He went around to his side, and they drove into the night. I looked over at Rachel.

"Is that her husband?"

"No wonder she didn't bring him in. There would have been dozens of ladies trying to get his attention."

Rachel smiled.

"Yeah, myself included," she laughed.

We watched the Jaguar disappear. Rene was dabbing his eyes with a white handkerchief.

"Oh, that stinks, everyone gets a surprise or laid, and I will go home empty-handed."

I signaled Rachel with a nod. Claire, Ms. B. and I watched Rachel as she walked over to Rene, kissed him on the cheek and reached into her blazer to retrieve a Louis Vuitton wallet containing five one hundred dollar bills. Rene screamed. We laughed.

90

The view of the pacific coast was crystal clear. The head of the organization, a well-built man that could pose as a Sean Connery look-alike, wearing a gray suit and white collared shirt, stood on the balcony breathing in the cool air of twilight. The Queen Ann mansion stood majestically along the coast. The tall, slim faced limousine driver sat in a stuffed old English-style chair and propped his feet on a matching ottoman.

The man standing said, "I want the slate cleaned by the end of next week. We have to move on. A new program will begin this summer."

He puffed on a Cuban cigar and gestured to the leather chair beside his desk. On it was a box, long and thin enough to hold a 14X18 painting. Surely it was the one he was expecting to be from Mr. Brooks' office.

"The two bitches said that this is the last piece of the puzzle. Once this is gone, so is any evidence of our clients," he said in between puffs.

He walked over to the chair, picked up the box and, using a long lighter he had retrieved from his desk, set the corner of the box on fire. When it began to burn, he walked over and tossed it in the fireplace. He never even opened the box. He stood there, puffing on his cigar and watched the box burn. The box was making a crunching noise green and crimson flames danced over it as it burned.

The well-built man said, "The skinny bitch did something right for a change. I wonder how they are enjoying their vacation," he laughed sarcastically.

A knock was heard at the door.

"Si pasale, come in," the man holding the cigar said as he turned toward the door.

The housemaid, wearing a black skirt and white shirt adorned with a red ribbon tie, slowly rolled a black chrome cart holding a bottle of brandy and two crystal glasses into the room.

He looked at her and asked, "You are new here si?"

The housemaid smiled and replied, "Si."

It was not uncommon for his regular maid to take time off and appoint a replacement while she was out.

That was not the case in this matter. What happened was that the maid received a letter containing $600.00 addressed from her employer, letting her know she would not be needed for the next two weeks and that she was receiving time off with pay.

This maid was pretty and busty. He couldn't help holding his gaze on her very full, voluptuous breasts. She smiled and poured two glasses of brandy that she placed on the tray. She smiled and turned to leave the room as professionally and quietly as she had entered.

The older man took the two glasses from the tray and handed one to his slim driver.

"Salud! May the tiny bastards line my pockets with money for many more years to come."

"Si, si!" the other man said, and they raised their glasses in unison.

They both took long, hard swallows and enjoyed the smoothness that a $500.00 bottle of brandy is sure to provide. Ten seconds passed, and the men looked at one another in horror, grasping at their throats. In one minute, they were both numb and completely paralyzed, but could feel their body shutting down. Three minutes later, their bowels surrendered and released foul from their bodies. Four minutes after that, both men lay dead. Downstairs, the housemaid turned on the sound system that echoed Beethoven's 9 symphonies.

She exited the beautiful mansion that would now serve as a tomb. She set the alarm using the key pad by the door. She locked the heavy doors and left the keys under a planter that was kept by the large front door. She looked up at the mansion, smiled, and took a deep breath of relief.

"This is for the children. May your souls burn in hell."

She climbed in her convertible, took the sunglasses from her glove compartment and drove away from the mansion down a winding driveway. At the end of the driveway, she drove out and stopped to place a heavy chain on the gate to keep intruders from entering the property. She returned to her car and drove away. Turning onto a turnpike with the ocean on one side and a canyon on the other, she removed her flesh-colored latex gloves and tossed them out and away.

"Best $600.00 I have ever spent," she said and smiled big.

91

We danced the night away, laughing, kissing, and making plans for our future. Grant held me as we slow danced.

"I am the luckiest man on earth," he murmured into my ear as he nipped at my neck.

He looked into my eyes and kissed my head. He held me, afraid, that if he didn't, I would disappear. He held me close in a protective embrace. We were in love. Nothing would come between us, and I was finally happy.

In time, I would reveal my strange skills to Grant, but for now, I just wanted to enjoy a romantic evening with friends and the one I love. I wanted this evening to move slowly in time so that I could savor every precious moment of celebration.

We arrived at my apartment arm in arm, kissing every 3 feet as we walked upstairs. Grant and I had discussed where we would be spending the evening. Because I have Chloe and Kayla and I hated leaving them alone, we decided to return to my place. I had not unlocked the door, and Grant was already attempting to pounce on me like a tiger on his pray. The door opened, and we walked in. I tossed my keys in the bowl on the table.

Grant leaned down to meet my lips, and I welcomed his warm, soft kiss. He began to unzip my dress and it fell to the floor. I slipped out of my shoes as Grant picked me up like a groom would carry his new bride. He laid me on the bed and unbuttoned his shirt, joining me on the bed and laying by my side. He kissed me passionately and very skillfully unfastened my front snap bra. He nipped at my neck and fondled my breasts with his firm hand. I lay back as he slid his hand to feel the moistness between my legs. He removed my panties and unbuckled his slacks. His body was hard and ready to enter me. We moved in perfect rhythm. My body responded with his every thrust. He placed his full mouth on my breast and sucked gently. The pleasure brought me to climax and convulsive orgasms. When he sensed me climbing, he thrust himself into me wildly and moaned. We were both exhausted.

"I love you," Grant whispered and pushed my hair behind my ear as I laid my head on his chest.

"I love you too," I said and kissed him again before placing my head on his chest once more.

I wanted to fall sleep in his arms.

Tomorrow we would begin to plan our lives together. I was imagining a life with children, a dog, and a house-made into a loving home. I was ready to be Mrs. Monroe. I had so many plans for a happy future. This night was the second happiest night of my life. My happiest evening will be when I say, "I do."

I could feel Grant's chest rising and falling as I lay next to him.

I was sound asleep when I awoke to a knock at the door and wondered who could be at my door this late. I quickly put on my robe and looked through the peephole on the door. I could see a uniformed officer standing there. I opened the door.

"Yes, can I help you? What's wrong? Are my friends, okay?"

"Everything is fine, ma'am, the officer said. "Are you Ms. Jennifer Knoes?"

"Yes, I am."

Suddenly I was staring into the barrel of a gun. A shot rang out.

"Beep! Beep! Beep!" My morning alarm went off at 6:00 am.

Printed by Libri Plureos GmbH in Hamburg, Germany